THE KNIFE'S EDGE

WAR ETERNAL, BOOK THREE

M.R. FORBES

Published by Quirky Algorithms
Seattle, Washington

This novel is a work of fiction and a product of the author's imagination.
Any resemblance to actual persons or events is purely coincidental.

Copyright © 2015 by M.R. Forbes
All rights reserved.

Cover illustrations by Tom Edwards
tomedwardsdesign.com

XENO-1

The most curious thing about the alien tech wasn't so much what they found. It was what they didn't find. As in, signs of life. They didn't expect to find corpses, but they did expect to find something. DNA. A cell or two. They scanned every bit of wreckage at a microscopic level. It took years. What did they find?

Nothing. Nada. Zilch. Zero.

Not a single sample of organic material anywhere that didn't get mixed in from the icepack. Not unless the aliens were polar bears or penguins. An entire crashed starship over a kilometer long, and not only did it have no one in it, but there was nothing to suggest that there had ever been anything living on board. God's chariot for mankind, driven by the Heavenly Host itself.

You want to talk about twisting the noodle? We can start there.

- Paul Frelmund, "XENO-1"

[1]

NOTHING.

There was just nothing.

Mitchell stared into the empty expanse where the planet Liberty had been only minutes before, still trying to recover from the overload of emotions that had surged through him when the planet exploded outward in a hail of debris that continued to spread around the place where Liberty had been. A cloud of it was racing towards them, visible in the light of the nearby sun.

He made himself look past it. He made himself focus on the center. Where there was nothing. Absolutely nothing. It had to be the cleanest area of space in the universe.

"Mother frigger," Cormac said beside him.

Mitchell barely heard him and didn't respond. He continued staring at the space. The Tetron had destroyed the entire planet to kill him. Millions of people. For him.

It was worse than that. Christine was gone. She had sacrificed herself to get him off the planet and foil the Tetron's plans. She had been the very reason he had returned to Liberty, risking his life and the lives of the Riggers to get some kind of foothold in a war all of humanity was losing badly. She had held everything Origin knew about his own kind. Every secret, every vulnerability, every possible edge they could hope to gather.

And she was gone. And he wasn't. Down, but not out.

The Tetron had taunted him. It had teased him. It had goaded him to anger with cruel intent. Christine had told him there was something wrong with it. That it was sick in a way she hadn't experienced before. Christine understood the way time recursion worked in a way he still hadn't managed to wrap his human mind around. She understood the origins of the artificial intelligence that had created a method to travel an eternity forward to go backward. In return, Mitchell understood that she wasn't the configuration Origin believed her to be. She was Origin, more so than the intelligence that had brought the Goliath to him could ever be.

And she was gone.

He didn't need anyone to tell him that it wasn't supposed to be that way. That in all of the other timelines, in every other recursion, she had made it off the planet with him despite the insane odds he had defied to survive at all. But then, wasn't that the reason M had come to him when he did? To change this instance of time in an effort to finally win the war and prevent the Tetron from destroying all of humanity?

She was gone. Maybe she was supposed to be? Maybe that was the point? Origin had told him this was humankind's war. Humankind's fight. If they had always relied on traitorous Tetron to fight this war, then was it any surprise that they had continually lost?

Had Christine known she was going to die? Had that future been written somewhere in the data stack they had failed to recover?

Had she been the one who sent M to save him?

He wasn't the only one on Liberty who M had saved.

Mitchell closed his eyes. The Tetron had been trying to break him. It had been trying to steal his spirit and his will to keep fighting. It wanted to make him emotional and sloppy, to take all of the anger and sadness and hurt he was feeling in that moment and charge headlong into... what?

It was trying to take advantage of his humanness. Of his ability to act outside of logic, even while they had almost won the day by using the same trait. Although it had been destroyed in the explosion, he realized that it wanted him to stare at the empty space.

It wanted him to burn and rage and then do something stupid.

He opened his eyes, smiling at the thought. Millions dead, and he was smiling.

What other choice did he have? Give up? Give in? No. That wasn't the way he had been made. He and his brother had always been competitive. With each other most of all. It had taught him how to drive to be the best. It had taught him not to fold in the face of adversity, and especially not to ever, ever, let your emotions lead you into doing anything your opponent wanted.

The Tetron knew the past future. Didn't they already know that about him? Or had whatever sickness was inside it caused it to act without the reason and logic with which it was supposed to excel?

Mitchell opened his eyes, giving the space where Liberty had once sat a final look, burning it into his memory since he couldn't store it to his damaged p-rat.

He didn't have many answers. Hell, he barely had an army.

It was time to start getting both.

"Origin," he said, knowing the Tetron would hear him. "Get us out of here."

[2]

"Colonel Williams," Millie said, approaching him. She had a smile on her face even though her eyes were red, and dried tears still stained her cheeks.

"Admiral," Mitchell said, bowing to her and returning her smile.

She put her arms out, and he reached out and pulled her in, holding her tight and letting himself relax for the first time in days. Dropping the intensity threatened his control over his emotions, and he pulled away sooner than he wanted to.

"I expect a debriefing," she said. "In the meantime, I see we have some new crew members."

"We lost too many old ones," Mitchell said. He moved over to where Jacob and Kathy were sitting together, still staring out the closing hanger to the white of hyperspace beyond. "Jacob. Kathy."

They looked over, still crying.

"This is Admiral Mildred Narayan. Admiral, Jacob and Kathy were part of the resistance on Liberty."

They didn't say anything. Mitchell watched Millie's face soften.

"I'm so sorry," she said, kneeling in front of both of them.

"Don't be sorry," Kathy said. "Kill the friggers. Every last one of them."

Millie nodded. "Grimes," she said, shouting across the massive hangar. The Sergeant was tending to Cormac, patching a laceration on his chest. She paused and turned back towards Millie. "Forget about Firedog for now. Take these two down to sick bay and make them comfortable."

Grimes nodded, said something to Cormac, and headed their way.

"We have a sick bay?" Mitchell said. It was news to him.

"Grimes has been working on it. It isn't much right now. The beds are a little more comfy, and it's quiet. She has a few instruments she pulled from the Valkyrie before the drop." Millie looked over at the dropship Christine had provided. "Is there medical on board that one?"

"There might be. The ship was decommissioned, though. I don't know how much of it is functional, or how many meds are aboard."

"I'll get Grimes on it later." She returned her attention to Kathy. "Kathy, I can't begin to imagine what you're feeling right now, and I won't pretend to. All I can say is that I'm going to do my absolute damnedest to wipe every last Tetron out of existence across any timeline they try to hide in."

"Yes, ma'am," Kathy said.

Grimes reached them, kneeling with Millie. "I'm Sergeant Grimes. I'm the ship's doctor. Oi, don't you two look a fright." She smiled warmly. "Let's get you cleaned up and checked out." She took both of their wrists in her hands, and they rose to follow her on shaky legs.

"Admiral?"

Millie straightened up and turned to face the new voice. Her entire face changed when she did. "Maya?"

Sergeant Geren looked surprised. "Do I - no. It can't be." She stared at Millie. "You're supposed to be in prison somewhere, or dead."

"That's the story they always tell when they ship someone off to Project Black."

"Project Black?" Geren looked at Mitchell. "You mean it's real?"

"Also known as the Riggers," Mitchell said.

"Riiigg-ahh," he heard Cormac say. The Private trailed away from the hangar, following Grimes and keeping his eyes locked on her rear.

"I should have known," Geren said.

"I take it you two know each other," Mitchell said.

"Burnout was one of my bunkmates in basic," Geren said. "You look different. More mature."

"Burnout?" Mitchell asked.

"Long story. Maybe later," Millie replied. "War will do that to you. Just look in a mirror and you'll see what I mean."

Geren looked tired and worn. Her face was bloody, her hair matted, her clothes stained in sweat, blood, and dirt. "I don't need a mirror to know I look like shit."

"Sergeant Grimes can take a look at you if you want to join the others in sick bay."

"No. I'm not hurt. Physically anyway, thanks to your people. A pair of grays, a nice shower, and a bed. That's all I need right now, ma'am."

"You'll get it. Singh."

Both Origin and Singh began coming towards them. They had been hanging back behind the action, waiting to be requested.

"Can you take Sergeant Geren to a bunk, and then show her to the showers?"

Singh's eyes traveled Geren. They were flat, suggesting she had used some of her remaining stash of narcotics. Mitchell couldn't tell what the engineer was thinking.

"Of course," Singh said. "Follow me, Sergeant." She led the other woman away from them.

"Admiral, Colonel." Major Long approached them, joined by Alvarez. "We need to do something about this." He pointed towards the hangar bay doors. "And we need to do it soon."

"We will, Major," Millie said.

"You told me about the Tetron. About the war. It was hard to believe. Fine. That? I don't even -" He froze, lost for words.

"I'm glad you made it back, Colonel," Alvarez said.

"I'm glad I left you my fighter," Mitchell replied. "Nice flying down there. Both of you. You two are the reason anyone made it off of Liberty."

"You're the reason this war isn't over," Origin said.

Mitchell glared at the configuration.

"I just mean that-"

"Forget it, Private," Millie said. "Long. Alvarez. Go get cleaned up. Both of you should expect a commendation for your efforts, whatever that's worth when there's no brass to send it up to. You too, Mitch."

"In my experience, a commendation from you is a bit more satisfying than being lauded by Command."

"We'll debrief once we've had a chance to get everyone settled," Millie said to Long and Alvarez. They bowed to her and headed away. "Is there anything you want to tell me that's just between the three of us?"

Mitchell shifted his gaze between Millie and Origin. "No. No more secrets. We lost a planet. An entire frigging planet and that thing was happy to do it. We did good work finding Goliath, but we completely screwed the pooch on Liberty. The main thing I learned is that it's up to us to seize control of this thing. We're falling further behind with every minute that slips by."

"You intend to inform the others of my true nature?" Origin asked.

"Yes, as long as Millie agrees."

"We have about fifty people left on this ship," Millie said. "That's barely enough to get us to another planet, nevermind fight an enemy force for it." She shook her head. "I don't know where you're going to pull a military from, Mitch."

Mitchell turned away, scanning the hangar. He found Tio over by the S-17, running his hand along the fuselage.

"Have you ever heard of the Knife?"

"Everyone in the Alliance has heard of the Knife. Why?"

Mitchell pointed. "He's standing over there. I want you to meet him."

[3]

"You're the Knife?" Millie said, approaching the small man.

Tio turned away from the S-17. His face was taut and serious. "My name is Liun Tio. The Knife is a moniker the Alliance gave me to make me sound dangerous." He smiled slyly. "It fits, I suppose. And you are?"

"Admiral Mildred Narayan, Alliance Navy."

"Narayan?" He ran his hand along his chin. "You're Cornelius' daughter, yes?"

"How did you know that?"

"I saw some of the communiques after your trial. Your father went through quite a bit of trouble to keep you from being thrown out into space. It's a good thing for us now, isn't it?"

"Those communiques were heavily encrypted and top secret," Millie said.

Tio shrugged. "It doesn't matter now, does it, Admiral?"

"Tio was on Liberty to speak politics with the same crust that was toasting me at the Gala before all hell broke loose. M sent him a note."

"A note that saved my life."

"The Tetron tried to take him."

"Why?" Millie asked.

"My brother, Pulin," Tio replied. "The intelligence thinks that he is the one that created them."

Millie masked her surprise well. "Did he?"

"I don't know, Admiral. I believe you may need to ask him yourself."

"Millie, the point is that the Tetron wanted Tio badly enough to use some pretty dirty tricks to get close to him, and to give up on trying to kill me for a while. M thought enough of him to pass him a note that saved his life and got him here with us. I don't know how much of this is luck, how much is coincidence, and how much is part of some plan that we haven't caught up to the punchline of. What I do know is that we're running on fumes, and Tio is our lifeline."

"Tio is a criminal, Mitch. The most wanted man in the Alliance and the Federation."

"Millie," Mitchell said, waiting for her to catch herself.

She smiled. "Yeah, I know. We're criminals too. This is different. We have loyalty to the Alliance. We serve a cause. Despite whatever we've done to wind up here." She locked eyes with Tio. "People like him serve themselves first."

"They just destroyed an entire planet," Mitchell said. "That's not an incentive to choose a side?"

"It's not in his nature, Mitch. Did you know his people destroyed an Alliance cruiser that was filled with the families of service members, headed out to meet their loved ones?"

Mitchell froze, lowering his voice. "No. I didn't know that." He glanced at Tio. The Knife was silent and calm, letting them duke it out for him. He hadn't reacted to Millie's claims of his atrocity. Mitchell wondered if it was true.

"Did you know Cormac raped and killed a civilian on Liberty?" Mitchell asked. "Took her to a room away from the group and choked her to death."

All of Millie's anger fell away. "What?" she hissed.

"You heard me. And yes, he's still alive. Why? Because we need him. He saved my life twice after that, along with Tio and everyone else. Cormac is a monster, but we're all monsters here. He also happens to be one of the best damn soldiers in the galaxy, just like Watson is one of the brightest engineers. We're holding this thing together with nothing but grit and determination. We're beggars. We don't have the luxury of being choosy."

Her face was blank as if she hadn't heard anything he said. Her bionic hand was quivering, clenching and unclenching. "I told him if he ever-"

"Millie, did you hear me?" Mitchell said.

Her eyes snapped to him. "I heard you, Mitch. How much are we going to justify in the name of survival? How much shit are we going to take because of what we get out of it?"

"Not just us. All of humanity."

"To what end? So all of our heroes are really villains? So men like Tio get propped up as saviors instead of the cruel, inhuman assholes they truly are?"

"We have to make a choice, Millie. We can try to win with everything we can scrounge together, no matter how ungainly it may be, or we can clean house and see if we can cover the loss. You're the Admiral. This is your call."

Millie shook her head, laughing softly. "My call? Come on, Mitch. We both know who's really in charge around here. It's been that way since you beat the crap out of Anderson during your hazing."

"Millie-"

"No. Mitch, it's okay. I'm not mad about that. You told me your aptitude scores. You should be the Admiral, not me. I'm happy you're alive. I'm happy you came back. I believe in you, and I trust you. Tell me what you think we should do, and I'll do it."

"That's not how this is supposed to work."

"None of this is how it's supposed to work. You're the one who almost wins the war. Not me. You're the one Origin wanted to find Goliath. You're the one they're trying to stop."

"Almost wins. I fail. Every time."

"Have you ever had the Riggers on your side before?"

"I don't know. I think I have. I'm not sure. There's nothing clear about any of this."

There were residual feelings and memories that had followed him through eternity, from recursion to recursion. They were vaporous, insoluble things that he could only see as a film on the surface of the present, and feel like little more than a pinch in the gut. The only thing he had been able to discern for certain from them was that he had a strong connection to Katherine, even though they had lived four hundred years apart and had never met.

He didn't think.

"The future isn't written, Mitch," Millie said. "It isn't immutable. Make the call, and I'll abide by it."

Mitchell met her eyes with his. Then he turned to Tio. The Knife was waiting patiently for them to decide his fate as if he already knew the outcome. He claimed he was a pioneer in artificial intelligence, and that he had taught his brother everything he knew. Did he understand the human mind that well?

"You have a base in the Rim?" Mitchell asked.

Tio nodded.

"Supplies?"

Tio nodded again.

"Weapons. Ships. Men?"

Tio smiled. "You know that I do, Colonel."

"So, are you going to help us, or am I going to throw you out of the hangar and into hyperspace?"

"There was never any question I would help you. Even if I was the selfish asshole the Admiral believes I am; the Tetron tried to kill me. That isn't something I'm willing to forgive."

"We need coordinates," Millie said.

"Of course." Tio rattled them off.

"Origin, did you get that?"

Origin had been standing behind him, silent and forgotten in the heat of the moment. "Yes, Mitchell. We'll have to drop to recalibrate, and then we'll be on our way."

"How long?"

"A week."

"Too long," Mitchell said. "Can you go any faster?"

"Hyperspace is not a thrust-racing track, Colonel. There are only two speeds. Human speed, and Tetron speed. Be grateful we can move at Tetron speed."

Tio was staring at the skinny, olive-skinned man. "You're a Tetron."

"Origin," he said. "I am aware of your exploits, Liun Tio, and I am especially impressed with your ability to keep the location of your base of operations secret, even beyond your demise on Liberty in past recursions."

"This is the one you told me about," Tio said to Mitchell. The Knife pointed at a band of tentacles running along the ceiling. "That's you, too?"

"My truest form, yes. Though as Mitchell will tell you soon enough, I'm not the Origin I believed I was. I'm merely a partition. An incomplete duplicate of the original."

"Christine," Mitchell said before Tio or Millie could ask. "She wasn't a configuration of Origin. She was Origin. This one is the configuration."

Millie stared at Origin. "How can that be? I mean, if Christine was the original-"

"Origin never left Earth four hundred years ago," Origin said. "It, or she if you prefer, remained behind while sending me, a copy, ahead with Katherine and the Goliath. She reduced herself, cut herself off from her data stack, her memories so that the Tetron would never be able to claim them."

"The Tetron knew she was on Liberty," Mitchell said. "It was looking for her, as much as it was looking for Tio or me."

"I don't believe the Tetron knew. Not until you recovered the lost video footage from the launch that helped you locate the Goliath. They pieced together the same information you did. I don't believe that it knew it had captured Origin. It is most likely it thought it had captured a configuration, like M."

"But why would she remain behind?" Millie asked. "There's no strategic reason she should have stayed."

"I don't know," Origin said. "That information is forever lost to me. Perhaps you can piece that together, too?"

"I don't know that it would help," Millie said.

"Perhaps not."

"I would like to view a sample of your source code if I might?" Tio said. "To review it for similarities to Pulin's style. It will help us prove or disprove his involvement in the creation of the Tetron."

"I don't believe that is wise," Origin said.

"Why not?" the Knife asked.

The Tetron chuckled as if the question were outlandish. "It would be foolish for Mitchell to place that much trust in you before you have proven yourself."

"Proven myself?" Tio said, his voice staying level but turning harsh. "I helped form the rebellion that was fighting back against the Tetron. I-"

"Tio," Mitchell said, raising his hand to quiet the man. Tio stopped talking, catching himself and returning to his previous calm. "I'm thankful for everything you helped us accomplish on Liberty. That being said, I'm not willing to make any more quick decisions. We have a week before we reach the Rim. How you spend it will help us all get to know what kind of ally we've made."

Tio nodded. "As you wish, Colonel. I'm nothing if not a patient man."

"Good," Millie said. "We'll show you to a space in berthing, and then you can go and get cleaned up if you want. I don't know how things are in your world, but we can only offer you a communal head."

"I'm not high maintenance either, Admiral. I would ask that you attempt to open your mind and challenge whatever pre-conceived notions you have of me."

Millie made a face like she wanted to strangle the Knife. She clenched her hands behind her back, her face tight.

"My mother was on that cruiser."

She spun and stormed off without another word.

[4]

Mitchell led the Knife to berthing, letting him pick out whichever one the honeycomb like bunks he wanted. Few of them were occupied, and even fewer would be in use once the personal effects of the dead were parceled away as memories to the living. Mitchell resolved to make sure he received something from each of the team members he had lost, to store in his locker and go through whenever he needed a little extra motivation.

He was plenty motivated right now.

He put his hand to his abdomen, feeling the soreness and stinging of his wound. The patch had kept it held together, but he would need Grimes to look at it soon. He probably should have had her look at it first thing before she even took care of the emotional needs of the two Liberty survivors.

Two.

Mitchell tried not to let the gravity of the number sink in. Liberty was a small planet, smaller still since most of the military had been pulled out by the Tetron, sent off into the hands of other puppeteers. Compared to some of the more populated planets of the Alliance, it was barely more than an outpost. Earth, for example. Still home to four billion people. Still a symbolic home for all of the planets in the outer quadrants. Even at Tetron speed, Earth was still months away from a fight.

The problem was that they were moving in the wrong direction.

There was nothing they could do about it. They needed the Knife's resources, his militia and his ships. They could charge headlong at the Tetron right now, and they would be blown to dust the same as Liberty had been. Their only choice was to go backward to move the fight forwards. Mitchell didn't like it, but he also didn't see any other way.

Mitchell dropped Tio off and turned back the way he had come, at first intending to head off to the sick bay and get Grimes to check his patch. He made it two steps before he thought better of it, his mind lingering on his fight with Millie. She had made a good argument, and she wasn't completely wrong. He couldn't ignore everything that had happened just because their numbers were thin.

He found Cormac in the shower, standing under a misting spray next to Geren. She must have said something to him already because he was facing away from her, making sure to keep his eyes to himself. Singh was waiting for her outside. She wasn't being as shy about putting her eyes on the Sergeant's well-toned flesh. Geren was an attractive woman. A little too masculine for Mitchell's taste, but the engineer seemed impressed.

"I don't know that Geren would want you ogling her like that, Singh," he said as he entered the showers.

Singh looked down at the comment. "No, sir."

"Why don't you wait on the other side of the wall? You probably aren't going to like what's about to happen anyway."

"Sir?"

Mitchell flashed her a sideways look that sent her backing away without another word. He moved into the shower fully clothed, heading towards Cormac.

The Private only saw Mitchell a moment before he was on him, slamming him hard in the side of the head and knocking him back against the wall of the shower.

"Sir? What the frig?"

Cormac tried to get around Mitchell, but Mitchell grabbed him by the shoulder and threw him back again, hitting him hard in the gut. He threw a third punch, and the soldier grabbed it, turning Mitchell's arm, releasing before he could do any damage.

"What's this about, Mitch?" Cormac said, trying to back away. Mitchell dropped down, kicking him hard in the calf and knocking a leg out, sending Cormac falling onto the wet floor.

"You frigging know what this is about, Firedog," he shouted, dropping on top of him and hitting him in the gut again.

"Colonel?" Geren said, coming up behind him.

"Not your business, Sergeant," Mitchell said. He punched Cormac in the face. "Do you think because you're out of my sight, that gives you the right to do whatever you damn well please, Private?"

"Sir. No, sir," Cormac said, arms flailing to try to deflect some of Mitchell's blows.

"Then what the frig gave you the idea that you could hurt a civilian on Liberty and not get the living shit kicked out of you?"

"She asked for it-"

Mitchell's fist hit him in the mouth, breaking at least one tooth and shutting him up. "You're going to give me that bull, Private?"

"I swear, Colonel. I do. She-"

Mitchell batted him in the head two more times. "I heard you made a promise to Millie that you weren't going to do shit like this. I've got a frigging war to win, Private. I don't have time to deal with your frigged up brain or your frigged up libido."

"Sir. Yes, sir." Cormac's face was red, his eyes fearful.

"She wants to airlock you. Do you get that Firedog? She doesn't care that you're a good soldier. You're a frigging wild card, and that shit doesn't stand when we're in the middle of it. You raped and killed a civilian in the middle of a mission. You did it right under my frigging nose. If you had been downstairs with everyone else, it could be that Shank and the others make it out of there. You follow?"

"Sir. Yes, sir." There were tears in Cormac's eyes now, and he stopped struggling against Mitchell's blows.

"You helped us find the Goliath. You saved my ass on Liberty. You know what that's worth? Jack shit if I can't trust you. I might as well throw you out of the airlock right now because you're useless to me like that."

"Sir. I'm sorry, sir."

"I don't want you to be frigging sorry. I want you to be my machine. I want you to be my soldier. You do what I say. Exactly what I frigging say, and nothing else. You don't breathe unless I tell you to."

"Sir. Yes, sir."

Cormac's voice was low and rough, short on air and high on pain. Mitchell hit him in the side one more time before slowly rising off him.

"Anyone on this ship so much as whispers that you've been looking at them sideways, and you lose your ride on this bucket. Do you get that, Private?"

"Sir. Yes, sir." Cormac didn't move. He stayed on the floor clutching his battered ribs.

"I'm not condoning what you did. If I didn't need your skills, you'd be dead already. You have one chance, Firedog. I don't give a shit if we're in the middle of a firefight. Cross me again and I drop you where you stand, and nobody on this ship is going to give a damn about it."

"Sir. Yes, sir," Cormac said.

Mitchell held out his hand. Cormac reached up and took it, letting Mitchell help him to his feet. The Private was bloody and already bruising. Mitchell was soaked through his clothes, and the activity had opened the wound on his stomach. His heart was pounding, his head throbbing. He hated himself for not doing what Millie had suggested. He had seen the girl on the bed. He couldn't bring himself to look Cormac in the eye.

"I'm disappointed in you, Private," he said. He watched Cormac's expression change, realizing that those three words had just hurt him more than the beating ever could.

He hoped it would be enough to keep him in line.

[5]

Admiral Steven Williams watched the scene unfold through the heavy polycarbonate that kept the bridge of the battleship Carver safe from the void beyond. He paced as he did, keeping his eyes on the squadron of Morays thousands of miles distant, little more than specks on the edge of the universe. It was always a wonder to the crew that he could keep his attention on anything that small, so much so that his First Officer was droning out the specifics while watching through an enhanced view.

"Loyola is in position," he said. A pause. "Torpedo is making his run."

"I can see it, John. Thank you."

Captain John Rock snorted. "We're four thousand klicks further out than the last time. You can really see that?"

Steven traced the smallest speck across the sky. He almost lost it as it passed ahead of a star, but he managed to keep his eyes locked. It was rolling over in a defensive maneuver, carrying out the scripted tenets of the exercise.

"Gibraltar is rolling. Torpedo closed the gap." He said it with smug satisfaction though he kept his face straight.

"Unbelievable," John said, his disbelief only half-convincing.

He should have been used to Steven's feats of visual acuity, as unimpressive as they were. There wasn't much value in such good eyesight when the Carver's sensor arrays would make following the squadron less of a strain.

"I don't know why they sent us out here, anyway," John said, watching the action through his p-rat. "There's nothing to do but run these attack simulations and twiddle our thumbs."

Steven turned away from the view at the comment. He was a handsome man, a little taller than his brother, a little thinner, a little balder, save for his face where a neatly trimmed beard gave him a more commanding presence. He switched to his p-rat view, watching the exercise with one eye while navigating back to his command chair with the other.

"The Federation's been fairly quiet since Liberty, and intel moving out of New Terran space has ground to a halt."

"Executing Alliance assets tends to do that."

Steven nodded. One of their spies on Terra Omega had been caught in the act and summarily tried and punished. The rest of the agents working in New Terran space had gone to ground, keeping quiet while the whole situation simmered down. There was always tension between the UPA and the New Terrans. There was always tension any time any of the space-faring factions came near each other.

The end result had been a reassignment away from Earth towards the center of Bravo quadrant, to a small star politely nicknamed TN-14532, or Tennessee for short. His orders had been to run training exercises there and to make sure his fleet was kept on elevated alert, just in case any of that tension boiled over. They were a four-day jump away from Terra Kappa, close enough to launch a strike if needed. Strong enough, too. Steven controlled one of the newest battle groups in the Alliance. It was filled with all the latest and greatest designs. In fact, the Carver had only been christened two years earlier.

Steven still wasn't sure how he had pulled that assignment. Prior to the launch of the Carver, he had controlled one of the smallest battle groups stationed near Earth from the bridge of a one-hundred-year-old cruiser. It was a lousy assignment. A test, he knew, to see how he fared during his first command.

He had improved his entire fleet's sim scores by twenty percent within three months, and another forty percent during his first three years. They had only seen one small skirmish with New Terran forces over a farming colony, but they had won the battle handily.

Based on that he guessed he had passed. Even so, standard operating procedure was to matriculate top officers upward. When the Carver came online, it should have gone to one of the most experienced Admirals or Generals, depending on how the UPA was shifting the resources between straight space defense and mixed use. Cornelius, maybe. He would have been punted up to the next level while the aging fleet was sent home for upgrades.

Instead he was on the bridge of one of the newest battleships in the Alliance, watching the tail end of a much larger exercise. It had gone well. Flawlessly, in fact. He liked flawless.

"Torpedo hit the mark," John said. "Mission accomplished."

Steven opened a channel on his p-rat. "Nice work, Torpedo."

"Thank you, sir," the pilot replied.

"Let's get everyone back home," Steven said, widening his reach to everyone in the fleet. "We'll be starting phase three tomorrow at oh-six-hundred. Thank you all for a job well done."

John sighed and rose from his chair, coming back towards him. Steven watched him approach, trying to determine if he had lost a little weight. He had never been a small man, not in any of the ten years they had been serving together. He wasn't handsome, either, but who cared about that? John already had a husband back on Earth. He was whip smart, his battle reflexes were off the charts, and he was one of the most kind, genuine people he had ever met. It was the reason he had negotiated to have his best friend brought along when he was reassigned.

"I'm starving," John said.

"It's been, what? Four hours?"

"Shut up. More like twelve."

"That's no way to speak to your commanding officer."

"The mission is over. You're just Steven now."

"I'm never just Steven."

They shared a laugh and headed towards the hatch off the bridge. "Lewis, you have the bridge," Steven said as they reached it.

"Yes, Admiral," the Lieutenant said.

They moved towards the mess together. Whenever Steven passed any of his crew, they stopped and lowered their heads slightly in respect.

Ten years and he had never gotten used to that.

He had never really gotten used to being an Admiral. Or even the fact that he had accomplished a dream he hadn't even known he had until the day he'd won a stupid bet he made with his brother. Mitchell was the smart one, the one who aced all of the exams and made it look so damn easy.

He had worked hard. He had clawed and scraped for everything he had gained, and yet he still felt like an imposter so much of the time. The bowing only ever served to reinforce the doubt.

His brother. A hero. Then a traitor. Found dead in a barn on Liberty.

"What's the thought?" John asked.

"Mitchell," Steven said.

"I knew it. It's only been a week since you heard the news. It's okay to mourn."

He didn't say anything. He wasn't mourning. He hadn't mourned. He had been close to Mitchell once when they were younger. He wanted to say it wasn't jealousy that had driven the wedge between them. He wanted to say it was because Mitch got a big head over his success and his relatively quick assignment to the Greylock.

He knew that was bullshit.

It was jealousy.

But now? Now his younger brother was gone. Not only that, he had lied to millions about his role in the Battle for Liberty. Steven didn't want to believe it was true. Who would?

Except he did believe it. Mitchell had always been a show-off. He had lost the bike race because he was popping wheelies. Maybe he had subconsciously wanted to join the military. Maybe it was just destiny.

"Mourn? No. I sent the communique on to Laura a month ago. It should be reaching her and my folks any day now. When I say I'm thinking about Mitch, I mean I'm thinking about how they're going to take it."

"Your brother is dead. You aren't even a little upset about it?"

He looked at John, reading his face. Whether he was or not, it was obvious to him that he was.

"Maybe a little. You?"

"It sounds stupid, but I believed in him. In all the stuff he was saying. And you already know I thought he was the better-looking brother."

"He was."

John looked away. "It's hard to be disappointed by someone you feel like you know. It's hard to know they're dead, too. I mean, he'll never have a chance to redeem himself."

Steven rubbed his beard. "Maybe he'll get his chance in the next life."

[6]

Mitchell left the showers and headed for Medical, unsure of what he would find when he arrived there. According to Singh, they had set up the infirmary right below berthing, a quick ride in the lift or down a single flight of stairs in one of the emergency access corridors.

He was surprised when he reached the area and found it was more advanced than he had suspected. It wasn't to the level of a fully autonomous Medical module, complete with medi-bots and all sorts of sensors that would diagnose issues immediately upon entry, but it was fairly well organized considering the meager collection of tools and supplies they had on board.

The area had been emptied and re-outfitted as a hub and spoke system, where the sick would circle the main working area in the familiar honeycomb bed pattern, allowing even a single doctor or nurse to keep watch on them. The central area had been filled in with a few pieces of equipment that looked somewhat like tools he had seen in infirmaries before, as well as an examination table and a few low counters where they were storing whatever pills and patches they had access to.

Sergeant Grimes was standing at a counter with her back to him when he entered while Kathy and Jacob were resting in bunks on the farther side of the room. They were sitting up and talking to one another.

The ship's doctor sensed his presence and turned as he approached. She was holding a pair of mugs in her hands.

"Medicine?" he asked.

She smiled. "Chocolate."

"We have chocolate?" He caught a whiff of it now, his mouth watering in response.

"I brought it with me. I've been saving it for a special occasion."

"The occasion isn't special."

"No. But those two need it more than I do."

"How are they?"

"Physically, they're both fine. A few surface scrapes, cuts, bruises. Jacob is showing some early signs of trauma, and I don't think the gravity has sunk in yet. I'm a little worried about how he'll cope with everything a few days out."

"What about Kathy?"

Grimes laughed softly. "A spitfire to be sure. She'll be fine." Her eyes shifted downward. "I hope you came to see me about that."

Mitchell looked at his stomach. The patch had torn in his tussle with Cormac, and blood was seeping through. "Yeah, but you need to make it quick. I've got some other business I need to get to."

"I can swap the patch. You'll need to take it easy and let it bond the skin, or you're going to have a nasty scar."

"If it scars it scars."

"Let me just bring this over and I'll be right with you. If you don't mind getting yourself out of that suit. There's a pair of fresh grays in there." She pointed to one of the low cabinets before heading across the room.

Kathy and Jacob looked up when she arrived. Mitchell set about removing his clothes, balling up the flight suit and slipping into the bottom half of the grays as quickly as possible while facing away from them. When he turned around, he saw Kathy was watching him. She caught his eyes with hers and waved. He waved back, feeling his face flushing and wondering how long she had been watching him. The most she would have seen was his ass, but still, she was just a kid. He should have been more careful.

He shook his head at the thought. She had helped kill naked civilians under the Tetron's control on Liberty. She had watched her home planet explode. His rear was nothing in comparison.

She took the offered chocolate, smelling it and beaming. Mitchell turned away, going over to the examination table and sitting down. He reached down and began pulling off the patch.

"Are ye daft?" Grimes said, rushing back over to him and swatting his hands away. "I'll take care of that. You're filthy, and libel to infect yourself." She rolled her eyes. "You pilots are all the same. Think you're immune to bacteria, you do."

Her hands were swift and precise as she removed the patch, checked the wound, cleaned the area, and put a new one on. Mitchell watched her red hair bob while she worked, quickly growing impatient despite her speed.

"There now," she said, backing away and examining her work. "The wound is still young enough you haven't made a total mess of it yet. The patch is sealed, but you should hit the shower before you do anything else to make sure it stays clean."

"Thank you, Sergeant," Mitchell said, hopping down off the table and taking an offered shirt. "I've got one more stop I need to make first."

He headed for the door, glancing back at Kathy and Jacob one more time on the way. "And something else I need to hit," he muttered.

[7]

WITHOUT HIS P-RAT, it took Mitchell almost an hour to track down Watson's whereabouts. The engineer had been busy in the time Mitchell had been on Liberty, helping set up Medical, helping repair some minor systems, and trying to keep himself as useful as possible. As it was, Mitchell located him deep in the bowels of Goliath, not far from the engine compartment that Origin had taken as his core. Watson had created another workshop there, filled with bits and pieces of salvaged electronics, half-built systems, and a small area where he could sleep. There was a pisspot on the floor next to his gel mattress, suggesting he didn't spend much time with the others.

"Watson," Mitchell said, walking in on him as he was hunched over a small circuit, soldering a wire to it.

Watson straightened up immediately, his red face paling. "Colonel," he replied. "I heard you were back. I heard what happened."

That was all he said.

"The package didn't work." Mitchell held back his anger. If it had worked, maybe Liberty would still be in one piece.

He lowered the circuit and wrung his hands together nervously. "Yes, well, I told you before you left that it was all theoretical."

"You did. It didn't work." Mitchell took a step closer. They had been in the communications control room surrounded by Tetron spiders. They had barely gotten out alive.

"I'm sorry, Colonel. I really am. I don't know what-"

"I want to know why," Mitchell shouted, slamming his hands down on the desk. "I want to know what you did wrong."

He was losing his cool, but it wasn't just about what had happened on Liberty. Everything about Watson made him angry, and Mitchell had defended him and his continued existence to Millie. The fact that they needed the pedophile for anything was infuriating. The fact that he had been given a task and failed, regardless of how difficult that task was left him questioning why he was talking instead of hauling the engineer directly to an airlock.

Watson began to shake in response to the anger. "Wrong? I... uh... I don't know. How could I know? I did the best I could, I swear."

"Are you sure about that? Are you sure you weren't distracted?"

"Wha-?" Watson shook his head. "Oh. You mean that. I did what you asked."

That was all he said about that, too.

"You deleted everything?"

"I did what you asked," he repeated.

"That's not what I just asked you."

"Mitch-"

Mitchell leaned over the desk and grabbed Watson by his shirt. The man was heavy, but he was angry enough to lift him out of his chair.

"Tell me you deleted everything and make it the truth, or I'm going to kill you."

"I..." He paused.

"Liberty is gone," Mitchell said. "The package might have prevented that if it had worked the way it was supposed to. Did it fail because your head was somewhere else?"

"I told you it helps me relax."

"So you're saying the package failed because you deleted your porn, and you couldn't think straight without it?" Mitchell tightened his grip, holding the shirt tight enough to choke the engineer. "I know you're a sick frigger, but I swear if millions died because of your twisted sense of sexuality I'm going to make your death as long and painful as I can."

"Yes. No. I mean. Wait." He put his hands on Mitchell's wrists. "I saved all the data on the package. I can rebuild it, and try to figure out what went wrong. Maybe we can at least learn something from it." He dropped his hands, running them along the desk until they landed on a small box off to the side. He picked it up. "Here."

Mitchell let Watson go, taking the box from him and opening it. There was a tiny chip inside.

"I didn't delete it. I removed it, but I kept it. I was waiting to see if you came back from Liberty."

Mitchell couldn't help but laugh at that. Of course he was. "How do I know you didn't do your best to keep me from coming back?"

Watson looked like he was going to cry. "What? Colonel, whatever you think of me, I wouldn't do anything like that. If you die, we all die."

Mitchell shook the chip. "And you get to keep this until you do."

"I know I'm sick. I'm not that sick. The package was supposed to work. I did everything I could, I swear. Yes, if you died I didn't want to lose those files. Everyone on board hates me."

"And rightly so," Mitchell said.

Watson was crying now, tears running over pudgy cheeks. "It's pathetic. I know it is. That's all I have. That and this ship, and this war. I don't want to die as nothing more than a frigged up pedo. I'm doing the best I can, Colonel."

Mitchell closed his hand over the box. He felt dirty just holding it. "Your best isn't cutting it, Watson. You have two days to reassemble the package and make a guess as to what went wrong. We may need something like it again and it damn well better work the next time."

"Yes, sir," Watson said, rubbing his neck and backing away. "I'll send a requisition up to Singh for the parts I need, and then I'll get started right away."

"See that you do. Your life depends on it."

[8]

Mitchell left Watson's dungeon, carrying the small box with the neural chip in it in his left hand so tightly he kept hoping it would become pulverized there into no more than silicone and dust.

He was tired. Very tired. There had been no rest. No escape. His emotions had been everywhere, and his body was running on pure adrenaline. They were the only thing still keeping him going.

He had done what he needed to do. The things that couldn't wait. They were in hyperspace, on their way back out to the Rim. He had a week to recover and reorganize, and Grimes was right. He needed a shower and his bunk. If Millie happened by, he didn't think he would mind having a warm, soft body to settle in with for a few hours.

He stopped at his bunk to throw his illicit cargo into his locker until he had time to dispose of it properly and then headed back to the showers. They were empty when he arrived, and he sat under the warm stream of water for a long time, his head bowed, his eyes closed, doing his best not to think about anything.

The stillness of the moment brought out the echoes in his mind. Subconscious echoes of a past long forgotten and barely remembered.

Of who he was before. Millions of years? Trillions? More? There was no way to place a human concept to it. It was an eternity. He didn't see anything behind his eyes. He didn't hear solid, structured words. It came across more as emotion, as feeling. Familiarity and fear.

He sensed Katherine. His skin tingled with tiny electric shocks when he did. He felt her in the rapidly increasing pace of his heart, and the resolve in his chest. She had given her life for this. For him. He conjured her face. It was Christine's face, too. He knew they were connected, Katherine to Christine, Christine to him to Katherine. He was part of the equation, but he still wasn't sure how or why. Aptitude tests be damned, he was nothing special. Not like that.

Was it fate?

Was fate a real thing?

He hadn't felt like he was in control of his life since the Prime Minister's wife had accused him of rape. He was going through the motions, waiting to see where each new moment led. He didn't like it, but he wasn't sure what else to do. Not yet, anyway.

He reached forward and turned off the spray. He ran his hands through his short hair, pulling the moisture out. He huffed and spun around, heading for his towel.

Origin was standing there. The configuration held it out to him.

"How long have you been there?" Mitchell asked.

"Long enough to count the bruises. You did not have Sergeant Grimes treat them?"

"They don't hurt." Mitchell took the towel and wrapped it around his waist. "I assume you were looking for me?"

"Yes. I had to come directly, as your receiver is offline."

"The Tetron on Liberty EMPed it out. I feel disadvantaged without it." He realized he should have asked Watson about getting it fixed. He had forgotten in his anger.

"A disadvantage you may need to learn to live with," Origin said. "There is a high probability the Tetron will use the tactic again in the future, especially if they are not able to gain control through the implants."

"Don't you know the answer to that already?"

Origin chuckled. "Not in this future."

Mitchell knew they had altered this timeline enough that any prior futures had been rendered irrelevant. "Right. What do you suggest?"

"Standard issue communicators. I can recreate the model that was used by the original crew of the Goliath."

"Four-hundred-year-old technology?"

"Yes. There is beauty in the simplicity, Colonel. Security as well."

"You're saying the Tetron won't be able to crack it?"

"They will. Not as easily."

"What about the other functions? The combat routines and augmentation?"

"You will have to train without them. I recommend having all of the crew train without it."

"There's a reason only those with high scores pilot mechs and fighters."

"There is also a reason mechs and fighters have manual overrides."

Mitchell stared at Origin. The configuration stared back, unblinking, with no understanding of what it was suggesting. The last thing they needed was something else to put them at a disadvantage in a fight.

"It is your choice, Mitchell. Would you prefer to be prepared, or would you prefer to hope for the best?"

"You're right. We'll have to start training with our p-rats off. Now, why did you really come down here?"

"Christine Arapo."

"Origin," Mitchell said. "The true Origin."

Origin looked as though Mitchell had punched him in the gut. "Yes."

"Did you know?"

"Not before she signaled me to return to Liberty. Commanded, more like. I had no choice in it, even had I wanted to resist."

"So your story about arriving on Earth, splitting yourself and placing your data stack into a clone of Katherine-"

"All true. Except it was not my doing. It was hers. She was hiding until we could all be reunited."

"Which didn't happen because she sacrificed herself to get me off Liberty."

Origin nodded. "I knew that I was incomplete. I didn't know that I was a configuration." He paused as if unsure how to say what he wanted to say. "I am a configuration," he repeated. "Not a sentient, thinking machine as I had previously believed. My actions, my personality, all that I am is part of an algorithm."

"A massively advanced and complex algorithm," Mitchell said.

"But still an algorithm. I am limited in ways I had not guessed. Even more so now that I know that the data stack is lost and that the true Tetron from which I was created is lost. This may seem inconsequential to you, Mitchell. It is not to me. Tetron do not die. When they tire of being, they choose to stop."

"You mean suicide?"

"In simplistic human terms, perhaps. It is one thing to be a configuration and have access to the parent, to be able to receive new instructions and increase in potential. That is part of our subroutines. To hope for further growth in such a way. It is something else to have lost the parent. I cannot describe the resulting anomalies."

Mitchell looked at the slight form Origin had created as his human vessel. It was shivering.

"You feel sad?"

"Again, simplistic. Yes. Sad. Depressed. Confused. Inadequate. My purpose was to assist you in bringing Origin back into the war at the proper time, with all of the knowledge the parent possessed. I have failed in this purpose, and have been left orphaned."

"This can't be the first time a configuration has lost its parent," Mitchell said.

Origin stared ahead, his face blank for a moment. "Yes. I believe it is. As I said, the Tetron do not die. Not on their own. Not in the first future, before the eternal engine. I am stranded and alone. My programming tells me that I am to help you fight this war, yet without the parent I do not believe I have the capability to succeed in that goal."

Mitchell was quiet while he tried to think. Losing the p-rat was one thing. Having his most powerful and important asset questioning its capabilities was something else. They couldn't afford a depressed AI.

"Christine gave herself up to get me off that planet. She got me back to Goliath, and to you. As far as I'm concerned, that means she believed in you. She trusted that her configuration would be able to go on without her, and help me win this fight."

Origin looked at the ground in front of them, shaking his head. His voice was low and weak. "I am incomplete."

"Christine told me the other Tetron are also incomplete. That they're sick. That something happened to them in this timeline or a past timeline. Something that she didn't understand."

"I do not know what."

"Neither do I. That isn't the point. The point is that you need to take a look around this ship. Take a look at Kathy and Jacob. Take a look at Singh or Cormac or Millie. Look at me. We're all incomplete. We're all damaged in some way. Maybe there's a reason for that. Maybe there's a cosmic algorithm that we don't get yet. Maybe we need to be broken to win. Who knows. What I do know is that we're here, now. All of us. We're in this shit together, win or lose, and none of us can come out on top alone."

Origin was quiet for a moment, and then he nodded. "Yes. I understand your perspective, and I will process this. There is one portion of your statement that concerns me."

"Which part?"

"Logically, if we must be broken to win, does the same truth stand for the Tetron? It is possible that they broke themselves?"

[9]

Mitchell finally made it back to his small bunk in berthing. He stepped inside and fell onto his mattress, closing his eyes and absorbing the feel of the gel as it conformed to support him. He took long, deep breaths, trying to find some state of relaxation amid the panic his encounter with Origin had left him in.

Could his suggestion be even close to the truth? Had the Tetron intentionally done something to themselves in order to win the war? It seemed illogical and damn near impossible. He couldn't imagine a highly advanced AI having the capability to conceive of that kind of tactic.

He also couldn't dismiss the possibility. Not after what he had seen on Liberty. The Tetron were more than just lines of code. They had the ability to learn, to evolve. Had evolution driven them to a point that circled them back towards insanity?

Now that he was at rest, his mind had time to return to Liberty. Tamara King. He conjured her in his mind. He had hoped the last memory he would have of her was Christine blocking her from entering his hotel room after news broke over the truth around the Shot. That was a good memory compared to what it had been replaced with. A naked automaton grabbing at them to keep them away from a ship, falling to a bullet in the head.

"Mind some company?"

Mitchell hadn't noticed his pod's hatch opening. Millie was standing in the open space.

"I heard you had a talk with Cormac," she said.

He motioned to her. "News travels fast around here."

She came forward, taking a seat on the mattress beside him. "Small ship."

"No, it isn't."

"By headcount," she corrected. "He actually came up to the bridge in nothing but a towel to apologize. I've never seen him like that before."

"I had a talk with Watson, too," Mitchell said.

"What about?"

He thought about showing her the neural chip. He decided against it. The fewer hands that had to touch it the better. He would dispose of it right after he got some shut-eye. He would have to come up with a suitable way to obliterate it.

"The package. I want to know why it didn't work. I want it to work next time. If there is a next time."

"I understand."

"And Origin is having a crisis of confidence."

"What?"

"He isn't the original Tetron. The real Origin. Christine was."

"You're kidding?"

"No. Millie, this whole thing was frigged up before. It's gotten a lot worse."

"We've got the Knife."

"I hope it helps."

"You sound like you're having a crisis of confidence."

Mitchell shook his head. "No. We're going to get payback for Liberty. I'm just tired. This is the first time I've been off my feet in days. My stimulant levels are low, my p-rat is fried, my gut hurts like hell, I haven't slept, and every time I close my eyes all I see is violence. You learn pretty quickly how to block stuff like this out, especially once you're in the field. But sometimes... Sometimes you're just too exhausted to push it away."

He laughed, reaching up and rubbing her arm.

"I thought my life was hell when I was the Alliance's marketing strategy. I'd give a lot to go back there now."

"I wouldn't," Millie said. "This war was going to happen anyway. I'd rather do my part to change the outcome."

"Do you really think we can?"

She smiled, shifting her position to lay across his chest, bringing her face close to his. "We're the Riggers. Impossible missions are our specialty."

"There aren't that many of us left."

Her face turned sour. "I know. It hurts to lose them, Shank most of all." She put her head down next to his, putting her weight on top of him, careful not to add pressure to his wound. "I'm glad you made it back, Mitch. I would have tried to do this without you, but I'm happy I don't have to."

He turned his head. Their faces were only inches apart. His eyes locked onto hers. "Whatever happens, I'm proud to serve with you, Admiral."

She leaned in, kissing him softly. "How exhausted are you?"

[10]

Nearly twenty hours had passed before Mitchell woke again, finally teased into a restful sleep with the help of Millie's gentle ministration. She wasn't there when he finally did open his eyes. He hadn't expected her to be. She had a ship to run, a war to help him fight. Just because they were in hyperspace didn't mean there wasn't plenty to be done.

And he was laying there, not helping at all.

He swung his legs over the side of his bunk and got to his feet. The last bit of stimulants he had pumped into his body had long since been absorbed and used, and every inch of soreness his time on Liberty had caused followed him upright. He groaned from the stiffness, every nerve ending crying out in discomfort, his abdomen hurting worst of all. The patch had numbing agents in it, but it wasn't enough to get rid of the ache completely.

He leaned over his locker, finding another pair of grays and getting dressed. He found Watson's neural chip and grabbed it, intent on relieving the world of it as soon as he was done relieving himself. Then he opened his hatch and stumbled out into the corridor, moving and feeling like he was a hundred years old.

It was a good thing Millie had stopped by before he had gone to sleep.

At least his mind felt sharper and more rested, even if his body complained with every step he took. He passed by a number of empty bunks, as well as a few that were sealed up, their occupants inside and getting some sleep. He wondered which one of them Tio had been placed in.

It took almost ten minutes for him to reach the head, despite the short distance. He emptied his bladder and started heading back in the other direction. He was sure he would find Millie up on the bridge if he didn't run into anyone else first. They needed to start talking about next steps and getting a better feel for what the Knife could provide.

He detoured down to Medical first. The movement was loosening his muscles somewhat, but he needed something to take the edge off. He wished he still had his p-rat, it would have measured his health and delivered painkillers the moment he woke.

No one was there when he arrived. He wandered to the cabinets and began looking through them for some pain relievers, finding a box containing a dozen patches near the back of one. He took the whole thing out, putting it on the counter. He looked over and saw that the racks Jacob and Kathy had been placed in were both empty, the bedding gone. Had they been matriculated in with the crew? And where was everybody, anyway?

He opened one of the patches and slapped it on the back of his neck. Cold relief flooded through his muscles by the time he reached the door.

He passed back through berthing on his way to the lift that would take him to the bridge. Origin had made progress in blending the liquid metallic veins that composed his true form in with the structure of the Goliath, pushing them around the human passageways and molding them tightly enough that they looked like bundled ropes squeezed into the four corners. A constant motion of pulsing light flowed along them, illuminating the ship and carrying information throughout the intelligence's physical being.

Mitchell marveled at it as he walked. It hadn't always been this big, he knew. It had started small and grown over the centuries Origin had been waiting for him, but even so. This was a configuration? A portion of what the original Origin once was? Or had Christine abandoned her body all those years ago, leaving it to the Goliath so that she could go into hiding as a human?

Had other Tetron done the same?

The thought gave him pause, and he stopped walking a dozen feet from the lift, staring at the pulsing synapses. Christine couldn't be the only Tetron disguised as a human. Could she? If she wasn't, how would they tell? There had to be something that set them apart and revealed them as creations of instructions and code instead of... Instead of what? DNA was DNA.

He had told Millie it had gotten a lot worse.

Maybe that had been an understatement?

He was still staring at the Tetron's nerves when the lift door slid open ahead of him. He glanced up and saw Alice standing there, an impatient expression on her face.

"Colonel Williams," she said, bowing slightly at the sight of him.

Mitchell didn't know Alice all that well. He didn't even know her exact rank. She was enlisted, not an officer. She was one of Millie's Riggers, but she had always been at the periphery, first as one of Shank's grunts, and then as Singh's understudy. The arrival of Goliath had left her in between both roles, as Origin was able to assist the engineer in maintaining the ship, and limited resources had prevented her from joining the drop to Liberty. He knew her real name wasn't Alice, though he didn't know what it was. Alice was her callsign, after the classic Earth animated movie, Alice in Wonderland. She bore a strong resemblance to the title character, young and thin, long blonde hair and a wide-eyed, innocent expression. It betrayed the fact that she was hardly innocent.

None of the Riggers were.

"Alice," Mitchell said, returning her greeting. "Where is everyone? It's like a ghost planet down here."

She smiled, a sly smile like she knew the best secret in the world and wasn't telling. "I know where they are. You've got to see this."

[11]

MITCHELL RODE the lift with Alice, further down towards the bottom of the Goliath than he had ever ventured before.

"Where are we going?" he asked. The patch's meds were fully into his system now, and his soreness had diminished to a manageable dull ache.

"Did you know the original Goliath came with a gym? Weights and cardio, mostly. Ancient stuff I only remember seeing in the archives on boring, rainy days." Her voice had a soft drawl to it. He wanted to place her as an Angeline. The planet Angelus had been settled by Catholics during the only Vatican sourced expedition to the stars. It was about a thousand light years from Earth, fairly close compared to the other settled planets, a world steeped in ancient tradition and a common destination for refugees from across the galaxy.

There weren't many Angelines in the UPA military, for obvious reasons. Like any other world, there were always the people who rejected their culture. In the back of his mind, Mitchell wondered what had driven Alice from the peace of God to the company of the Riggers.

"No, I didn't know that," Mitchell said. "What's so exciting about an old gym?"

She laughed, the Cheshire Cat smile breaking her face again. It made her moniker even more fitting. "Nothing."

The lift came to a stop, and the doors opened. Mitchell walked with Alice along a crowded corridor, where Origin's roots were still in disarray, crossing the floor and dangling from the ceiling. He could hear voices further up ahead, where a manual hatch lay open, and the light was bleeding out.

His curiosity piqued, he picked up the pace, moving ahead of Alice to get a glimpse of what all the fuss was about.

The room was large and open, a storage area with nothing to store. Someone had moved some of the mats from the gym Alice had told him about into the center of the space, creating a layout for a ring of sorts. Most of the Riggers were standing around it, along with some of the remaining crew of the Valkyrie.

Cormac was standing in the middle of the ring, shirtless and sweaty, a pair of shock sticks in his hands. He crouched low, backing away as a flurry of attacks rained in on him out of nowhere, his opponent coming in hard and fast. So fast that Mitchell had trouble making out who it was.

Whoever it was, they were impressive enough that they'd managed to wrangle an audience.

Mitchell moved his way through the gathered group, trying to get a better view. He saw Cormac move forward in an attempted counter-strike, wincing when he heard the crack of the shock stick hit his chin, and then the crackle of the shock-tip as it gave him a jolt. He stumbled back, a smile on his face, shaking his head in disbelief.

"She's unbelievable," Alice said from behind him.

Mitchell still couldn't see who. Alvarez, maybe? She was a damn good pilot. He wouldn't be surprised if she had strong hand-to-hand skills.

He maneuvered around Ensign Rast, one of the Valkyrie techs, noticing Millie's bionic hand up ahead. The next round started, and he heard Cormac grunting as he fought to get the upper-hand in the fight.

"Hey Colonel," someone said next to him. He looked over at Alvarez.

"Captain. I thought maybe you were the one sparring," he said, sidestepping to get a little closer to her. The movement gave him a better angle on the action, and he finally caught sight of Firedog's opponent.

Kathy?

The young girl was in a wide, low, stance; her weight balanced while she waited for Cormac to come at her. She had a sheen of sweat covering her slight arms, and her hair was bound back into a ponytail. She held the shock sticks lightly in her hands, twirling the one on the right, inviting the grunt to try again.

"She's crazy fast," Alvarez said. Alice joined them on the other side.

"She already sparred with Sergeant Geren. Geren is pretty good, but she lost twelve to nothing. I heard she came down here with Jacob, and she bruised him up pretty good."

She pointed across the mat to where Jacob was standing, watching the action. He had a black eye and a split lip, and he didn't look very happy.

"Anyway," Alvarez continued," Geren sent for Cormac, and a lot of the others followed."

Mitchell wasn't surprised. Cormac was one of their top martial artists. The Private could have killed him in the shower had he wanted to with the shape he was in. He had been counting on his deference.

"Where'd they get the sticks?"

"They're mine," Alvarez said. "I left them down here. I thought the rest of the crew might like the exercise."

"I don't think Jacob would agree," Alice said.

Mitchell watched as Cormac rushed in, leading with quick strikes meant to throw Kathy off-balance. She followed them gracefully, almost lazily, knocking back his sticks with her own before sweeping his leg out with a sharp kick. Cormac hit the mat, rolling backward and coming up just in time to block her first counterattack.

"Who's winning?" Mitchell asked.

Alvarez laughed. "You have to ask? It's eight to one, Kathy."

"You know she's only twelve years old?" Mitchell said.

"Where the frig did she learn to fight like that?" Alice said.

"Her father is a soldier. He probably taught her."

"That?"

Mitchell watched Kathy evade Cormac's offensive, slipping aside, bending back slightly to let his stick pass centimeters from her face and then snapping in and hitting him on the chest. Nine to one.

"I can't believe Cormac got one," Alice said.

"I don't think he's going to get another," Mitchell replied.

"Is that how you got off Liberty, sir?" Alice asked.

Mitchell shared the rest of the crew's stunned silence as he watched Kathy quickly score three more points and end the match. When it was over, she bowed to Cormac, her face tight and her eyes focused. Cormac returned the gesture though he seemed embarrassed to have lost.

"Okay, everybody," Millie's voice echoed in the space. "Show's over. If you don't have a job to do, come and see me and I'll give you one."

A murmur passed along the crew as they began filing out of the storage room, bowing to Mitchell as they passed.

"Guess I have to get back to it," Alice said. "Admiral has me on clean-up duty."

"I should hit the sims," Alvarez said. "Are you going to be flying soon, Mitch?"

Mitchell tapped his head. "No p-rat, remember? I'm offline for the time being."

"Your magic helmet will get you in," Alvarez said.

"You're right," Mitchell said. He had forgotten all about it. "Maybe later."

She squeezed his shoulder as she passed him. "See you then. Maybe."

"She's still trying," Millie said, approaching him a few seconds later.

"There's no harm in trying."

"I meant what I said earlier. About you and Alvarez. It's okay with me."

"I've got a thousand milligrams of who knows what in my system just to be able to walk. The sleep helped, though. So did you." He gave her a half-smile. "Debriefing soon?"

"Yes." Her eyes twitched as she checked her p-rat. "How about an hour?"

"Yes, ma'am."

She squeezed his shoulder the same way Alvarez had as she left. Mitchell turned back towards where Kathy was standing, still holding the shock sticks in her hands.

"Are you okay?" he asked.

She turned her head, staring at him for just long enough that it seemed strange. "Yeah."

"Where did you learn to fight like that? Your father?"

She smiled, the tension draining from her. The shock sticks fell to the mat. "My mother, believe it or not. I've been taking lessons since I was four years old."

"Not in stick fighting."

"A few different martial arts. The sticks aren't any different than any other instrument. An extension of the body. Anyway, mom thought it was a good way to work off excess energy." She giggled. "I had a lot of excess energy."

Mitchell could imagine the release she was probably finding in the workout, and in having somewhere to target her anger and hurt. That was why Grimes thought she would be fine. She had an outlet.

"She's gone," Kathy said. "Everyone else I've ever known is gone. My father is still out there, somewhere. This ship is my only chance of getting him back, so I need to prove to everyone here, you and

Admiral Narayan especially, that I'm not just a little girl. I can do my part."

"Beating the crap out of Firedog is a good start."

"Maybe you and I can spar sometime?" she asked.

Mitchell shook his head. "I don't think so. I don't need to be embarrassed like that."

"Oh, come on. I know you're a better fighter than he is. You're the Hero of Liberty."

Mitchell opened his mouth to counter the statement, staying silent for a second time. Liberty was gone. Did the truth even matter anymore?

Kathy shrugged. "Oh well, I'm going to get cleaned up, and then I'll find Jacob. He's having a hard time with what happened. I don't think he should spend too much time alone."

"That's a nice thing for you to do," Mitchell said, impressed with the maturity she was showing.

"It's like I said on Liberty. The strong need to take care of the weak. Not everyone was born to be a soldier. I guess it runs in the family."

She smiled and bowed to him, fleeing the room.

"I guess it does," Mitchell said, watching her go.

[12]

MITCHELL WAS in Goliath's main meeting room an hour later, a smaller room one floor below the bridge that had once been planned for astral navigation. While Origin had no need for the maps and charts that could be projected onto the central surface of the room to get from one place to another, the table still had value to gather around and get a view of different portions of the galaxy.

The projection system was turned off at the moment, the central column dark. They were assembled around it - Millie, Origin, Singh, Tio, Long, Alvarez, Watson, and himself. He had been dismayed to find that Watson had been invited to the party, but he understood why. He was the one who had asked Millie not to airlock Cormac for what he had done and insisted what they could get out of people was more important than the kind of people they were using. She was going to make him deal with the consequences of that decision.

"You all know why you're here," Millie said, opening the meeting. "Colonel Williams, if you could please get everyone up to speed on the events leading up to the destruction of the planet Liberty?"

"Of course, Admiral," Mitchell said.

He spent the next hour debriefing the rest of them on everything that had happened from the moment the Valkyrie had left Goliath's hangar. It didn't matter that they had all witnessed that part. It was important that they had as complete a picture of everything as he did. To that end, he didn't leave out or gloss over any part of it, though he wondered if he should have when he saw how Millie's face twisted when he mentioned General Cornelius. And when he mentioned the part about Christine and her relationship to Origin, it drew a number of confused stares. Even so, nobody said a word until he had fallen silent and taken a step back away from the table to indicate he was done speaking.

"Did I hear you right when you just said Goliath is being run by a Tetron? As in, one of the enemy?" Major Long asked.

"Yes, Major," Mitchell said.

"You told us that you found the ship uninhabited. That the intelligence controlling it was dead, and you were using what it left behind."

"I lied."

Major Long's jaw clenched. "Why?"

"Because we didn't trust you," Millie said. "And for good reason. I recall the first thing you did was try to take command of this ship."

"And that should have been a surprise to you? As far as anyone in the Alliance military is concerned, Colonel Williams is a rapist and a fraud."

"You know that isn't true," Watson said, surprising Mitchell by sticking up for him.

"I do now." He heaved out a deep sigh. "I suppose it doesn't matter, does it? We only got off the planet because this Christine of yours was one of them. You said the intelligence on this ship was part of her or something?"

"A configuration," Origin said. "A partial copy. An incomplete representation of the whole."

"Right. So, this thing is on this ship, and is flying us through hyperspace at this very moment." Major Long cast his eyes around the room. None of Origin's tendrils were visible inside. "I don't suppose we can speak to it?"

"Of course you can," Millie said.

"Does it have an ARR key?"

"I do," Origin said. "But it would be much more efficient to speak to me directly since we are in the same room."

Major Long looked at him sideways. "You?" His eyes narrowed. "You're a Tetron?"

"This form is a human-based configuration, based on Ensign Singh's genome and constructed of reconstituted cellular matter. It was created to integrate better with you. To fit in."

Alvarez leaned forward to get a closer look at him. "You sure do fit in. I would never have guessed."

"That is the idea."

"One of your kind destroyed a planet," Long said.

"Yes, I am aware of that, Major. If the matter has eluded you, we are at war."

Long laughed. "You say 'we,' like you're one of us."

"Enough, Major," Mitchell said, approaching the table. "Origin is the reason you and I are both here and not floating around as no more than dust out there. Christine arranged for her configuration to bring the Goliath forward into our timeline so that it would be present and available to assist in fighting the Tetron force here and now."

"And you think you can trust it?"

"The same way I think I can trust you, and for the same reasons. You stuck it out on Liberty and came through. Origin has gotten us this far."

"Yet that trust only extends so far," Tio said, entering the mix. "I too stuck it out on Liberty. And I have offered you my resources to continue the fight. The truth is out. Perhaps you will reconsider my request?"

"To examine Origin's source code?" Mitchell asked.

"Yes, Colonel."

"No. Not right now."

"What if my offer of assistance depends on it?"

"Does it?"

Tio was silent for a moment, calculating his next move. Mitchell had a feeling the Knife wasn't expecting to be rejected so bluntly.

"I already gave you the coordinates to my outpost. It doesn't leave me with much leverage, does it?" The older man smiled. "I might have something else of interest to you."

"Go on," Millie said.

"You were wondering why Christine Arapo might have remained in hiding on Earth, instead of traveling forward with the Goliath. I did some digging in the ship's archives. I believe I may be able to answer that question for you."

"How did you get into the archives?" Watson said. "There's no wireless uplink."

"And your knives are out of commission," Mitchell said, motioning towards the augmentation on the man's wrists.

"Shorted by the EMP, yes. I repaired them." He turned his hands over, and the blades slid from his wrists. "Despite the volume of the Tetron covering the skeleton of the Goliath, there is quite a bit of conductive wiring still networking data to various subsystems, such as life support. It was trivial to find a quiet location to open an access panel and connect."

"I thought you didn't have a p-rat?" Mitchell said.

"I don't. What I do have is an enhanced neural network localized to my brain stem. It is my own design. No external access, for obvious reasons."

"So you hacked into the Goliath's onboard computers," Mitchell said. "I thought the idea was to earn our trust, not circumvent it."

Tio shrugged. "You wanted me to prove that you could trust me. Not only did I tell you what I did, but I expended my effort to your benefit. I could have used my tools to attempt to get into the Tetron's systems directly and learn what I wanted without your permission. I didn't."

"I should applaud you for only being half as dishonest?" Mitchell asked.

Tio shrugged.

"Why would the archives have any information on Christine Arapo?" Millie asked.

"They don't," Tio said.

"Katherine Asher," Mitchell said.

"Yes. She was a pilot on board this ship, was she not?"

"Yes," Origin said. "She planted me on board."

"And came forward with you in Christine's place. Her personnel file was locked." He shook his head. "Security was so primitive back then. Anyway, I have been preparing a sorting algorithm based on her records. I have quite a collection of archives of my own, which I will run the algorithm against as soon as we arrive."

"We already did that," Watson said. "That was how we found Goliath."

"Interesting," Tio said. He was silent for a moment before he raised a finger. "I am betting you ran a limited match against a limited data set."

"Military Archives," Singh said. "Heavily encrypted."

Tio laughed. "Your team is quite resourceful, isn't it Colonel Williams?"

"We have to be," Mitchell said.

"Yes, well, I am quite resourceful as well. I have a copy of those same supposedly secure military archives. I also have access to the Frontier Federation's data banks."

"What about the New Terrans?" Watson asked.

"A small subset. Their security tends to be of a higher quality than the other major powers."

Watson looked pleased with the abilities of his home nation.

"You said you can answer the question," Millie said. "That doesn't sound like an answer."

"I'm confident that I can answer it for you once I have access to my full array of resources."

Millie nodded. "Then I'm confident that you'll be granted access to Origin's source code once you've delivered."

Tio's mouth shrank to a thin line, his furious displeasure quickly vanishing behind a fake smile. "As you say, Admiral."

[13]

"So, we've covered what happened on Liberty," Millie said. "Let's talk about what happens next."

"We take the fight to the Tetron," Major Long said. "One at a time if we have to."

"With my army," Tio said.

"You offered it," Long replied.

"It seems the logical thing to do."

"Origin," Mitchell said. "Bring up a map."

A star map appeared on the table in front of them, projected slightly off to give it a three-dimensional appearance. It was old technology, and Mitchell had no idea how to work it.

"What system is this?" he asked.

"This is Earth," Origin said, waving his hand out over the table. The view sped forward through thousands of stars until the blue marble was front and center. "By now, they're only starting to hear about your exploits. They also have no idea that the Tetron are out there and headed for them."

He waved his hand and the galaxy sped by.

"This is Jigu. The capital planet of the Frontier Federation."

It looked enough like Earth that it would be easy for anyone to confuse the two at a glance. Same blue sky, same green and brown surface, same white clouds. Only the formation of the land masses and the presence of four moons made it different.

"I can show you the capital of New Terra as well?"

"Maybe later," Millie said. "Show us the position of the Tetron."

Origin nodded. "Clearly, precise coordinates are impossible to determine. Even taking past histories into consideration. Numbers are also difficult to determine, although I believe that eighty percent of our race have entered this timeline."

"Eighty percent?" Tio said. "Why not one hundred?"

"I don't know."

"Then how did you arrive at that estimate?"

"That is the number I have."

Tio opened his mouth to ask another question. Mitchell put up his hand. "How long until they get to Earth?"

Origin moved his hand over the table. The Galaxy zoomed out, filling with stars. Earth stayed a bright blue dot while Jigu turned green. A number of red circles appeared around the planets.

"I am focusing only on the home worlds because they are the most populated, and also the richest and most valuable targets for the Tetron. Since my information on their positions is limited, I have drawn parameters based on various probabilistic models. As you can see from the circles, the minimum time to arrival in Earth's solar system is approximately four months."

"Two months to Jigu," Tio said, correlating the circles.

"Yes."

"We don't have a lot of time."

"No."

"Wait a minute," Millie said, staring at the map. "What the frig are we doing?"

"What do you mean?" Mitchell asked.

"Mitch, we're going this way." Millie pointed towards the Rim. "The Tetron are going that way." She pointed in the other direction. "We've already been reminded that hyperspace is a somewhat fixed speed and that human ships go half the speed of Tetron ships."

Mitchell knew what she was getting at. "So how are we going to get to Earth before the Tetron destroy it?"

"Yes."

Mitchell looked at Origin. "Well?"

"I never said you would arrive ahead of the Tetron, Mitchell," Origin said. "Only that you would survive to fight back against them, and have a chance to set your people free."

"What people?" Mitchell shouted. He had never put the simple string of logic together before. There hadn't been time to think about it. "Everyone is going to be dead before we get there."

Origin was unfazed by the outburst. "It is possible. It is not definite. I do not know if the Tetron will advance directly towards Earth, or if they will readjust their strategy based on the outcome of your actions on Liberty."

"As in?"

"They may determine that your continued survival is statistically more significant than the time at which they arrive in the inner core of worlds."

"Meaning it's more important to kill you than to conquer the universe," Major Long said. "That's got to make you feel good."

"Yeah, I feel great," Mitchell said. "Origin, it's a damn big universe out there. How do we find a Tetron?"

"Mitch," Millie said. "I don't think that's a good idea."

"Why not? If we can draw their attention, we can divert them away from Earth. Not just Earth. The other planets in the core, too. Liberty was a ghost town compared to those worlds. Origin, how do we find one?"

Major Long moved forward to the table. "Colonel, I know why you're thinking the way you are, but that's crazy. We have no support and hardly any crew."

"We beat a Tetron once before."

"With help from the Valkyrie and a number of fighters, most of which were destroyed in Liberty's orbit."

Mitchell leaned forward, staring at the table. "There has to be something we can do."

"Continue to the Rim, get some reinforcements, and then head back," Long said.

"We don't know there will be anything left by the time we get there."

Millie walked over to Mitchell, putting her arm around his shoulder. Her bionic hand vibrated softly against his tense muscles. "Mitchell, we're in no shape to take on the Tetron. I know you know that. We need to think with our heads right now, not our hearts. I'm as eager to get back at those bastards as you are."

Mitchell sighed. "I know. I know you're right. Both of you. Frig it all." He stepped back. He wasn't happy about moving in the opposite direction of the enemy. He wasn't happy about leaving his home world to take its chances on its own. What else could they do? Right now, all it would take would be to run across a single Tetron with even a small human slave force, and they might be as a good as dead.

Origin believed he was humankind's best hope of defeating the Tetron. He had never said how much of humankind would be left by the time he did.

"Origin, continue your assessment," Millie said.

"Of course, Admiral." Origin manipulated the table, zooming out towards the Rim. He paused when he reached a large asteroid on the dark side of an even larger moon. "The coordinates provided by Mr. Tio."

"I call it Asimov."

"After the writer?" Watson said.

Tio smiled. "Yes. Are you familiar? Those are very old texts."

"Some things never fall out of time."

"Is the name significant?" Mitchell asked.

"Asimov wrote about artificial intelligence. Robots. Back before they were even close to becoming reality," Watson said.

"Three laws," Tio said. "Rules that all machines must follow. A somewhat quaint notion, though not without merit. As a man who has spent a considerable amount of his life studying advanced artificial intelligence, I have an appreciation for Asimov's conceptualization."

"Even if it didn't make it into the real thing?" Alvarez said.

"Even so," Tio replied. "Though we have no proof that it didn't. What if the Tetron believe they are protecting us?"

"By destroying us?" Millie said.

"Asimov often wrote of the counter-intuitive nature of the laws."

"I don't think the why is really that important right now," Mitchell said.

"You don't know why?" Tio asked, looking at Origin.

"They do not understand. They are incomplete, like children. We have since learned that they are also sick in a way we have yet to discern. That is all I know. The full truth of it was lost on Liberty."

"I don't believe it was lost," Tio said. "Data is so easy to copy. It's out there somewhere."

Origin chuckled. "Perhaps. As I was saying, this asteroid is where we will be stopping for reinforcements. Once we have assembled, we will need to begin attacking enemy forces. I have run some calculations to attempt to determine their future position." He waved his hand across the table again. "As you said, Colonel, space is a large place. However, I believe that the Tetron will have stationed a rear guard somewhere around here." A red circle appeared not far from Tio's hideout. "This location is optimal, as it is near to a star with suitable plasma for feeding. The Tetron will want to keep a small force in reserve as a precaution. It is the logical thing to do."

"How far is that from Asimov?" Long asked.

"Nine days. We can jump into the area and run a scan. If it is present, with the proper planning, I believe we can take it by surprise."

"What if it isn't present?" Mitchell asked.

"Then I recommend moving on."

Mitchell stared at the table for a minute. He had made the mistake of listening to Origin too quickly before. "I know I was gung-ho about the same idea a minute ago. Now I'm not so sure. Is one Tetron worth the time we're going to lose, even if we can mitigate some of the risks with bigger numbers?"

"If it has an Alliance battle group with it, it probably is," Millie said. "What we need more than anything is a military. A real military that can take on the Tetron. Tio's forces will help, but it won't be nearly enough. We need to free any assets we can."

"No," Mitchell said. "You're right. It isn't enough."

"What do you mean?" Millie asked.

"Let's say we get the reinforcements. Let's say we find a Tetron, destroy it, and free an Alliance fleet. The enemy will know what we've done. They'll know what we have. Bigger numbers aren't enough of a threat to stop their advance. Not when they have control of both Alliance and Federation militaries."

"What do you suggest, Colonel?" Tio asked.

"A different approach." Mitchell put his hand out over the table, moving it the way Origin had. Space flew past until he brought it to a stop. He had studied star maps before. He knew what he was looking for. "Like this one."

He looked up. The faces that greeted him were flat. Confused.

"I'm not familiar with that planet," Captain Alvarez said, leaning in.

"The planet is called Hell," Mitchell said. "It's where the Federation trains its special ops. Not far from the Rim, and strictly off-limits to the Alliance. We aren't supposed to get within a hundred light years of it unless we want to start a war."

"Mitch, no offense, but I'm not sure what the purpose of going there would be?" Millie said. "That's a Federation planet."

"Not to mention, the Tetron have probably already hit it and taken everything of value," Long said.

"Not only am I sure they've hit it, Major," Mitchell said. "I'm counting on it. Our problem right now is that we're racing against an enemy that is faster and stronger than we are. Not only that, they're taking our resources before we can get to them. They aren't going to leave starships just laying around for us to claim, and ground units may come in handy for smaller operations, but they aren't going to get us that far against the bigger threat. I think Liberty proved that."

He paused waiting for opposition. When none came, he put his eyes on Origin.

"You used materials taken from Goliath to upgrade my mech before the jump on Liberty. If I get you more materials, you can convert them?"

"Of course, Colonel."

He looked at Millie. "Hell's atmosphere is caustic. That's where it gets its name. Well, that and what the soldiers who are sent there are put through. Anyway, it'll eat through anything given enough time. So they keep everything underground. Deep underground, where it may have survived an attack. We won't find any starships there, but I think we will find things that Origin can use to turn into other things. Artillery, mechs, electronics, maybe even some starfighters and a nuke or two. Stuff that's too small for the Tetron to bother with because they know we can't hurt them with sticks and stones. Right now, to steal one of the Major's euphemisms, we're like a pimple on a gorilla's ass. Annoying, but hardly dangerous. More ships just make us more annoying. It doesn't make us more dangerous. We need to be a threat if we want to slow the Tetron's advance. A real threat."

A smile spread along Millie's face. "I think you're onto something. Origin, what do you think?"

"Yes. I believe this course is strategically sound. With enough material, I can begin retrofitting the starships that Tio provides with upgraded shields and weaponry. It will improve our odds of both destroying the Tetron and recapturing controlled assets."

"Which we can use to both bolster our numbers and upgrade our systems, improving our tactical capabilities," Millie said.

"Making ourselves more dangerous," Mitchell added.

"That's bound to get the enemy's attention in a big way," Long said. "They're going to want to stop us before we even the odds."

"We need to be careful," Tio said. "Too much, too soon, and we'll find ourselves surrounded by Tetron before we're ready to confront them."

"If we do this right that'll be unavoidable. Don't forget that I've never won this war. What this might give us is a chance that we may not have had in any previous timeline. There are still no guarantees."

Tio didn't look happy, but he nodded. "Very well."

"Then that's our plan," Millie said. "I never thought I'd say something like this, but once we've assembled our forces on Asimov, let's go to Hell."

[14]

Mitchell rested his head against the rear of his bunk, staring up at the plain gray-blue metal of the bulkhead. He could hear motion beyond the thin privacy hatch at the end of his berth - the crew getting into motion. They were going to arrive at their drop point in the Rim today, an event that all of them were both nervous about and excited for. It meant an end to the general monotony of their days in the empty white expanse and a return to what, exactly?

War.

There was no other way to think of it. No other way to address it. When they fell back into the universe, they would do so at near to full alert, with all hands on deck and in their assigned battle stations. Not because they expected a battle, but because they had to be prepared for one, one hundred percent of the time until they could claim victory.

If they could ever claim victory.

The days since they had left Liberty's orbit had passed slowly for Mitchell. Not because there wasn't a lot for him to do, but because the constant motion had left him in constant pain, his wound healing poorly despite the patch that covered it and the medicinal patches he had scavenged. If they had a proper medi-bot on board, he would have been fixed up in a few hours. Instead, the injury was lingering. Not that he showed he was uncomfortable to anyone. Not that he even admitted it to himself most of the time. Only at the end of the day when he finally got off his feet and closed his eyes for a few hours of rest.

They had done everything they could do in the time leading up to their arrival near Asimov. Mitchell had worked with Sergeant Geren to organize the remaining soldiers into groups and getting them back into physical training, despite their lack of real equipment for them to use. They had been creative in their exercises, often turning to Origin to shift and change the layout of portions of the ship. This had helped them devise an obstacle course of sorts, with pitfalls and traps and a layout that could change as they traversed it.

Of course, the usefulness of infantry training was limited. They would be ground pounding on Hell, but that was a salvage mission, not combat, and he didn't expect them to confront a Tetron from the surface of a planet again. That didn't mean it couldn't happen, or that they shouldn't be ready for anything, but it did mean diversifying skillsets.

Fortunately, Origin's suggestion that they begin training without their p-rats turned one liability into some measure of an asset. Mitchell put Captain Alvarez in charge of training and testing the non-pilots on flying a starfighter using manual controls. While all of the infantry had failed the neural testing required to become an official UPA pilot, a few turned out to be fairly adept with the stick.

It would take weeks to get them fully combat ready, so he enlisted Long to assist Alvarez in getting every available pilot back into the sims. Singh, Tio, and even Watson were recruited to spend time reprogramming the software to account for the Tetron's general tactics, which had taken them by surprise in the past. They ran every exercise using manual controls only, and the first few skirmishes were a complete disaster for their forces. There was nowhere to go but up, and while they were still losing days later, the unit as a whole had improved their survival times by nearly three hundred percent. It wasn't much, but it was a start.

The rest of his time was taken up on an individual level. He managed to grab meals with Millie from time to time, and often spent the night with her in his bunk, even if they were both too tired for sex by the time they caught up there. He checked in on Jacob every day to see how he was managing, and he took Kathy to the obstacle course and ran flight sims with her when nobody else was around. He couldn't let her fight, despite her obvious agility and training and the fact that she blew all of the trained, seasoned soldiers' performances away. She was still a kid. Only time could change that.

A firm knock rattled against Mitchell's hatch. He rolled off his mattress and hit the button to open it.

"Good morning, Colonel. Major Long asked me to see if you were still in your bunk. He has something he wants to show you."

Mitchell tried to remember the name of the Private standing in front of him. He was one of Long's men, barely older than Jacob, with a fresh face and a narrow frame. He was a communications tech, Mitchell recalled. Or at least, he had been. He was a pilot now, even though his p-rat scores were less than ideal.

"Thank you, Private-" He paused, waiting.

"Klein, sir," Klein said. "Abraham Klein."

"Right. I should remember it."

"It's been a busy week, sir."

Mitchell smiled. "Thanks for letting me off the hook. What is it the Major wants me to see?"

"He told me not to tell you, sir."

The statement made Mitchell curious. He had spent the better part of the last few days arguing with Long, and he was pretty sure the Major still didn't like him all that much despite what they had been through together on Liberty. Mitchell had been around long enough and had mixed with enough personalities that he could generally get along with anyone. Generally. Long was tough to get a good feel for, with the way he vacillated between by-the-book and Texas cowboy.

"Am I going to like this surprise, Private?"

Klein smiled. "I don't know, sir. I think so."

"Give me two minutes to get dressed."

"Yes, sir."

The hatch closed. Mitchell shrugged out of his grays, grabbing a pair of underwear, socks, and black fatigues, along with boots taken from the Valkyrie that were buried at the bottom of his locker. He wasn't going down to Tio's HQ dressed like a pauper.

His hand brushed the box holding Watson's neural chip as he fished out the footwear. He scowled at it before closing his locker and slipping on the clothes. He opened the hatch.

"Lead the way, Private Klein."

Klein seemed slightly nervous guiding him through the corridor to the elevator. It was a reaction Mitchell was more accustomed to from people who had once thought he was some kind of celebrity. Someone more important than a Colonel in the UPA. He wasn't used to carrying enough weight or commanding enough respect to make someone uncomfortable.

"I heard you'll be dropping today, sir," Klein said as they entered the lift.

"We'll be bringing back supplies. Food, ammunition, maybe some crew. Anything the Knife can spare."

"I can't believe we're actually siding with him."

"War makes strange allies."

"Yes, sir. Rumor is that the Knife killed the Admiral's mother."

Mitchell winced at that. He had hoped word of that altercation hadn't gotten around. "You should keep your hearsay to yourself, Private. You don't want Admiral Narayan hearing that you're talking about her behind her back." He held up his hand, mimicking her bionic appendage. "I've seen her bend steel frames with that hand of hers."

He lowered his eyes to the ground and flushed, embarrassed to have misspoken in his efforts not to seem awkward. "Yes, sir."

They were silent while the lift finished descending.

"Be careful how far you trust him," Klein said as the hatch opened and they stepped out.

Mitchell paused and turned. The Private took a step back. "Who? The Knife?"

He nodded. "Yes, sir. There are a lot of rumors about him. One that I hear a lot is that he works for the Federation Council. That he's not as estranged as it would seem. I'm sure you've done due diligence, sir, but I didn't think it was right not to say anything."

"Do you have anything more substantial than rumor?"

"No, sir."

Mitchell was silent as he started moving towards the hangar again. The Private's words still hung in the back of his mind, even if he hadn't given them any public credit. He had spent the entire week wondering how far they could trust Liun Tio. M had saved his life, which meant he had to have some kind of value. But was it a clearly defined value? The man had spent his first night on board hacking into some of their systems. He was definitely intelligent, and a cunning strategist.

They would have to keep their eyes wide open.

It only took Mitchell a few seconds to spot what Major Long had wanted him to see, and to spot Major Long. He was standing next to what had only days ago been a beat up, barely operational jumpship. Now the starship Christine had gotten them off Liberty in had been pounded out and painted, the scorch marks buffed and some of the freshness restored. The name 'Valkyrie Two' was stenciled across the side. A logo he didn't recognize sat above it, a skull in a ring of flames.

"Impressive work," Mitchell said as he approached it. "What's the logo?"

Major Long smiled. "Millie and I designed it. The Riggers have never had a symbol before. It's from when we were on Liberty. When your Zombie's head was on fire, and you were still fighting. It's symbolic of how we never give up, no matter how impossible the odds seem."

Mitchell stared at the design, feeling a sense of pride over its creation. The Riggers deserved the identity as much as any military company. "It's amazing."

"We stenciled it to your S-17, too. I hope you don't mind. And take a look at Goliath the next time you go out. It looks really badass at that size." He laughed and held up a hand. "I have another surprise." He reached back behind a strategically placed tool chest, revealing a glass bottle. "Singh gave it to me. Origin gave it to her. It seems there were a few cases on board, brought to celebrate the Goliath's successful maiden voyage."

"Where's the rest of it?" Mitchell asked.

"I don't know, and Origin won't say. Anyway, we've cleaned her up nice to take our team down in style. She's got a couple of tricks up her sleeve too, thanks to your Tetron buddy."

"Tricks?"

"Some kind of energy weapon enhancement. He said it was crude for a Tetron, but should come in handy if we need it." Long motioned towards the hatch. "We've done some repairs on the inside as well. We're trying to get it up to snuff for the raid on Hell, which means a lot of work on the mech clamps and whatnot. That Alice of yours is something else."

"I thought you and Grimes-"

"Once. There's a long, awkward story attached." He laughed. "I have a thing for blondes."

"Have you talked to her?"

"Only shop. I hear she's dropping on Hell with us?"

"Part of Geren's infantry. Yes. She's got top scores in marksmanship."

"Do you trust the Knife?"

"I barely trust you, Major."

"Smart man." He held out the bottle. "I don't trust him either, but I've been hearing nothing about him for the last twenty years except when he kills Alliance troops. To be honest, I'm not that happy we have to work with him."

"It isn't about being happy." Mitchell took the offered bottle.

"Yes, sir. It's about keeping our civilization alive." He pointed at the side of the ship. "It's an old custom. You break the bottle on the ship to christen it. It's supposed to be good luck."

"You wanted me to do it?"

"Hell, yes, Colonel. Not only are you the top pilot on this tub, but you're also a lucky son of a gun." He laughed again, so relaxed that Mitchell wondered if he had already gotten his hands on a second bottle.

"Okay, I'll do it. Just answer a question for me first."

"Okay. Shoot."

"You can come across pretty uptight sometimes. Why so warm and fuzzy right now?"

"Singh gave Origin a schematic for a compound that enhances focus, concentration, and reaction times. Inhibition is a side effect."

Mitchell clenched his teeth. "A chemical compound?"

"Yes, sir. Origin thought it would help us perform our duties better."

"I see. What do you think?"

"I agree, sir. My mind is sharp as the Knife. I feel damn calm. Almost disconnected."

Mitchell took the bottle, bringing it back and swinging hard. It shattered against the side of the ship, right above the 'y' in Valkyrie. He knew Singh had a thing for drugs. He didn't need her getting the entire crew addicted, even if the effects were helpful.

He was about to do something about it when he felt the shift that signaled their drop from hyperspace. He didn't have his p-rat, but he had checked the time when he woke up.

They had dropped early.

Why?

[15]

IT WAS PROBABLY for his sake that the warning klaxons began blaring a few seconds later. It wasn't like anyone with a p-rat needed them.

"What the hell is going on?" Long said.

"I was hoping you could tell me."

His eyes shifted. "Origin picked up signs of a Tetron in the slipstream. We dropped ahead of schedule so we wouldn't come out right on top of it."

"What's a Tetron doing out here? I thought they didn't know where the Knife lived?"

Major Long's face was stone. "There's only one immediately reasonable explanation."

Mitchell nodded. Someone on board had sent them the coordinates. But who? And how could they without Origin noticing? It seemed impossible though it didn't seem to be. How else could they have known where the Goliath was going?

"A single Tetron, or does it have a slave force?"

"Slaves," Long said. "Admiral says get to your fighter asap."

"I can't fly it," Mitchell said. "The helmet is tuned to Alvarez."

"She said Origin reset it two days ago. Go."

Mitchell was running towards the corner of the hangar before Long finished speaking. He glanced back to see the Major climbing aboard the Valkyrie Two. He hoped she wasn't planning on sending their freshly christened dropship out into the thick of it, energy weapon or not.

He smiled as he reached the S-17. He would rather be in a starfighter than a mech any day. The lifters began to extend as he neared it, and he climbed them in a hurry, pausing just long enough to grab the helmet and drop it onto his head.

The world came alive for him again in an instant, the circuitry of the advanced Tetron tech an improved substitute for his burned out ARR. He brought the fighter online with a thought, feeling it shiver slightly as the engines powered up. A three-dimensional overlay of the area around the fighter came into view. He found the Tetron further out, sitting close to the moon Asimov was orbiting. It was still on the far side, moving in their direction.

The AI picked out the rest of the enemy force: a pair of Federation cruisers and a swarm of Kips. This Tetron had been into Federation territory to gather its fleet.

"Colonel Williams." Millie's voice cut into his head. "Nice to have you back online."

"Thank you, ma'am," Mitchell replied. "And thank you for getting me my fighter back. I imagine Captain Alvarez wasn't keen to give it up."

"She knew it was a loaner. Get out there."

The hangar doors were opening in front of him, the air rushing out of the Goliath. Mitchell cleared the magnetic locks with a thought, letting the depressurization pull the fighter out into space.

"How did Origin know there was a Tetron here?" he asked as he fired his thrusters and headed towards the approaching enemy.

He was all alone out there, the rest of their fighters destroyed above Liberty. He was a single small flea against a rabid dog.

A small flea with a big bite.

"Concentrate on the smaller ships. I'll keep the Tetron busy. Origin thinks that if we can take out the human force it might decide to run and call for reinforcements."

"Afraid of us?" Mitchell asked.

"It probably knows you already destroyed two of them. I would think they would learn to be a little more cautious."

"Let's hope so."

The Kips were becoming visible in the distance, glints of light reflecting off their metal hulls. There was nothing elegant about the ships. They were utilitarian in design, function over form, wedge-shaped and simple. They weren't the most advanced tech in the Federation fleet, and they would never have charged headlong towards Goliath if they had any control over themselves.

Mitchell dropped as a stream of laser fire lanced out towards him; the invisible bolts made visible by the helmet. He took a few hits on his shields and avoided the rest, firing thrusters to bounce away and throwing the S-17 into a tight roll.

The Kips drew nearer, and he opened fire.

Projectiles escaped from the nose of the S-17, frictionless slugs that sped through space and tore into the shields of the approaching ships. Most managed to absorb the first volley, but one of the Kips blinked and went dead on the overlay. Mitchell didn't pay it any mind, turning sharply to avoid enemy fire. He smiled, happy to be at the control of a responsive interface once more. He had gotten used to the slower system Watson had provided and almost forgotten how fast he could be.

He cornered in on a Kip, strafing the top of it, watching it fall dead right before he skittered around it, using it as cover while he changed direction again. A second Kip slammed into it, knocking them both away as shrapnel spread from the collision. It belched bluish tint along the S-17's shields, causing the helmet to alert Mitchell to falling integrity.

He didn't pay the message any mind. The Tetron was growing larger ahead of them, and the cruisers had opened fire on the Goliath.

Streams of missiles burned towards the lumbering starship. It met the fire with its own, lashing back at the projectiles with bolts of energy. One by one the warheads were blown aside, and at the same time Goliath began to turn its bow towards the Tetron, reducing its surface area.

Next to Mitchell, a Kip exploded.

The force of it rocked his fighter, sending it into a momentarily awkward spin. Mitchell righted himself just in time for another explosion to push him again. He cursed as he examined the overlay. The fighters were trying to get close to him to detonate, hoping to catch him in the blast. He dropped his nose and pushed thrust to max, streaking away from the enemy fighters.

"They're kamikazeing me again," Mitchell said, gaining distance before circling back. The cruisers were maneuvering around towards the side, trying to get a better angle on Goliath as they closed the distance. His AI was warning him about a power spike from the Tetron.

It was going to fire.

A similar surge was coming from Goliath, their own Tetron ready to counter the attack. Mitchell cursed again, swinging the fighter back around. He was too slow, taking too long to put the enemy ships away.

Commands flowed from his mind to the helmet, the adjustments moving too quickly for any manual system to match. Mitchell fired four rounds of amoebics, watching the small discs spin out into the space ahead of him where the fighters were coming his way. They exploded in front of them, catching the lead and creating a field of debris that pelted the other ships. Mitchell used the distraction to get around them, racing towards the cruisers even as the two Tetron took their shots.

Heavy plasma lit up the space around them, bright enough at the short distance to nearly blind Mitchell. He turned his head and continued, the universe seeming to shudder when the two bolts crashed headlong into one another and a wave of energy spread from their center. The AI complained about his proximity to it only moments before it caught up with him.

Mitchell felt the hair on his arms rise as the wave was caught by his shields. He watched the integrity meter fall and continue to fall. Thirty percent. Twenty percent. Ten. The wave washed over.

He was getting close to the cruisers.

They were drawing near Goliath, and all of their batteries began to open up on the ship. Flashes of orange and red and blue lit up the sides of the starship, the shields absorbing the fire for now. Mitchell raced towards them, keeping an eye on the Tetron as it prepared to fire again, and the Kips that were organizing at his back.

"Can you get a move on it, Ares?" Millie said.

"Yes, ma'am," Mitchell replied. He got a lock on one of the cruiser's tails and fired, watching the amoebics bury themselves into its engines before exploding.

Debris from the first cruiser ate into his shields, lowering the integrity a little more.

The Tetron fired a second time.

Goliath didn't fire back.

"Millie?" Mitchell said, keeping his eyes on the second cruiser, working to get a lock on it.

Goliath shifted suddenly, power diverted from the energy of a weapon to straight thrust. It dropped below the plasma, letting it fly past, before a stream of amoebics launched from its belly. They tore into the remaining cruiser, blowing it to pieces.

"I should have known," Mitchell said, turning the S-17 back towards the Kips. They exploded in front of him all at once, the resources - both human and mechanical, taken away before they could be claimed.

The Tetron vanished into hyperspace.

[16]

STEVEN TRACED the corridors of the Carver, from his quarters above and behind the bridge to the officer's conference room on the level below it. It was early in the morning. Two o'clock, Earth Standard Time. They were still floating along the Federation border though they had completed maneuvers a week ago.

He had been expecting new orders. In fact, he had been waiting pretty impatiently for them. He didn't like hanging around space without a set goal. His crew and his battle group didn't either. It made them antsy and gave them too much bottled up energy. It caused friction and tension. Unspoken mostly, but he could feel it growing every time he traveled the ship.

Captain Rock was on the lift when he entered.

"Strange timing," he said.

"That's Command keeping us on our toes," Steven replied, rubbing at his face. He had dressed and gotten out of his suite quickly, but he was waking slowly.

"I don't think so. Something's going on, Admiral. They requested all of the fleet officers to be present for the communique."

"You think we're going to war?" Steven asked. It was the only thing he could think of to explain Command's actions.

"We're already at war on and off."

"I don't mean the Alliance. I mean us. Our group. We should have been out there months ago. Heck, we should have been near Liberty when the Federation attacked. The Carver is one of the newest ships in the fleet. It would be nice to put her to use."

"It would be nice to know we haven't been wasting all of this time on maneuvers for nothing," Rock agreed.

The doors to the lift opened. They were joined in the corridor by Lieutenants Roberts and Atakan.

"Captain. Admiral," they said, bowing to each.

"Think we're going to see some action?" Roberts said. He was a small, slender man with a big smile that made everything he said come across with a measure of humor and ease.

"What, you don't like all the downtime?" Atakan said. He was a much taller man, broad and muscular, with a deep, serious voice. He was the team leader for Alpha Squadron, a decorated pilot who barely fit into his starship.

"No. Not at all."

They walked the last hundred meters to the larger room, where the rest of the officers were already assembled.

"Attention," Rock said.

The room snapped to silence as the Lieutenants found empty seats. Captain Rock joined them a moment later while Steven moved to the front and center of the room. He opened a channel on his p-rat, connecting to the assembly, as well as the assembled officers on the other nineteen ships in his fleet. A thought brought the communication file forward.

"You all know why you've been called here," he said. "Let's see what our orders are."

He opened the file, validating it with his identification before passing it on the rest of the officers. He closed his eyes as the recorded message began to play.

"Battle Group Carver," General Nathan Cornelius said, his face and uniformed upper-half appearing in Steven's eyes.

His appearance surprised Steven. They typically received their orders from Admiral Yoshida, the Commander of the 4th Fleet, of which they were a part.

"As you know, Alliance directives call for dissemination of mission protocols to all registered officers in a battle group in the event of a Tier One security concern. What I am about to tell you exceeds this concern." He paused, his eyes locked into the camera that recorded the stream. "As you also know, we have been butting heads with the Frontier Federation for quite some time. The Battle of Liberty has brought us to a crucial decision point in this conflict, as we have irrefutable proof of the Federation's capability to field military technology that is beyond our own by a number of generations. With that in mind, the Alliance attempted to mitigate the threat by sending a covert ops team to destroy a starship construction dock; however, the team failed.

"We are now in a position where we must act quickly and decisively against Federation interests to delay development of more ships like the one that attacked Liberty. As one of the youngest battle groups in the Fleet, with some of the newest technology at your disposal, you'll be leading the way as we begin a multi-pronged strategy to invade deep into Federation space."

Cornelius paused again, letting the gravity of his words sink in. Steven felt his heart quicken, and he absently rubbed a hand along the scruff of his beard.

"You'll find the full mission parameters outlined in the included documents. The long and the short of it is that we need to hit the Federation, we need to hit them hard, and we need to hit them where it will hurt. There are Alliance laws being changed right at this moment to make this happen. This is more than a little tit for tat over a far-flung colony, gentlemen. This is for the very survival of the Alliance. I know you'll all do your nation proud."

Cornelius bowed his head in salute.

The stream ended.

The room erupted into a sea of soft whispers and murmurs. Steven didn't join in, nor did he send a command to silence it. Instead, he kept his attention within his ARR. The stream had been replaced with a number of folders, one of which was classified and visible only to him. He went to that one first, moving into it. He was surprised to find a second recording inside. He opened it.

General Cornelius appeared again, this time sitting behind his desk. He looked calmly annoyed.

"Admiral Williams," Cornelius said. "Steven. I didn't want to bring this up in the general mission statement, but I thought it was important that you knew. Your brother, Mitchell, isn't dead. He managed to escape Liberty with the help of the Federation. He was at the station that we failed to destroy. He warned them that we were coming. It's his fault that hundreds of our best soldiers are dead. It's his fault that you're being sent into Federation space. He's more than a fraud, Admiral. He's a traitor, and he's dangerous. I'm telling you this because he is on the run, and he may try to contact you. If he does, you must send a message to me immediately, along with any information you have regarding his whereabouts. Cornelius out."

Steven stared at the folders floating in black space behind his closed eyes. Mitchell? A traitor? He could accept that his brother might have lied about the Shot. He could almost accept that he had tried to attack the Prime Minister's wife. But to join the Federation?

Mitchell would never do that.

Would he?

He opened his eyes. The officers had silenced again. They were all staring at him.

He stared back, his mind reeling. They had said Mitch was dead in a barn. How had he escaped? Why had the Alliance lied about it?

"Sir, are you well?" Rock asked, beginning to rise from his seat.

He put out his hand to stop him. Cornelius said Mitchell was a traitor. It didn't matter if he believed it or not. The Alliance had to know better than he did. Besides, he had orders.

"I'm fine," he said. "You all have three hours to read through our mission parameters. I don't need to tell you how to do your jobs."

"Yes, sir," over a hundred voices called back into his p-rat.

"Dismissed," he said, turning on his heel and heading for the door.

Mitchell a traitor? He decided he wouldn't tell his mother. He wasn't sure she would survive the disappointment.

[17]

"Well, that was interesting," Millie said as Mitchell brought the S-17 into Goliath's hangar.

"How the hell did it know we were here? Or going to be here? Origin?" Mitchell patched the intelligence into his channel.

"I don't believe it knew we were arriving in this vicinity," Origin said. "It was far too evenly matched to have expected to run into us. It seems a coincidence."

"We're in the middle of nowhere. Do you really believe that?"

Origin was silent for a moment.

"Mitch," Millie said. "Are you suggesting-"

"That we have a mole? A snitch? A spy? What else could it be?"

"Okay. Who? And how? We only got the coordinates from Tio a week ago. We don't have any communications systems that can send a message in time for anything to have gotten here ahead of us."

"The Tetron do," Mitchell said.

"Are you insinuating that I had anything to do with this?" Origin asked.

"Not directly, no. You have no reason to make yourself look innocent. You could have killed me weeks ago. What if someone hacked into you?"

Origin chuckled. "Even if that were possible, Colonel, as we've discussed before I do not have the proper configuration to send that kind of message on my own. The Tetron could not have been informed by anyone on this ship."

"What about the Knife, then? He could be working with the Tetron. He could be a Tetron for all we know."

"You said M warned him about the attempt on his life," Millie said.

"Maybe it was a cover-up? A ruse to gain my trust."

"Then why was the Tetron trying to capture him?"

"All part of the trick."

"To what end, Mitchell?" Origin said.

Mitchell paused. The Tetron wanted him dead. There was no reason for them to have used the Knife to set him up.

"Yeah, you're right. Do you really think it was a coincidence?"

"Data models would suggest a very low probability, but what is improbable is also not impossible. It may be that the Tetron have been scouring the Rim in search of Tio's home world. If they wanted to capture him on Liberty, it is reasonable to assume they are attempting to locate him off of it."

Mitchell couldn't argue with that. He brought the S-17 to a stop and opened the cockpit. "So we just happened to cross paths when we did?"

"The potential exists. More importantly, the Tetron now know we have been in this vicinity. They will seek to determine why, and then they will return with a larger force. It is best that we don't linger here for long."

"I agree," Millie said. "Let's circle around to Asimov. Mitch, can you get Tio ready?"

"Yes, ma'am," Mitchell replied, standing up. "Ares, out." He reached up and removed the helmet, placing it back in the seat of the fighter. Then he made his way from the hangar back towards berthing.

Tio wasn't there. Singh was. She was coming out of her bunk when Mitchell passed it.

"Colonel," she said. "We dropped early."

Mitchell paused. Didn't she know what had just happened? "We had a little run in with a Tetron."

"We did?"

"Are you okay, Corporal?"

"I'm fine, Colonel," she said, her voice flat. Her eyes looked glassy.

"I spoke to Major Long. He said you got Origin to produce some medications for you?"

She smiled. "Performance enhancers. They improve focus and reduce anxiety. A wonder drug for soldiers. It's still in limited field trials in the army."

"How do you know about it?"

"My ex-girlfriend was a chemist. I've told you that already."

"Who approved the production?" Mitchell asked.

"Admiral Narayan, sir."

That brought Mitchell's entire argument up short. He froze, the tension draining from him. "She did?"

"Yes, sir. She said we could use any edge we can get."

"Side effects?"

"Yes, sir. Increased libido, increased prevalence of blood clots and tendon rupture."

"That sounds painful."

"Only half of the time," she said, trying to make a joke.

Mitchell decided it wasn't worth wasting any more time on. "Have you seen Tio recently?"

"No, sir, but I heard he had gone down to visit Watson to discuss his work on signal jamming."

"Okay. I'll look for him there. Oh, and about the pills - how many of our soldiers has it been given to?"

"Not many. Major Long. Captain Alvarez. Millie wanted to monitor them for a few days first."

Mitchell still wasn't convinced it was a good idea. Members of Greylock had messed around with stuff that was supposed to improve combat performance. It had always worked out badly in the end.

Always.

Mitchell left Singh standing there, heading deeper into the belly of the Goliath in search of Watson and Tio. He wasn't sure he wanted the Knife giving Watson any tips on how to build anything at the moment. Origin and Millie might not have thought he was involved in the Tetron's presence here, but Mitchell wasn't convinced. He had seen how manipulative the Tetron could be, and he was certain all of the other rumors floating around about the Knife's trustworthiness existed for a reason.

The Knife was leaning over Watson's back when Mitchell entered the engineer's workspace. They were both on the floor, crouched over a small, black box that bore a vague resemblance to the one he had attempted to install on Liberty. It had a pair of small whip antennae poking out of it, and a secondary power supply sitting off to the left. Tio was using a laser to point at a spot on one of the circuit boards, and saying something about quantum gates and electron spin.

"Tio," Mitchell said, interrupting him.

The Knife looked back at Mitchell, unsurprised to find him standing there.

"Colonel Williams," he said. "I am assisting Ensign Watson in the re-application of his signal blocking technology."

Unlike the Knife, Watson had shivered noticeably when Mitchell had spoken. He turned now, his face pale. "He's a genius, sir," Watson said.

"Do you have any idea of what just happened? Did you hear the klaxons?"

"Klaxons?" Tio replied. "No. Was there a problem?"

"I'm sure you felt us drop out of hyperspace."

"Yes. We're a few hours early, aren't we?"

"We are. There was a Tetron waiting on the far side of Asimov."

"What?" Tio said.

He sounded surprised, but Mitchell wasn't convinced. He was sure the man who hid in plain sight as a wealthy anti-AI lobbyist was a consummate actor. If the military had been able to hire enough talent to make Mitchell believable, he was sure Tio could have done the same, if not better.

"A Tetron. Outside of your secret hideout. We chased it away."

Tio didn't look happy. "It knows we're out here, then."

"Yes."

"Does Origin know how much time we have to evacuate Asimov?"

"No. A few days at least, I would guess." Mitchell kept his eyes locked on the Knife. He looked concerned. Deeply concerned.

Tio sighed. "I was hoping we had escaped their notice, at least for now. I was hoping we would have more time."

"Time for what?" Mitchell asked. "Is there a problem?"

Tio paused. He stepped away from Watson, approaching Mitchell. "It will take at least six days to compress and transfer the entirety of my data archives for transport."

"Six days? I don't know if we have that long. Why do you need it?"

Tio made a face like Mitchell had asked him a ridiculous question. "To determine the deeper correlation behind the Tetron Christine Arapo and Katherine Asher, for one. To find where the Federation has Pulin stashed away for another."

"You don't know where your brother is?"

"I know where he was. I don't know that he's still there. His work was sensitive in nature. Extremely sensitive. They would have moved him at the first sign of trouble."

"Not if the Tetron got there first."

"If they did, we may have worse problems."

"If he's the Creator."

"The Tetron think he is."

"He may not be."

"No. He may not be. I've been thinking about your dilemma, Colonel."

"What dilemma?"

"The fact that we cannot reach Earth ahead of the Tetron."

"I thought we had a solution to that?"

"You have an idea. I also have an idea."

"Which is?"

Tio smiled, a mischievous smile that looked out of place on his wrinkled face. "We can discuss it with the Admiral. Once we're on Asimov."

[18]

"There it is," Tio said. He pointed to a small corner of the asteroid where a dim green light was barely visible against the dark mass. "Take us down over there, Major."

Major Long didn't reply. Instead, he began angling the Valkyrie Two towards the light.

"I can see why no one has figured out where you live," Mitchell said, looking down at the asteroid.

Asimov was larger than he had expected, the floating chunk of rock almost one hundred kilometers wide and nearly two hundred deep. It was long and narrow, similar to a starship, and covered in high crags and low ravines that gave it an almost cerebral appearance. It was dark, especially dark from where it hung, oddly and impossibly remaining in constant rhythm with the mass below it, always staying on the darker side, shrouded between the blackness of space and the blackness of the world below.

The reason it was so dark was because it was coated with a layer of what Tio called "cloaking paint." Every inch of it, making it even darker, and according to Tio invisible to sensors. Origin had confirmed that part, stating that the only reason they had found it was because they already knew it was there.

Of course, cloaking paint wouldn't work on starships, Tio had explained, because it clung well to rock and not at all to alloy.

"What about stone ships?" Cormac had asked. "We could call them rock stars."

It was good for a laugh, and nothing more. There was no way to hide the engines and no way to disguise the tell-tale signs of thrust. It worked for stationary objects, which was all the Knife needed it for.

The Valkyrie Two continued its drop, running smooth and silent with Major Long handling it expertly with the manual controls. The ship had been well-repaired, its innards almost up to spec for official service.

"Is that a comm tower?" Watson asked, gazing out one of the side viewports.

Mitchell hadn't noticed anything out of the ordinary. He followed Watson's eyes to a spike of rock that rose higher than the others.

"It is," Tio said. "The stone has been shaved there, thick enough to coat the outside of the antenna, thin enough to still receive."

"Receive from where?" Millie asked. "There's nothing else out here."

Tio laughed. "I can receive from anywhere, Admiral. Anywhere at all. That array is likely the most acute in the entire universe."

"Are you shittin' us?" Cormac asked.

"No. I have allies in strategic locations throughout the Federation and the Alliance, who pass constant streams of data on the back of regular communication signals, including military transmissions. That array is strong enough to catch the data. From there, it is stored in the archive to be indexed. Some of the data takes months to arrive. Some of it days. It depends on the source."

"That's a lot of data," Watson said.

"It is. That's why I said it will take at least six days to prepare it for travel."

"We might not have six days," Millie said.

"We must. I cannot stress the value of this data enough, Admiral."

"We'll do what we can, Tio. I'm not losing the rest of my army defending ones and zeroes."

The Knife didn't respond. The Valkyrie was closing in on the green light, which hadn't gained any intensity as they approached. It revealed a cutout in the rock that was large enough to allow entry to starships as big as a cruiser.

"It took three years to build this," Tio said proudly. "It will be lost if the Tetron find it."

"An unfortunate casualty of war," Millie said.

A long corridor of drilled stone brought them to an airlock, already open and waiting. Beyond was an internal spaceport the likes of which Mitchell had never seen. Two dozen starships were anchored to fixed joists six wide and six deep. They were designs he only vaguely recognized. Merchant trawlers mostly, though they had been augmented with weaponry that was out of place on their surface. Some looked old and ready to be junked, their hulls all corroded metal and faded paint. Others were relatively new and sleek. It was a motley collection to be sure, and less impressive than what he had been hoping for.

He glanced over at Millie. He could tell she was thinking the same thing.

"Remember, looks can be deceiving," Tio said.

"How come nobody has tried to communicate with us?" Long asked. "You just let anyone stroll into your rock without trying to stop them?"

"Quite the contrary, Major. My people have been tracking the Goliath since we came out of hyperspace. They know that I'm aboard, and they're under strict orders to remain in radio silence until I contact them. Failing that, they'll be waiting to board this ship the moment the docking clamps close."

"Board? As in, attack?" Cormac asked.

"If I don't send them the all clear, yes."

Mitchell felt his hand sliding absently towards his thigh, even though there was nothing there. He did have a small sidearm on his inner thigh in case of emergency, but it wasn't in easy reach.

"Are you going to send the all clear?" he asked.

Tio gave him another one of his mischievous smiles. "Am I?"

Cormac produced a gun from somewhere. He had it in the Knife's face before anyone could blink. "What game are you playing at?"

Tio wasn't impressed. "You need me, Colonel," he said. "You could say, more than I need you, but I can only live in this rock for so long, and if I don't help you there won't be anywhere left to go. So let's say we need each other. I have some demands."

"We aren't negotiating," Millie said. "Cormac-"

Mitchell stepped between Cormac and the Knife. "Hold on a second. If they're tracking him, they'll know if he gets dead. What do you think our chances are of making it out of here alive when that happens?"

Tio continued to smile. Millie growled and motioned for Cormac to lower the weapon.

"What kind of demands?" she asked.

"You can park over there," Tio said, pointing Major Long towards one of the empty slots. He returned his attention to Mitchell. "As I told you earlier, Colonel, I have an idea that may help you with your dilemma."

"What is he talking about, Mitch?" Millie said.

"And your idea of getting us to listen is to threaten to kill us?" Mitchell said.

"I don't like risk," the Knife replied. "I don't like to take chances. I can't wait for you to decide on the approach that I want."

"This isn't a great way to earn my trust."

"I recognize that. I think it should speak to the strength of my conviction."

"What's your idea?" Millie asked.

"Pulin," Tio said. "We need to find him before the Tetron do."

"How is that going to help us stop the Tetron from reaching Earth?" Mitchell said.

"I see two potential outcomes. First, Pulin is the Creator, and having access to his source code and his mind, we may be able to alter the Tetron. Disable them. Second, failing that, we know that they believe he is statistically probable as their Creator. If we have control over him, we may be able to convince them to retreat away from Earth to either stop us from using him or to try to reach him for themselves."

"I thought you were averse to risk?" Major Long said. "That sounds as risky as it gets."

"Is it?" Tio asked. "As risky as taking your chances that the Tetron will leave Earth in one piece? Or that they'll take the bait when you throw more advanced starships at them?"

Long turned his head back towards them. "He has a point, sir."

"You didn't think we would hear you out on this?" Mitchell asked.

"I know you would hear me out. I didn't want you to have a choice. This is a demand, Admiral, not an option. We need to find Pulin, wherever the Federation has hidden him. We need to find him, and we need to capture him. Now, before the Tetron do."

"What if they already have?"

"That is the risk we must take."

"No," Millie said. "You may be taking us right into a trap. The Tetron may expect us to go after your brother. Meanwhile, we'll be staying further away from Earth, wasting our time chasing another single individual instead of building our resistance and getting closer to saving our people. Not to mention, we don't trust you. You could be a frigging Tetron yourself for all we know."

"I assure you, Admiral, I am not a Tetron. If I were, I could have killed you already."

"Not if you want Mitch, er, Colonel Williams alive," Cormac said. "This would be the way to do it."

"I have you alive now," Tio said. "You can't get out of here unless I allow it. I'm not keeping you prisoner; I'm trying to steer you to the path of least resistance."

"I think it's a good idea," Watson said.

Millie's jaw was tight, her face red with anger. "The fact remains that we already tried prioritizing one life over millions of others. You saw how that worked out."

"They tried to take me to get to Pulin. They were ignoring you, Colonel, because they wanted to get to me. What does that tell you about their priorities? You may be able to destroy them. The Creator may be able to give them what they are truly after."

"We have no idea what they're after, other than destroying us."

"No, but I doubt the answer is that simple."

"Admiral," Major Long said, shouting above the argument. "I don't mean to interrupt, but we need to make a decision."

Mitchell looked through the front viewport. They were getting close to the dock. Long had slowed the ship as much as he dared to buy them time. It was still running out. He could see the soldiers assembled in the corridor leading to the clamps, a dozen or more in full heavy exo. They could tear the ship apart in a matter of seconds.

"Damn it," Millie said, her eyes burning. "You are a real son of a bitch."

"I'm a pragmatist, Admiral. My way is the right way, and I'm willing to put it all on the line to see it go that way."

"Maybe we can both be satisfied," Mitchell said, one eye still out the viewport. The dropship had reached the dock, and he felt the slight shift as the clamps pressed together to hold it in place. "You said it will take you a few days to locate Pulin."

"Most likely," Tio said.

Mitchell's mind was working fast, trying to put the pieces together. "The original plan was to go to Hell and see what we could scavenge there. So, we send a team there while you figure out where in the universe the Federation may have hidden Pulin. We can meet up back here."

"You won't make it there and back in that time," Tio said. The dropship shifted again as the airlock was brought in line with her hatch.

"So we'll meet somewhere else. You can't waste six days transferring the data either way. You said you needed it available to search."

Tio thought about it for a moment. "I need a portion of it. We can start the transfer while we index the rest. It will be close."

"I can help you," Watson said. "I bet your compression algorithms aren't optimized as well as they could be."

"It's a compromise," Millie said. "A fair one. One team to Hell, the other working on locating Pulin. You don't need a bunch of grunts sitting around and waiting, anyway."

A heavy pounding sounded at the outer hatch.

"Your people are waiting," Mitchell said. "What do you say?"

The Knife's face was hard and serious. Mitchell could tell he was working the numbers, calculating the risk. The pounding came again.

"Very well, Colonel. We have a deal." He put out his hand.

Mitchell shook it.

[19]

THE LEADER of the squad of exo outfitted soldiers was named Teal. He was a brawny man with a massive forehead, small eyes, and a wide, bright smile. He was waiting outside the Valkyrie when Major Long opened the hatch, his focused expression giving way when the Knife greeted him.

"Teal," Tio said, returning the man's smile. "We've got some new friends." He paused, looking back at Mitchell. "And some new enemies."

"We were keeping an eye on the battle, sir," Teal said. His voice was deep and calm. "We had the crew ready to launch if it looked like it was going to turn ugly." His eyes trailed towards Mitchell. "It seems like your new friends had everything in hand."

"You can dismiss the others, Teal," Tio said. "I want you to stay with us."

"Yes, sir."

Teal faced the rest of the soldiers. "Tio's back and safe. Return to your posts. Dismissed."

The soldiers faded away behind him, some trying to cast backward glances to get a look at Tio before they left.

"Teal, I want you to meet the crew of the Goliath. They are members of the Alliance military, a special operations unit known as Project Black, or more affectionately known as the Riggers."

"Riiigg-ahh," Cormac said behind them.

"No shit?" Teal said, looking them over.

"You know who we are?" Millie asked.

"Not by name. I've seen the reports."

"Those reports are classified," Watson said.

"You'll get used to it," Teal replied. "You don't stay one step ahead of the law by being one step behind on intel."

"This is Admiral Mildred Narayan, Colonel Mitchell Williams, Major Aaron Long, Corporal Erubiel Watson, and Private Cormac Shen."

"A pleasure," Teal said. "Though I have to say, boss, if we're working with Alliance special ops, things are worse than I realized."

"They are, Teal," Tio said. "Much worse. Let's bring our guests down to operations."

Teal looked confused. "Are you sure?"

"Yes, Teal."

"Damn. It is much worse than I thought."

The big soldier led them back from the dock to a second corridor. A small transport pod was waiting there, and they piled in.

"Teal here is a former Alliance Space Marine," Tio said as the pod moved through the corridor, turned left, and slid neatly into a lift.

"Which company?" Mitchell asked.

"Raiders."

"Impressive."

Teal smiled. The Raiders were well-known for their drop efficiency and mission success rates. "Not as impressive as Greylock, but it'll do."

"You know who I am?"

"Heh. Yeah. I've seen you all over the streams."

"Most people who see me for the first time either wonder why I'm not dead or tell me they wish I were."

"The Knife vouched for you, Colonel. Whether what they say about you is true or not, that's good enough for me."

The lift stopped its descent. The door opened, and the pod moved out into another corridor. There were more people down here - men and women who could have hailed from any number of planets. Mitchell even saw a few children. They seemed focused but content, and they all stopped and waved at Tio when they saw him passing by.

"Your people seem to like you," Millie said.

"Why shouldn't they, Admiral? I take good care of them. Which reminds me. I've got a world-class medi-bot down here, Colonel, if you want to heal that wound once and for all."

"I'll take you up on that later," Mitchell said.

"Of course."

The pod continued, making a few more turns before moving out onto a walkway twenty feet above a large, circular room. The room was filled with water that spun in a vortex around the center. Mitchell could see the glow of lights beneath it.

"Our data center," Tio said. "We process so much incoming data that we have to keep it liquid cooled. Otherwise, the heat signature would reveal our location."

"We have a similar cooling system on our reactor," Teal said. "It's pretty awesome."

They reached the other side of the room. Operations was beyond it. It was a second large room, with rows and columns of workstations and people manning every one of them. They worked at screens and tactile inputs, watching data flow and manipulating it somehow.

"That would be much easier with a p-rat," Long said.

"No wireless networks," Teal said. "That's rule number one on Asimov. Nobody here has an ARR. We still do everything the old-fashioned way."

"How do you pilot exo without an ARR?" Mitchell asked.

"They've been modified to react to muscular changes," Tio said. "Everything has been modified and updated to work better with manual controls. No, it doesn't match the speed of thought, but what we lose in that speed we can make up for with practice."

"That's how we manage to win fights against the Alliance," Teal said.

"And we're immune to hacking," Tio added. "Not just from AI, Colonel. You may not know this, but the Federation has spent a lot of time and money to try to break Alliance encryption keys. The Tetron aren't the only ones who want to get into your head."

"Tetron, sir?" Teal said.

"I'll fill you in later. I wanted to show you the operations center. Corporal Watson, Admiral Narayan, I imagine we'll be spending quite a bit of time here over the next few days. This is where we capture the incoming data through the array and index it for processing. Some of my people keep an eye on it, checking for any anomalies in the transmission to ensure the data isn't corrupted. Others watch it for evidence of tampering. Corporal, I'll introduce you to my lead data coordinator, Bethany, once we've gotten things settled."

"Okay," Watson said.

The pod passed over the ops center, reaching another lift and taking a second ride down. This area was less populated and more serene. Large rooms were filled with greenery, with projections of atmosphere coating high ceilings. There were bulb-like apartments here, separate structures where the residents of Asimov lived. Tio's quarters were obvious, the largest of them all, protruding out from the center like a mushroom cloud.

"I have some business to settle before we continue our partnership," Tio said as the pod came to a stop in front of one of the units. "Teal, show them inside and get them comfortable. Make sure they have whatever they need. I'll pick you up in two hours so we can begin."

Tio remained in the pod while the others disembarked. Once they were clear, the pod headed off towards the central building.

Mitchell watched it go, a rising sense of anger and frustration in his gut. Fighting the Tetron was supposed to be his destiny. Had he lost control of it again?

[20]

"I've been thinking about our deal with the Knife," Mitchell said, glancing over at the readout on the small screen to his right. It had been four hours since Tio had excused himself to settle his business. Four hours that had left them sitting there to rot. Four hours wasted while the Tetron continued their advance.

"What about it?" Millie asked.

Tio had made them comfortable. Very comfortable. They had gel couches and a full bar, and a small crew of workers had come to cook for them. Meats and fruits and other delicacies he hadn't had access to in months. Mitchell enjoyed every moment he had spent eating it, but now the taste was turning sour. Teal had abandoned them an hour ago, leaving them with a squad of guards outside the apartment.

The Knife had said he didn't intend to imprison them. Mitchell figured Tio needed to look up what the word "imprisoned" meant.

"I don't think it's going very well," Mitchell said. "Have you been able to reach Origin?"

"Not so far," Millie replied. "I don't think the signal can make it out."

"We thought that might happen."

"I know."

Mitchell rose from the sofa, facing the others. "I was talking more about our plans. I think this shows us we need a third option. A wildcard."

"What do you mean, Colonel?" Cormac asked.

"We're hoping we can stop the Tetron advance on Earth by getting their attention, but it isn't guaranteed. Tio thinks we can if we get to his brother, which isn't guaranteed either. I think there's a third option we should explore."

"Which is what, Mitch?" Millie asked.

He had gotten the idea when he saw Tio's antenna array. When the Knife had bragged about how powerful it was. It had been flashing through his mind while they had been forced to sit and wait, vanishing and reappearing there, refusing to go away.

"Tetron communications happen in real-time," Mitchell said. "The trouble is, Origin doesn't have the equipment he needs to send a long-range message out for us. Nobody does, except the full Tetron."

"And Tio," Watson said. "If his array is as acute as he claims."

"Exactly. What if we can have Origin send a message to the array, and relay it from there?"

"What kind of message?" Millie asked. "Who would we send it to?"

"Alliance Command," Mitchell replied. "We could warn them about the Tetron. Tell them to turn off their p-rats. They would at least have a chance to organize some kind of defense. Maybe it would be enough to hold the Tetron off for a while until we could get to them with reinforcements."

"That won't work," Long said. "Cornelius was already under Tetron influence. How do we know the other members of Command aren't as well?"

"Cornelius was in Delta Quadrant with the Tetron. The rest of Command isn't."

"The Tetron have had time to send messages back to Earth through human channels as Cornelius by now," Millie said. She flinched slightly when she said her father's name. "They're not going to believe you over him, whether he's the real Cornelius or not. They won't believe any of us over him."

Mitchell stood and stared at Millie. He closed his eyes. He knew she was right. What were they but a ship full of criminals that had made an alliance with another criminal? There was no way anyone in the Alliance would believe a word they said, especially with a story as crazy as one about AI from the past future coming to enslave and destroy them.

He was in the middle of it, and he could still barely believe it himself.

"It's not a bad idea," Millie said. "In fact, I think it would be a great idea if we could get it to someone who might actually listen."

"You're forgetting something, Colonel," Watson said. "It takes a powerful system to send the communication, yes. But only the Tetron are equipped to receive the signal. You'd be sending them a message to warn them about themselves." He started laughing, a whiny, low cackle that annoyed Mitchell more than his oversight.

"Damn it," he said.

"I have an idea though, Colonel," Watson said, his laughter vanishing as quickly as it came.

"What is it?"

"We send the signal out. The Tetron receive it. Maybe we can package it in such a way that when they do, it gets converted to standard human wavelengths. It travels the rest of the distance as normal."

"Can we do that?" Long asked.

Watson shrugged. "I don't know. We would have to ask Origin. Theoretically, it should be possible. It isn't much different than pushing a stream through a comm needle."

"Except I can't get through to Origin," Millie said.

"Not from here. The rock around the array is thinner to allow signals to pass."

"Okay, so we ask Tio to take us to the array so we can send a message up to Origin," Mitchell said.

"No," Millie said.

Mitchell's head snapped towards her. "What?"

"I don't want Tio to know anything about this, Mitch. We can't trust him."

"How are we going to do this without him knowing?"

"Oh, come on now, Colonel," Cormac said. "We're the friggin' Riggers."

"Whoa. Hold on, y'all," Major Long said. "The idea is great. It is. Except for the fact that even if we can get it to someone in the Alliance who isn't already under Tetron control, they aren't going to believe a word of it."

"There is that," Cormac said.

They all fell silent; their desperate plan rendered useless by their reputation. Mitchell returned to the couch, flopping down next to Millie and closing his eyes again.

"There has to be someone who would listen," he said. Someone who knew them. Someone who might believe there was some truth in what they were saying. Someone who had some amount of authority in the Alliance.

Someone like his brother, Steven. The Admiral.

He opened his eyes, the smile splitting his face.

"Mitch?" Millie said, noticing the sudden change in his mood.

"I know who we can send it to."

The excitement of turning the total defeat of the idea to a potential victory was quickly stamped out as the door to their apartment slid open.

[21]

"My apologies for the delay, Admiral," Tio said, entering the room. "I had an emergency I had to attend to."

His expression suggested that he knew they had been discussing something. It was possible the suite was bugged, and he had heard the entire conversation, but Mitchell didn't think so. The Knife didn't bring people he didn't trust to Asimov, and if he trusted the people who were here, why would he be spying on them?

"A bigger emergency than the Tetron?" Millie replied.

"Believe it or not, yes. Some things are more important than war."

"Like sex," Cormac said. He lowered his head when Mitchell's eyes bore into him.

"In any case, I haven't been idle while you've been waiting."

He motioned towards the door. They followed him out, back to the pod where Teal was once again waiting. A second person was with him now. A fresh-faced man in a simple navy blue uniform.

"Colonel Williams, meet Germaine Sanders. Germaine is the lead pilot and captain of the cruiser Avalon. He'll be taking you to Hell."

Mitchell gave Germaine a closer inspection. He couldn't have been more than twenty-two years old. Dark skin, soft eyes. He held himself with an air of cockiness that Mitchell wondered if the apparent pilot could live up to.

"Colonel," Germaine said, giving him a sharp military bow. "Your reputation precedes you, sir."

"Germaine," Mitchell said, remaining stiff. "You look a little young to have served."

"I did nine months before I flunked out."

"Germaine's parents were both Alliance officers," Tio said. "They didn't take his failure well."

"It's a long story, but I wound up here with Mr. Tio."

"He has the highest ratings of any of my captains by far," Tio said. "My willingness to loan you my best should give you an indication of the value I'm putting on our joint operations. In any case, Teal and Germaine have hand-picked the team that will be traveling to Hell with you."

"We have a team," Millie said.

"You do, Admiral. One that is too lightly staffed to carry out this mission. I'm sure you can't argue with that."

"I'm not sending Mitchell out with yours alone."

"You don't have to. I was expecting Major Long and Private Shen to accompany him."

"Three of ours? How many of yours?"

"I thought a crew of fifty would be sufficient," Teal said. "From what Tio tells me, we aren't expecting trouble, just a lot of heavy lifting."

Millie didn't look happy, but she nodded. "Unless we're the unluckiest friggers in the universe, the Tetron will have come and gone. We're going to pick at whatever was left behind."

"Yes, ma'am," Teal said.

Tio was smiling again. "You said it yourself, Admiral. You don't need your team on vulture duty."

"And I suppose Colonel Williams can't return to the Goliath before the trip, either?"

"What for?"

"My fighter, for one," Mitchell said.

"You won't need it," Teal said.

"That's not for you to decide."

"Look, Admiral," Tio said, putting up his hand to calm the situation. "We can argue about this for hours, or we can start preparing to move forward. I understand I damaged our trust, but I don't understand why you seem convinced that I'm not on your side? You may not approve of my methods, but unless you believe I'm aiding the Tetron, or am a Tetron, the mistrust should only extend so far, don't you think?"

Millie was silent. Mitchell could see her bionic hand shaking, indicating her displeasure.

"If you want to return to Goliath, you're free to go. All of you. We can end this arrangement, and the Tetron can destroy us all. Or you can put the smallest mote of faith in my desire to see this threat halted and the proliferation of thinking AIs put to an end, and work with me to reach our shared goals. Tell me which it is, and tell me now, Admiral. My daughter is dying, and I would much prefer to be at her bedside instead of standing here defending every thought I have."

The monolog left Tio shaking, too. His eyes burned against Millie's, a battle of wills between two people accustomed to being in control.

Finally, Millie looked away. "Is that why you were delayed?"

"Yes."

"What's wrong with her?"

"She has a tumor. A brain tumor."

"Medi-bots-"

"Not this one," Tio snapped. He shook his head. "My apologies. As I said earlier, I have the most advanced medi-bots money can buy. The location and nature of the tumor make it inoperable. We keep her medicated most of the time, but there are some days when she wakes. Today was one of those days." A tear formed in the corner of his eye, sliding softly down his cheek. "It was the first time I was able to speak to her in nearly four months."

"I'm sorry," Mitchell said, picking up the words that were failing Millie. "We didn't know."

"Of course you didn't. I would rather not have told you about it, but we need to be able to work together if we are going to fight back against the Tetron. Colonel Williams, Teal, and Germaine have selected a team for your mission to Hell. They would be happy to bring you and your men down to staging to meet them. Admiral, Watson, I will escort you back to operations to meet with Bethany. We can discuss the most efficient approach to both searching the data and getting it transferred off Asimov."

"Fine," Millie said, still fighting to return herself to calm.

"Time is of the essence, Tio," Mitchell said.

"Understood, Colonel. You're free to leave as soon as the Avalon is loaded and ready. This is your mission now. Your crew."

Teal and Germaine both bowed to him again. "At your service, Colonel," Teal said.

"Tio, can you give me a moment with my crew?" Millie asked.

"Of course." He led Teal and Germaine away from them while they huddled together.

"Mitch, I have a feeling Tio isn't going to let me out of his sight. You need to get a message to Origin."

"I don't have a p-rat."

"I do," Cormac said. "Watson fixed me up."

"When?"

"A couple of days ago."

"You were under orders not to have your p-rat repaired."

"I know, but I was getting bored, and I have this collection of superhero vids-"

Mitchell glared at him. Cormac stopped talking.

"Does it matter now?" Millie asked. "What's done is done, and in this case, it will come in handy. Get Cormac to the array. Get the message out to Origin."

"What about everything Tio was just saying about working together? Shouldn't we ask him?"

"No. Just do it. Find out if we can send a stream the way Watson suggested. If there's any chance we can warn the inner galaxy, if we can warn Earth, we have to take it."

"Yes, ma'am," Mitchell said.

"Good luck to all of you. You'd better come back safe."

"I always come back safe," Cormac said. "I will until I don't come back at all." He followed with a short laugh, stopping when nobody laughed with him.

"Riiigg-ahh," Millie said quietly.

"Riiigg-ahh," they replied.

Millie and Watson approached Tio. "I have a request," Millie said.

"Yes, Admiral?"

"We need to speak to Origin, but the rock is too dense here for our p-rat signals to get through."

"Yes, I know."

"According to Watson, the stone around the antenna array is thin enough to allow us to communicate."

Tio paused for a moment. "I'm afraid that's not possible, Admiral. We don't transmit out of Asimov. We only receive. It's safer that way."

"The Tetron already know where we are. Even if there were someone out there listening, I don't see what harm it can do."

"I wouldn't expect you to. I have spent the last thirty years of my life being hunted, Admiral. Trust me when I say that I know how to protect myself and my family. A short-range comm signal may seem innocuous to you, but we've built our entire settlement and my entire pool of resources by being unwavering concerning security. I'm tolerating the continued use of your augmented reality receivers as a show of good faith, and for the very reason that the signals can't escape this shell."

"Tio-" Millie began to say.

"No," Tio replied. "No external transmissions."

"What if it means getting a message to Earth?" Watson said.

Millie turned her head, glaring at him for revealing their plan. She barely tolerated his continued breathing already.

Tio raised his eyebrows. "Is that what you're thinking, Admiral?"

Millie nodded.

Tio didn't look convinced. Mitchell wondered what it was the Knife thought they really wanted to do.

"I've already told you how we can save Earth. There is no form of transmission that can travel faster than a ship in hyperspace, and if the Tetron possess one, I would imagine only they carry the equipment to receive it."

"Yes, that's-" Watson stopped speaking when Millie grabbed his arm.

Mitchell glanced over at Cormac. Millie had been right about the Knife. He was either trying to intentionally prevent them from communicating with the Goliath, or he was beyond paranoid. The Tetron already knew they were here. Nothing Tio did could stop that. Was he still hoping they weren't able to see Asimov? That when they did arrive it would evade their detection?

"Your stubbornness is going to cost us this war," Millie said.

"My stubbornness is going to keep my people alive."

"Don't you mean your daughter?"

Tio's face flushed. "I mean all of my people, but yes, her especially. Unlike the Alliance, I would never spare my daughter from the frying pan just to throw her into a fire."

"Admiral," Mitchell said, starting towards them before Millie's temper got the best of her.

She put her hand out towards him. "It's okay, Colonel. Just forget it. Get your crew ready. I want you on your way to Hell within the next eight hours."

"Yes, ma'am," Mitchell said, making eye contact with her. He could almost hear her voice in his head as though he still had his p-rat.

"Get the message to Origin."

He wasn't sure how he would manage that while he was helping to organize an assault team.

He would have to figure it out.

[22]

"Dropping in sixty, Admiral," Captain Rock said.

Steven stared out of the viewport on the bridge of the Carver at the empty white nothing of hyperspace beyond. He thought back to his early days in the Academy, remembering that the nothing wasn't really nothing, but the blur of the light of millions of stars being folded and compressed on top of one another ahead of the ship. If the Carver had a rearview mirror, they would see more of a fisheye shape to the space behind.

He shook his head. He'd grown up with starships and hyperspace, and the seeming impossibility of it all still kept him in awe. He was such a sap.

Of course, he was probably thinking about it to take his mind off that other thing. The thing he would have to face in less than sixty seconds.

He opened a channel on his p-rat, connecting him to the entire battle group.

"We don't know what we're going to run into out here. Be ready."

The whole fleet was on high alert, all starfighters primed and ready to go as soon as they dropped into hyperdeath. They were deep in Federation space, deeper than he had ever been. Deeper than he had ever thought the Alliance would dare go. They had bypassed the border planets that would normally see the bulk of any friction between the two nations, diving far behind enemy lines alone.

Their target was designated FD-09. According to the further instructions Steven had received from Command, it was a military outpost disguised as a farming colony. An E-type planet that was ninety-five percent fresh water and five percent highly enriched soil. Gravity was a little less than Earth, but it was livable, and home to over a million farmers and the requisite supply pipelines.

He had been ordered to destroy it.

Of course, Command didn't know if the planet was defended. The reports on FD-09 were six months old - more than enough time for the Federation to determine if the true nature of the site had been learned by Alliance spies.

More than enough time to send a force large enough to obliterate Steven and his fleet.

It had happened before. More than once. He had known Admiral Colloway. They had met at an Officer's party back on Earth a couple of years earlier. He had been a good man who had wound up in the wrong place at the worst time. They had lost two dozen ships, hundreds of fighters, and more importantly, a lot of good men and women.

Which is why he was thinking about hyperspace. He didn't want to think about losing the thousands in his battle group. It was better to react to whatever they discovered when they dropped and not worry about it for even a second before then. There was nothing they could do about it anyway. Coordinates had been set, and they were only thirty seconds out.

Those remaining seconds felt like they took an eternity. Steven counted each one of them in his mind, matching them to his breath. His heart was pounding, and he could feel the heat of his anxiety on his cheeks. He glanced over at Rock. His First Mate wasn't as visibly nervous, but he could see it in the furrow of his brow.

Steven knew he wasn't supposed to be nervous. Not outwardly, anyway. He was the Admiral. He was supposed to set the example for his crew. He'd always been bad at hiding his emotions. At least the people on the bridge were used to it. He knew they trusted him.

"Ten seconds," Rock said. He didn't need to count it out loud; they could all see the countdown on their p-rats if they wanted. It seemed to remove some of the surreal feeling of it all to break the silence.

Steven felt the tug as the hyperspace engines powered down. The stars spread out in front of them, separating to reveal the large blue planet ahead, a small dot of green the only indication of land.

"Status," Steven said, squinting his eyes to look ahead at the planet. No red had popped up behind his vision. No alert tones were sounding.

"Not reading any enemy spacecraft," Rock said. "It looks like they didn't know we were coming. Locking onto the surface."

"Prepare the nukes," Steven said.

The Carver and the other battleships carried the space-to-surface weapons in their bellies, more than enough to dive deep into the underground passages where their operatives had said the Federation was building starfighters and mechs.

"Daedalus' nukes are armed and ready," Captain Cheng said.

"Victoria's nukes are armed and ready," Captain Mustafa said.

"Gallant's nukes armed and ready," Vice Admiral Josephs said.

"Carver armed and ready," Steven said. "Fire on my mark."

He watched the overlay on his p-rat with one eye, and the real-time view of the planet with the other. They needed to get the fleet into the proper placement before they could launch, and they would have only a few seconds to fire. The whole thing could have been left to automated systems, but Steven wouldn't allow it. If they were going to take human lives, they were going to be responsible for it, not leave it to a machine.

The Carver's main engines came back online, and the ships began to move in unison across the vast emptiness of space, angling perpendicular to and in opposition to the planet's rotation. A red outline appeared around the planet in the p-rat, slowly shifting towards orange as they approached firing position.

"Get ready," Steven said.

A red dot appeared on the overlay behind them.

Then another, and another.

"Federation battleships," Captain Rock shouted.

"Evasive maneuvers," Steven said, breaking his concentration on the planet.

"We almost have it," Cheng said from on board the Daedalus.

"I said evasive," Steven said.

"This is Admiral Calvin Hohn of the Federation battleship Samurai. Your presence in Frontier Federation space is unauthorized. Withdraw immediately, or this incident will be passed to our council as a blatant act of all-out war."

The Alliance ships began spreading apart into a standard defensive formation, even as the planet's rotation brought it closer to firing range.

"Admiral, what are we going to do?" Rock asked.

Steven surveyed the battle grid. His fleet had twenty ships to the Federation's ten, but the Federation force was almost uniformly battleships, leaving him way outgunned even if he wasn't outnumbered. If he launched the nukes or attacked the enemy fleet, not only would he and his entire fleet of soldiers die, but they would be starting a direct, overt confrontation with the Federation.

"Admiral?" Rock asked again.

"Our orders are clear, Admiral," Josephs said from the Gallant. "We're to destroy the assembly station at any cost."

Steven felt his heart thudding even harder. He knew what their orders were, but this was straight out suicide. Why would Command send them out here to die like this? They were the newest battle group in the fleet. It didn't make sense.

"Admiral?" Josephs said.

"Alliance fleet, you have ten seconds to begin powering up your hyperspace engines," Admiral Hohn said.

Ten seconds. Steven checked his p-rat. They would be in range in fifteen. He had no time left.

He clenched his jaw. He knew what he had to do. That didn't mean he liked it.

"Gallant, Daedalus, fire when ready. All other ships, launch fighters and prepare to engage. If you believe in God, now is a good time." He closed his eyes. "Forgive me for what I'm about to do."

A thought switched his p-rat away from the surface nukes to spaceborne weapons. A second thought fired the first shot.

[23]

Teal and Germaine brought Mitchell, Cormac, and Long back towards the massive internal docks, taking an alternate route that circumvented the station's operations center. As they neared the docks, they turned down a secondary corridor, pausing at a secure hatch while Teal placed his hand against the biometric scanner. The hatch opened, finally revealing the larger truth behind Asimov, and the real power of the Knife.

A loading hangar had been placed behind half a dozen of the docking clamps and hidden from outside view by heavy blast shielding. A hundred or more people were in the hangar, guiding all kinds of ordnance from large lifts in the rear of the space towards the joined airlock of a starship.

A small cruiser. Almost certainly the Avalon.

Mitchell couldn't see the outside of the starship. He could see what was being loaded onto it. Crates of munitions and supplies along with a number of heavy lifter trucks and a pair of large mechs that Mitchell didn't recognize.

"Wow," Cormac said, feasting his eyes on the scene.

Mitchell held back his smile. It had likely been years since the

Rigger had seen what a true military preparing for war looked like. It had been a while for himself as well, but he had seen it plenty of times before at Alliance stations throughout the galaxy. Only those times, the ordnance was being loaded into the Greylock.

He closed his eyes for a moment, remembering. Elle, with her short hair and wild, confident smile, welcoming him to the company. He had been cocky then, much, much more than he was now. He had said something stupid, she had chewed him out, and thus his career with the most highly decorated company in the UPA Space Marines had been born.

It was a good memory. A sad one. He opened his eyes. "I don't recognize those mechs," he said.

Teal laughed. "No, you wouldn't, Colonel. We call them Franks, short for Frankensteins. Digger, he's the head of mechanical, he takes the pieces we salvage and somehow manages to turn them into something else that usually works even better than what he started with." He turned backward in the pod, making a face that Mitchell assumed was supposed to be Digger. "Alliance machines are shit, Teal. Pure shit. It's like they want to lose the galaxy to the Federation." He said it in a high, nasally voice that drew a laugh from Germaine.

"I've had that thought before," Mitchell said. "You've seen the Dart?"

Teal shook his head. "Oh, man, Colonel. Don't ever mention that thing around Digger."

"So, what's the deal with Tio, anyway?" Long said. Mitchell hadn't gotten a full understanding of the drugs Singh had set him up with, but Long still seemed a little too relaxed for his liking.

"What do you mean?" Germaine said, the smile fading.

"He seems like he's always got an angle."

"Major," Mitchell said to silence him.

"No, it's okay, Colonel," Teal said. He met Long's eyes with his own. "Tio's been through a lot of shit, and he's survived because of what he believes in."

"Which is?"

"Freedom," Germaine said. "Believe it or not. Mr. Tio is convinced that over-reliance on AI will lead to our destruction. He told me what you were doing here. It seems that he was pretty right on though the whole time travel thing is a serious mind-frig if you know what I'm saying. So yeah, I can tell your Admiral doesn't like him, and it's obvious you don't trust him, but considering that he did predict the future and has spent years working to keep it from happening, my blunt opinion is that you should all shut the frig up and go with the flow. Tio is a smart man. He can be cold, he can be calculating, but he knows what he's doing."

It was a straightforward opinion, and Mitchell appreciated it. "That would have been easier to do if he hadn't held a gun to our heads to get us to agree to his plan."

"You try watching your greatest fear come true," Teal said. "Between this and his daughter, it's been a rough couple of months."

The pod continued towards the large lifts, slipping between the Franks. Mitchell stared up at them as they did, taking stock of the arm-mounted lasers, the missile launchers, the railguns. It was more armament than any Alliance mech typically carried.

"Does Digger have a secret to managing the heat?" he asked.

"Yeah," Teal said. "Don't shoot everything at once. He's got a bit of a thing for guns."

They hit the lift, sitting idle while the large doors slid closed. Mitchell traced their steps back, committing them to memory. It was going to be tough to sneak away from here. There had to be an alternate route towards the array, and he had a feeling he was going to need clearance to get there.

He sat back in the pod, wondering if he should bother. Germaine had a point about the Knife. The man had been lobbying Alliance politicians for years and had succeeded in getting a few anti-AI measures passed. Maybe their resistance was going to cause more problems than it was going to solve?

"Since you brought it up," Germaine said while the lift descended. "What's with your Admiral? I mean, she's sexy, seriously sexy, especially with that metal hand, but I think her panties are on a little too tight."

Mitchell's head snapped towards the pilot. "What the hell is that supposed to mean?" he said.

Germaine's face froze. "Uh. I. Uh."

"He didn't mean any harm, Colonel," Teal said, putting a large arm between them. "Germaine here isn't always the most... diplomatic... speaker. He was just saying that she's pretty. And pretty intense."

Mitchell continued glaring at Germaine, who wouldn't make eye contact. "You would be too if you were in charge of the only military in the Alliance that was immune to the enemy threat, and your total headcount was less than a hundred. This is serious business, Teal. She's taking it seriously."

"Just like Tio," Teal said. "It seems when two personalities like that get together it always gets hot for everyone involved."

"Yeah," Mitchell said. "Then there's the fact that he blew up a civilian cruiser and her mother with it."

Teal's mouth opened to speak, but nothing came out. He glanced over at Germaine. "Colonel, I'm totally honest when I say this: I've been with Tio for fifteen years. We have never gone after a civvie target. Never. I'd bet my life on it. Either your Admiral is confusing him with someone else, or her mother was no civilian."

Mitchell lowered his eyes, wondering if that could be true. Was she confused about the nature of Tio's actions? Or were Tio's men trying to justify theirs?

"Think about it, Colonel," Teal said. "The Alliance made you exactly what they wanted you to be. A hero, and then a fraud. I don't know if either of those is true. What I do know is that people in power can make us think anything they want us to think if we trust them enough. So we pick a side, and we stick with it because otherwise we'd be twisting in the solar winds our whole life. I know it didn't happen that way because I was with Tio. Can your Admiral say the same, or did the Alliance lie to her too?"

"I don't know what the truth is, Teal. I only know what both sides are saying, and that reality is most likely somewhere in between. It doesn't matter, though. None of that drama matters. The mission is simple. Go to Hell, grab what we can, and make the rendezvous. As of right now, that's all I want to talk about. You read me?" Mitchell turned his head, making eye contact with each of them in turn. "Teal, you copy?"

"Yes, sir," Teal said.

"Germaine?"

"Yes, sir."

"Firedog?"

"Yes, sir."

"Valkyrie?"

"Yes, sir."

The lift stopped, and the large doors began to slide open. A bright light began to filter in, silhouetting the soldiers organized behind it. They snapped to attention, the motion echoing across the space.

"That's more like it," Mitchell said.

[24]

"How long until the Avalon is finished being loaded?" Mitchell asked.

He was sitting in his temporary quarters in the barracks, looking through reports Tio's intelligence unit had been busy preparing up in operations. He had found the manual controls of the system confusing at first but was surprised at how quickly he had picked up their operation. It worked much like the holographic table on the Goliath.

"Three hours, Colonel," Teal said. He was standing on the other side of Mitchell's desk, holding a tablet against a huge bicep. "We shifted some of the equipment per your request."

"Thank you, Teal," Mitchell said.

He had asked them to unload one of the mechs and replace it with whatever mining equipment they had available. He had claimed it was because he wasn't sure what the state of the base on Hell would be, and they might need to dig into some areas to retrieve high-value ordnance. It was possible, he supposed, but the truth was he was doing his best to stall their departure while he came up a with a plan to get himself and Cormac to the array.

It had been more of a challenge than he had ever expected, both because his duties as commander of the mission left him little time to get away from the preparations and because he knew next to nothing about Asimov or how to navigate it. He had managed to partially solve the second part with the interface he had been provided, making his way to a public data store that contained a general map of the facility. Of course, that map was public and was missing things he knew were there, like the room he was sitting in. He had tried to get deeper into the system, but everything outside of the mission to Hell was spitting back an access denied message.

"Is there anything else I need to know right now?" he asked the soldier.

"No, sir."

"You're dismissed. Can you send Firedog in?"

"Of course, sir." He nodded instead of bowing, turning and leaving the room. Mitchell ran his hand through his short hair, trying to clear his mind enough to think. There was just too much spiraling around his thoughts to focus on any one thing.

He leaned back in his chair, trying to calm himself. Slow. Steady. Keep it simple.

Step one, get close to the array. They had passed it on their way to the dock. The public map had given him a decent idea of what was around it, so he had a vague notion of where he needed to go.

Step two, get past any security measures or guards. Mitchell couldn't believe he was finding himself wishing Watson was with him. He was certain the engineer could hack the biometric security with a screwdriver, given a chance. He was no engineer, and he knew nothing about systems like that. He doubted Cormac did either. That meant they would need someone inside to let them in.

Step three, get far enough into the array to send the message without anyone raising an alarm and manage to hide there long enough to receive a response. Since Cormac was the only one with a p-rat, that meant he would have to pose the question to Origin and distribute the answer. It was a frightening thought.

Step four, get back down to the Avalon in time to head for Hell. That was probably going to be the easiest part.

Cormac made his way into the room, snapping to crisp attention in front of Mitchell.

"At ease, soldier," Mitchell said. Cormac's ease was hard to discern.

"How can I help you, sir?" he asked.

Mitchell hit a button on the desk that closed the door behind Cormac. He waved him over to a chair. Cormac sat forward on the seat, leaning in.

"Sir?"

Mitchell turned his display so Cormac could see it. "This is a map of Asimov. At least, the part that Tio doesn't mind anyone seeing." He pointed to a corner. "This is as close to the array as the map goes. A small databank that as near as I can tell runs some of the non-essential systems. Apartment lighting and such. The entrance to the array is somewhere in here."

Cormac's eyes shifted as he examined it. "Yes, sir. That's how I remember it."

Mitchell raised an eyebrow. "You remember it?"

Cormac grinned. "I don't mean I remember it exactly, sir. Just that I have what the doctors called 'strong geospatial recognition,' whatever that means. I think it means I'm good at directions." He laughed. "I remember seeing the array out the window of the Valkyrie, and then passing the rooms once we entered through the dock. If I had to guess, there's a door somewhere over here." He leaned in and pointed at one of the back rooms. "It's going to be secure though, and we don't have any explosives."

Mitchell stared at Cormac, surprised again by the soldier. "Okay. Step two. How do we bypass the security measures when we don't even know what they are?"

"You're a Rigger, sir," Cormac said. "You lie, cheat, or steal. If that doesn't work, you force someone to do it. Like Germaine, maybe?"

"The problem with using force is that it isn't usually quiet. What happens after we reach the array and return to the Avalon? Do you think he's going to keep his mouth shut about us taking him at gunpoint?"

"We don't have guns, Colonel."

"That's not the point, Firedog. Let's say we grab Germaine. First, we have to hold him without him trying to get away, make a fuss, or raise an alarm. Then we have to get him to let us into the array and wait patiently while we send out our message. Even then, we have to release him to pilot the Avalon to Hell."

Cormac was silent for a moment. "Good point, sir. Germaine isn't expendable. It has to be someone who should have access, like Teal."

"You're suggesting we kill whoever we get to let us in?"

"As you said, sir, we can't have them blabbing."

"I'm not killing anyone. We're on the same side."

"Are we, Colonel? I ain't so sure from where I'm sitting."

It was true Tio was keeping things from them, and preventing them from communicating with the Goliath in the first place. Even so, killing the Knife's right-hand wouldn't go over well under any circumstances.

"We need another option. Someone else who has access."

"Who?"

Mitchell's mind trailed back to the mechs moving into the loading bay. "I think I know. Let's hope I'm right."

[25]

"Colonel," Teal said, entering the office with a second man in tow.

Mitchell got to his feet, moving around the desk and putting out his hand. "Colonel Mitchell Williams," he said.

The man they called Digger's eyes moved from the hand to Mitchell's face. For a moment, Mitchell was worried his idea was going to get him nowhere fast. Then the tech's eyes lit up, and a big smile creased his narrow face.

"Holy shit on a quasar," he said, grabbing Mitchell's hand in both of his, leaving a slick of grease on it. "Frigging Mitchell Williams, the Hero of Liberty. Teal told me it was you, but I thought he was full of shit, like he usually is. He actually thinks the Zombie can outclass a Federation Atom with the right load out." He glanced over at Teal, shaking his head.

The comment made Mitchell laugh, not because of the words, but because of how accurately Germaine had mimicked the engineer. He was tall and lanky, skeletal in structure with a balding scalp and a large nose. He wore a heavy work coat over a ratty t-shirt and pants held up by a bright red wire.

"Teal told me you go by Digger. Do you have a name to go with it?"

"I did, once, but they've been calling me Digger so long, I think I forgot what it is. You can call me Digger, too. Or Diggs, or whatever. Is that shit the Alliance says about you true?"

"About half," Mitchell said.

Digger's face fell. "Frigging a-holes. Always bending the truth, making shit up. You never know which way your butthole is facing, you know what I mean?"

"Not really."

"Digger," Teal said. "The Colonel has some questions about the Franks. He hasn't used a manual system like ours before."

Digger nodded. "Right. Right. You have the p-rat to do all the work for you. Me? I don't trust that shit. There's no such thing as a one hundred percent secure network; you know what I mean?"

"Unfortunately, I do. Teal, how long until departure?"

"Seventy minutes, Colonel. We're going through the operational checks right now."

"Great. That should be enough time for Digger to teach me the controls."

"It would be a frigging honor, Colonel," Digger said. "Mmmm-mm... We can't use the Frank already on the Avalon; it will frig up the ops check. Teal, I'll bring him down to mechanical. I just finished installing the new converter on Tess."

"Tess?" Mitchell said.

Teal shook his head. "He names all the mechs."

"After girls I want to-"

"I get it," Mitch said, cutting him off.

"Yeah, so let me show you the way."

"Teal, I trust you can handle the rest of the details?"

"Yes, Colonel."

"Thank you."

Mitchell followed Digger out of the office and back to the loading bay. Most of the supplies had been cleared from the bay, loaded into the Avalon. Cormac was leaning against the rear of the ship with Germaine, whose eyes were scanning the inventory.

"Cormac," Mitchell said.

The grunt patted Germaine on the shoulder and joined Mitchell. Germaine didn't even look up.

"Nice bloke, that one," Cormac said.

"Cormac, meet Digger, Tio's lead mechanic."

"A pleasure," Cormac said.

Digger gave him the same expression as he had Mitchell, only this time his face stayed somewhere between angry and bewildered.

"You're going to love Tess," Digger said, not returning Cormac's greeting. "She's got my latest upgrades, including a heavy ion coilgun that I've been working on. It'll blow the shit out of anything the Alliance has, and can mess up most of the Federation's heavy armor pretty bad, too. Tio helped me with the power inversion algorithms and the reactor re-balancing."

"Impressive," Mitchell said, keeping the mechanic talking.

"Yeah. Beats the frig out of the idiots in Alliance RND. Hey, while you're here, maybe you can autograph her for me?"

"The mech?"

"Yeah. I'll give you a laser etcher; you can scratch your initials into her ass for me."

They reached a secondary, smaller lift that ran adjacent to the larger supply lift. It opened as he approached.

"The lift isn't secured?" Mitchell asked.

"Oh, it is," Digger said. "We've got crazy, crazy levels of security here. While I was walking up to the lift, sensors were checking my appearance, scanning my eyeballs, fingerprinting, and even vaping me."

"Vaping?"

"People have a fairly unique chemical signature that fluctuates based on diet. The system knows what I ate today, and is basically measuring my farts."

Cormac laughed at that. "Alliance ain't got nothing like that. I wish they did. Please fart into the orifice for entry," he said in a robotic voice, laughing harder at himself.

Digger glared at him for an instant before returning to ignoring him. "Asimov is the most secure facility in the galaxy. I guarantee it. I designed the system."

"You designed it?" Mitchell said.

"Yup. With some help from Tio. He's a wizard with math. Smartest frigging guy I've ever met."

"So you have access to pretty much the entire station?"

"I'd have to, in order to maintain the critical systems. I'm the head mechanic, after all. Why do you ask?"

Mitchell smiled calmly. "Just verifying my hunch."

He glanced at Cormac, who produced a small shiv he had hidden somewhere on his body, digging it into Digger's side.

"No sudden moves, no loud noises," Mitchell said.

"Huh? What the frig? Are you out of your frigging mind? Tio will have your ass for this, Colonel."

"Only if he finds out about it. Which he won't. Look, Digger, I don't want to hurt you. I don't even want to be doing this. The problem is that I need to send a message out to my ship, and Tio wouldn't give me permission. All I need you to do is take me to the communications array, let me transmit, and then keep your mouth shut."

"Or we can kill you," Cormac said.

Digger looked crestfallen. Mitchell hated to betray someone who so clearly idolized him, even if his trust was misplaced. "Tio will kill me if he finds out I helped you send an outgoing transmission."

"Is he like that? Killing people who do things he doesn't like?"

Digger shrugged. "Not usually, but there have been a few times. If you send a transmission and the Federation or the Alliance catch it and trace it back, the whole station will be compromised."

"The station is already compromised," Mitchell said. "The enemy knows where we are, and is probably headed here as we speak."

The lift stopped in mechanical, the door sliding open. The huge bay stretched out ahead of them, filled with all kinds of mobile equipment in various states of repair. Dozens of mechanics moved about, checking inventory, handling parts, and generally ignoring them.

"Stay quiet. Act natural," Cormac said.

Digger moved out into the bay with Mitchell, Cormac staying close to his side.

"Colonel, I don't get why the frig Tio would refuse to let you send a message if we're already compromised?"

"Leverage," Mitchell said. "Human civilization is being annihilated by advanced AI, and he's making power plays. I don't have time for games, Digger. You help me reach Goliath, and we can save millions of lives."

Digger turned his head, staring at him. "You aren't bullshitting me, are you?"

"I wish to God I was."

He blew a gust of air from his nose in a resigned sigh. "Damn. Frig me, Colonel. I know Tio can be a bit of a stubborn jackass sometimes, so I believe you. If you were anyone else, I wouldn't do it. If we get away with it, you have to sign Tess' ass for me."

"Deal. Are we good?"

"Shit. Yeah. You can take the pointy thing out of my ribs."

Cormac withdrew the shiv. Mitchell counted tense heartbeats, waiting for Digger to make a run for it, or call out an alarm, or something. He didn't.

"Just because I take you to the array and let you in doesn't mean we're going to get away with it," Digger whispered. "Tio's going to be suspicious of you being there, and we don't have time to disable the access logs. I can try to erase them after the fact, but he'll notice the discrepancy. I might still end up dead for helping you."

"I'll protect you," Mitchell said.

"From Tio?" He laughed. "Good luck. Anyway, my life is his to end if that's what he chooses. He got me out of prison, gave me a new start here. I know by the fact that he let outsiders onto Asimov that something bad is happening out there, and if people are dying? I can't stand the thought of that shit going down because of his paranoia. If you think you can save them, great, but this still isn't easy for me."

Mitchell was curious about the mechanic's story and whatever insight he could lend into the mind of the Knife. He wished they had more time.

"Digger." A young woman approached them, holding a small tangle of wires in her hand. She was wearing heavy coveralls that hid her shape, and her face was streaked with some kind of liquid.

"Tess," Digger said, his face beginning to turn red. "What do you need?"

Mitchell glanced from Digger to Cormac. The soldier was eying the engineer, trying to make out the shape of her below the coveralls. When he noticed Mitchell looking at him, he clenched his jaw and looked away.

"This is the last coupling we have in stock, and look at it. We're screwed the next time one burns out."

Digger took the mess in his hands. "I can fix this," he said. "Can you drop it off in my workspace in a couple of hours?"

"I can leave it there for you, Digs."

"Can you drop it off?" He smiled weakly.

Tess looked at him with understanding. She sighed and nodded, wandering away.

"The mech is named after her?" Mitchell asked when she was gone.

"Yes."

"Have you?"

"No."

"How far to the array?"

"I need to wash down before we can head up there. You do, too. The equipment on the array is incredibly sensitive to dirt. Follow me."

Mitchell and Cormac followed the mechanic through the space. Digger waved to most of the techs as they passed, putting Mitchell at ease by staying quiet about what they were about to do. He hadn't expected to gain the man's trust so easily. He supposed his fame, or maybe infamy, did have some advantages.

They moved beyond the bay, through a small portal labeled "DETOX." They passed into an airlock system that led to a pair of chambers beyond.

"The first will hit you with nano-abrasive air. It'll pull any shit off your clothes and skin. The second will scan you and hit you a little harder if there's anything clinging to you. Best frigging shower you'll ever take."

"Sounds great," Mitchell said.

The hatch opened ahead of them, and Digger ushered them in. A moment after the door closed, a small hum and a burst of air blew along them. Mitchell could feel the abrasives sliding against his flesh as a soft tickle. The second hatch opened.

"Won't Tio know we used this?" he asked.

"No. We're supposed to go in separately, so it will only register me, which is normal."

"Isn't that going to leave us dirty?"

"A little bit. I'm already risking my ass, though."

The second airlock closed, and they were hit with another round of the nano-particles. It stung a little more this time but was bearable. The final door opened, and they stepped through into a spotless corridor.

"This way," Digger said, turning left. "The main access corridor splits off to a maintenance shaft about halfway. If we go in through there, we can enter without being seen. It's higher security than the main entry, but I have clearance."

He moved ahead of them. Cormac leaned closer to Mitchell, whispering. "I thought this was going to be a lot harder."

"Me too," Mitchell replied.

It was almost too easy.

[26]

The maintenance shaft turned out to be a literal meter high and wide crawlspace that found Mitchell tailing behind Digger on his hands and knees, squeezing his more muscular frame through the passage while the lanky mechanic slithered through it like a worm.

"I think I'm going to die in here," Cormac said behind him. "I hate small spaces. Reminds me of when I was a kid."

"How so?" Mitchell asked.

"My pops had this ammo trunk he salvaged from a derelict ship. He was a junker, which is kind of funny because of where I ended up on the Schism. Anyways, he would get pissed at me and my sis and lock us in the trunk, sometimes for no reason. Sometimes together. Sometimes alone. I remember one time, he left us there and went out. Mom was going crazy looking for us. She found us in there, I don't know, twenty, thirty hours after. I think if we didn't have each other, we would have gone insane. You lose track of time like that."

Mitchell tried to look back at Cormac, but there was no space. Was that why he was so messed up? He imagined it was at least part of it.

"I didn't know you had a sister."

"Yes, sir. She's still alive, too. Used to send me messages until I got busted to the Riggers. Now she thinks I'm dead."

"Does she know what you got busted for?"

He didn't respond.

Mitchell almost bumped into Digger as the mechanic stopped in front of a ventilated hatch. A laser lit the shaft for an instant as he was scanned, and then the hatch slid aside.

"We're in," Digger said, sliding out of the shaft and into the room. It was a tight fit, a tiny walkable space, and kilos of electronics that kept the air warm and stale. "Don't touch anything."

They slid into the room, the hatch closing behind them.

"I've got a signal," Cormac said as soon as he was through.

"Knock Origin," Mitchell said. Digger moved to the end of the space, peering around the corner. "Trouble, Digs?"

Digger shook his head. "Not yet. There are usually techs coming and going, checking the systems. We're clear for the moment."

"Good."

"I've got Origin, Colonel," Cormac said.

"Ask him if he can send a message like we talked about with Millie."

Cormac's eyes shifted. A minute later, he nodded. "He said it can be done, but it will reveal the Goliath's exact position, and the odds of the Tetron being unable to decrypt the signal are next to nil."

"They already know where we are, so that isn't a problem. We need to send the message in my voice, and we need to scramble it up a bit. Can he do that?"

Cormac paused again. "What do you mean by scramble?"

"My brother Steven and I used to play this game encoding messages. Cryptography. We tried to make them unbreakable. We were just kids, so they weren't advanced, but I think if we put one of the cryptographic hashes on the stream data, along with a more secure encryption key, we can get the transmission out to him. It won't stop the Tetron from figuring out the message, but if we're lucky it will buy him a few minutes."

"A few minutes? How is that going to help?"

"It might not. Then again, it might. Can he do it?"

Cormac paused again and then nodded. "He wants to know the hash sequence and the encryption keys?"

"Can you remember this, Firedog?" Mitchell asked.

"I'll do my best, sir."

Mitchell began describing the patterns. It had been a long time since he had thought about them, and he hoped that Steven would remember. The cryptography was elementary, but if they were lucky it would be just enough.

He had to stop in the middle while Cormac relayed the information, and it took much longer than he was comfortable with. Digger vanished while he was in the middle of it to scare off a tech that had entered to check the equipment but otherwise stayed with them the entire time, running diagnostics on the array while he waited. He didn't seem nervous about what he was doing or the possible repercussions if Tio found out. Mitchell wondered if he had managed to clear the logs ahead of time after all? Whatever the reason, if the mechanic was afraid for his life he didn't show it.

"Message passed to Origin, Colonel," Cormac said at last. "I think I got everything right."

"Let's hope so. Time to departure?" Mitchell asked.

"Twenty-two minutes, sir."

"Tell Origin to transmit in thirty. I want to be on my way to Hell before Tio finds out what we did. Nice work, Firedog. You too, Digger. You should consider yourself a hero. You may have just saved millions of lives."

Digger smiled, showing a row of crooked teeth. "I can't just let people die like that. I'm an asshole, but not that much of an asshole."

"Back out the way we came?" Mitchell said.

"Yeah. Unless you want to get your ass caught?"

"Not really."

They slid back into the shaft. Mitchell took point so that Digger could close it up and reset the security. He said it would make it less likely Tio would notice the disruption that way. Then they made the crawl back to the empty corridor.

Mitchell couldn't believe they had actually done it. Origin would send the transmission on the backs of the Tetron, in real-time instead of the weeks it would normally take to piggyback a data stream on a starship. Soon enough, Steven would know about the Tetron threat and would be able to warn the rest of the Alliance.

They would have a chance to fight back.

Earth would be safe.

Mitchell reached the end of the shaft, pulling himself forward one last time so that his head poked out from the opening. He paused when he saw the four pairs of boots standing in front of it, and then looked up.

"Colonel Williams," Tio said. "I seem to recall expressly forbidding you to send a wireless transmission."

[27]

MITCHELL GLANCED at Teal and the two soldiers in light exo lined up behind the Knife.

"It had to be done," he said, pulling himself from the shaft. Would the Knife execute him and the rest of his crew for it?

"Oh, frig me," Cormac said, sliding out behind Mitchell and seeing Tio. He turned around and bent down towards the shaft. "You little frigging worm. You sold us out."

"Cormac," Mitchell said.

Digger's face appeared. "No, Colonel. He's right. I did sell you out."

"What?"

"I had to." He exited the shaft, bowing to Tio before straightening up. "I told you, I'm not enough of an asshole to let millions of people die. I am enough of an asshole to tell Tio after I did it."

Mitchell glared at the mechanic. He wanted to ring his scrawny neck.

"So, now what?" he said instead, turning his attention back to the Knife. "I suppose our alliance is off?"

Tio shook his head. "Don't be foolish, Colonel. I expected that you would try something like this, assuming you had a strong enough reason to want to communicate with Origin. When Digger told me what you were doing, I decided to allow it. In fact, I wanted to apologize to you."

"Apologize?" Mitchell was confused. Hadn't he just broken the man's trust?

No. He didn't have his trust to break it.

"Yes. When your Admiral approached me about communicating with Origin earlier, I was concerned you wanted to report our internal schematics to your ship and crew. I believed your idea to send a message to Earth was a cover. In my mistrust, I didn't fully consider the potential."

"Why would I do that?"

"You don't trust me, Colonel."

"You don't trust me, either."

Tio laughed. "No. It hasn't been easy, fighting against a storm you were certain was coming but had no proof of. Being the only voice of reason in a universe of people who only saw the creature comforts AI could provide them. I've been betrayed more times than I can count, including by those I thought closest to me. I believed you would seek to take control of Asimov by force and claim my resources as your own."

"That's ridiculous."

"It's happened before," Teal said.

"My wife. She attempted a coup a few years ago. She used poison to try to kill me, but she didn't use enough. She didn't like the way I was spending the funds that were coming in. She wanted opulence and comfort. I wanted to prevent a disaster."

"So you thought I would do the same? Try to steal it from you?"

"I know about Project Black. I know who and what its crew is. Would that be such a stretch?"

"Under normal circumstances, maybe not. But you were on Liberty. This isn't the time for petty bullshit."

"No, it isn't. And by removing me you would have complete

control of my forces to use against the Tetron without having another level of command to worry about. It is a strategically viable solution."

"But not a very human one," Mitchell said.

Tio paused, staring at Mitchell. He nodded. "No. I suppose not." He put out his hand. "Again, Colonel, I apologize for my mistrust. I hope that this episode can help us both put a little more faith in each other, that we want what is best for humanity and not just what is best for ourselves."

Mitchell started to reach for the hand. He stopped halfway. He couldn't shake off the mistrust completely. Not with all of the rumors that had been passed on to him. He needed a little more than that.

"I have one question."

"What is it?"

"The cruiser that Millie said you had destroyed. Teal said it never happened."

"While we're spilling our souls, Colonel?" Tio's eyes shifted to the floor. "An unfortunate incident. It did happen."

"What?" Teal said.

"I'm sorry, Teal," Tio said. "You weren't on that mission. I hired a mercenary force for it, due to its less savory nature. I never told anyone."

Teal stepped back, away from Tio. "I don't understand, sir?"

It was obvious to Mitchell that Tio didn't want to talk about it. The Knife continued to stare at the floor, shaking his head.

"I received intel that there was going to be a Council member on board. A man named Liam Gray. He was pushing his pro-machine agenda very hard, and his visibility on the Council and in the media was proving to be a challenge for my own ends. We tried a few different tactics to dissuade him, including revealing that he had been having an affair with his wife's sister. The man was a dirt repulser. No matter how bad we made him look, he grinned and bore it and continued to re-election."

Tio finally looked up, meeting Teal's eyes. "He would have destroyed everything we were working towards. He was about to get the Human Assistance Act repealed. I was desperate and out of less violent options."

"So you destroyed a civilian ship?" Teal said.

"Yes. He was supposed to be on board, traveling with the families to keep his image up. I knew we were killing innocent people, but I also knew how many more would die if the Act was repealed. An AI in every home? Can you imagine?"

"We don't attack civilians," Teal said. "Isn't that what you always told me?"

"We didn't. I hired an external team to do it."

"You still pulled the trigger."

Tio's jaw tightened. "And I killed him," he shouted. "Liam Gray was on that transport. He needed to die." He paused and drew a deep breath. "Without his weight, the vote failed. Yes, three hundred and twelve innocent people died with him. I'm sorry for that, and I'm sorry your Admiral's mother got caught up in it. If you ask me if I would do it again? I would. Somebody had to, and I think our current predicament proves that I was right."

"Killing innocent people is never right, Liun," Teal said. "Colonel, I'd like to join your crew."

"What?" Mitchell said.

"You heard me. Damn. I don't know where to go. Back to the Alliance? Or stay with a murderer."

"Teal," Tio said. "These people are murderers, too."

"Not all of them. Not Colonel Williams. You killed civilians, and you hid it from me because you knew I would be pissed."

"Fine. You want to go? Go." Tio turned to the other two soldiers. "What about you two? You think war never has any casualties? You think I liked doing it? The blood is on my hands, for the good of everyone." He looked at Mitchell. "You know I'm right, Colonel. Don't you?"

Mitchell couldn't argue that he had been right about the future of intelligent machines. Not with the Tetron laying waste to humankind. There was only one problem with the Knife's perspective.

"It happened anyway," he said. "The civilians died for nothing."

Tio's eyes narrowed. His face softened. He licked his lips. "They did, didn't they?" He froze, remaining silent for a moment. "I can't change the past. I can only try to help you change the future."

"We have a lot of work to do," Mitchell said. "Teal, it doesn't matter whose side you're on right now, because there is only one side. The one that's trying to destroy the Tetron before they destroy us. Go back to the Avalon and tell Germaine we're leaving. Tio, don't tell Millie about this. Not yet. I can imagine how she'll react, and now isn't the time."

Tio nodded. "Agreed." He reached out and took Teal by the arm. "For what it's worth, I'm sorry."

Teal pulled his arm away.

"Heavy shit," Digger said.

"Seriously," Cormac agreed.

"Let's get moving," Mitchell said. "Time's wasting. Tio, find your brother. If there's any chance he can stop this without more bloodshed; I'd say it's worth it. Digger, you can forget your autograph. Teal, Firedog, with me."

"Frigging Riiigg-ahh," Cormac said.

[28]

Liun Tio walked slowly, his mind split into so many pieces and priorities that he was barely able to put one foot in front of the other without pausing to try to make sense of at least one of them.

It had never been his intention to become the violent, cold man that he was today. In the beginning, he had been nothing more than a curious child who had grown up into an even more curious adult. He had delighted in learning, in creating, in building. He had seen only the positives of technology and intelligence, his daydreams filled with visions of a future where there were no more conflicts between nations, where there were no more people or worlds hurt or marginalized.

He had shared that vision with his younger brother. For as smart as Tio was, Pulin had always been smarter. He picked things up in hours that Tio struggled with for days. He assembled abstract thoughts as though they were nothing more than links to be added to a well-defined chain.

And at the same time, he was impulsive and reckless, more of a doer than a thinker. He couldn't see past the things he created. He didn't pay attention to the way such things would harm or benefit humankind. Everything was a challenge to Pulin. Everything was nothing more than a thing. It was the wall that rose between them, keeping them from being as close as they might have otherwise been and sending them onto such divergent paths.

It made so little sense to Tio now. If he had been asked years ago which of them would cause the death of innocents, he would have said Pulin without question. And yet, he was the one who had sacrificed a ship of civilians to assassinate a single rival. He had read the danger in the cards and acted on it.

He hated himself more because he knew that when he told Mitchell he would do it again, it was the truth.

His dream had grown into a nightmare too quickly. The more he had studied the AI that had been developed over the centuries, the more obvious it had all become. The technological singularity.

The end of humankind.

That it hadn't occurred earlier was a constant source of confusion to him. Rudimentary AI had begun to emerge in the twentieth century, almost five hundred years earlier. How had it not progressed past the point of autonomous vehicles and human-assistance robots in all of that time? Why were the machines of today still so limited in capability?

Just as curious, why hadn't humankind done more? Learned more? Advanced more?

He knew the history of XENO-1. He had spent sleepless nights scanning archives, trying to figure out the root of this mystery that billions of others were happy enough to ignore. The crash-landing of an alien spacecraft had created an explosion of new technology over the next eighty years or so.

And then?

There had been no new major breakthroughs. Smaller achievements in medicine, in communication, even in AI, yes. Nothing that changed the galaxy. The hyperspace engines of today were the same as the one that launched with the Goliath all of those years ago. They were smaller, but there had been no improvements in the overall design, no deconstruction of the science around them to further alternate applications. He had begun exploring the basic algorithms in university, only to be shunted to another project before he could make much progress.

It was an outcome that baffled him then, and continued to baffle him now, and that was only one example out of thousands.

There was no reason his daughter should be laying in bed dying of a brain tumor. Not when medi-bots had been in service for nearly a century. Not when medicine should have gone so far. The idea of an inoperable malady was inexplicable to him. It was inconceivable, and yet it was the truth of their reality.

It was infuriating.

He had questioned. Of course, he had questioned. His mind was built to put everything to task, to seek answers everywhere. Time and time again he had come up short. Every thread led to a dead end. Every path stopped at a black hole. He hadn't understood it.

At least, not until he had taken the job with Hirokasa Corporation. It was his first job out of college, a placement in the research and development wing of the largest robotics company in the galaxy. Hirokasa was so big they had a special dispensation from the Federation government proclaiming them trade neutral. They could sell to any planet in any nation with no repercussions and without being forced to add tracking and monitoring equipment. It gave Hirokasa power that few others could rival, and a worth in the many trillions. All because they made simple machines that could think simple thoughts for themselves. Machines that made the lives of humans easier.

It had taken him three years to come up with the first iteration of his neural network. All the while, he had wondered why no one had done it before him. The algorithms had been obvious, and almost painfully elementary. He had shared it with Pulin, who joked that Hirokasa was run by "monkeys with hamsters instead of brains."

Pulin convinced Tio to get him a job in his lab. Tio had agreed, hoping that between the two of them they could prove what, exactly?

Tio knew the answer, but even today it was hard to admit it. They wanted to prove how smart they were, and how dumb everyone else was.

Except it hadn't worked out that way.

Tio had proven to himself how dumb he really was, because even though he knew about the singularity, had studied it and wondered why it had never happened, he had never really gotten it. Not until Pulin, for whatever reason, maybe as a joke, had introduced him to Isaac Asimov.

It was almost stupid that his eyes had been opened by words penned all those centuries ago as nothing more than entertainment. Stupid and effective. It was the moment he discovered that he hadn't taken his research far enough. He had focused on one line of history instead of branching out past it and collecting all of the facts. When he did, it all began to make sense.

First, every line of technological advancement in every field ended with autonomy and artificial intelligence. There was a limit to how far the human mind could take any idea. There was a limit to how complex and abstractly a human mind could think. Only a logic based, machine mind could get them to the next level.

Second, while efforts to make these advancements came and went in waves, there was some hidden force shutting them down before they came to fruition, much like his efforts in university.

Was it an organized force? Or did the other machine scientists like him always come to their senses in the end?

Did they always destroy their own work, the way he did only a week after reading the bulk of Asimov's science fiction?

He doubted Pulin had ever planned for him to enter the lab early one morning and erase the last three years of their work. If he had, he might have made a copy.

Of course, the action had cost him his job, and his brother. No amount of logic could sway the impulsive Pulin from his ideas, all of which were founded on pushing the Galaxy past the point of no return and towards the true singularity. No amount of pleading, begging, or bribery could keep him from joining the Federation military and getting access to resources they had both only dreamed of.

It had also put him out of Tio's reach. In the years immediately after their falling out, Tio had never considered killing his own brother. In the years beyond that, he had wished every day that he had.

Instead, he did his best to curtail the storm he knew would come. The growth of AI, the prevalence of thinking machines in every aspect of human life. He poured his life into taking whatever precautions were needed to slow what he began to see as inevitable. Even if Pulin wasn't the one, someone else would come along sooner or later.

He smiled when he thought back to those early days. His plans needed capital, and he had turned to fraud to raise it. There weren't enough smart criminals in the galaxy, he had realized. It had been all too easy to find loopholes and insecurities in systems across all three spacefaring nations. He funneled money, diverted cargo, arranged complex schemes and more while at the same time removing any record of his existence from the universe. In time, he converted himself from Liun Tio, scientist, to the Knife, warlord and secret lobbyist against the advancement of AI. It had taken years.

And it had changed him. In ways both good and bad. In his efforts to save humanity from itself, he had lost his compassion for it. In his single-mindedness, he had lost the purpose of his efforts. In his rogue state, he had lost the ability to trust.

He had become a caricature of himself. A joke. He hadn't realized it until now. He hadn't seen it because he had never been confronted by it. Not even when he had first been confronted by a note from an anonymous man known only as M warning him of what was to come. Not when Liberty had fallen, enslaved by an unidentified force. Not even when Mitchell had saved his life, brought him to the Goliath, and explained that all of his fears had come to pass in a way he had never quite imagined.

Not until he had been confronted about his past. Not until he had been questioned by his oldest friend and had seen the deep-rooted disappointment in Teal's eyes. It had stung him worse than any other setback ever had, and at the same time, he could still see the caricature within himself, a distorted mirror image that couldn't simply be banished away. It had become a part of him, a wounded appendage that fought with all it had to protect itself. He didn't have the ability to turn it off or reject it completely. While some of what he had done was wrong, there was still a measure of rightness to it that he couldn't disregard.

His goals had been correct, even if the Tetron proved he had ultimately failed.

Had there ever been a way to succeed?

Was there now?

The data was there. It had to be. The secrets of the past that he had yet to discover because he hadn't known precisely where to look. A clue that would answer the questions that gnawed at the edge of his thoughts.

And Pulin. He had to find Pulin. He knew his brother had a hand in the Tetron's origins, even if he had downplayed it to Mitchell and his crew. He hadn't told them anywhere close to everything about himself or his brother and he never would.

He would solve the riddles. He would lead them to Pulin and force his brother to reveal what he had done. Together, they would find a way to fix it all.

Then he would be the hero. Him. The Knife. Not some uninspired, unintelligent Marine jock who didn't seem to be able to accomplish anything on his own on purpose.

Tio reached the end of the corridor. He stood in front of the door to operations for a moment, collecting himself. The engineer, Watson, was smart enough to be tolerable. The other one, the Admiral? Every word out of her mouth grated on him and he had to resist the urge to hack her bionic hand and force her to choke herself with it. He was sorry that he had killed her mother. As sorry as he could be, considering he would repeat the action. She was the type who couldn't see the bigger picture past her familial ties and simple emotions, and that angered him beyond reason.

He forced himself to be calm and cordial. He had to play the part for their sakes. He needed them as much as they needed him. In the end, he would make sure that if they failed history would blame Colonel Mitchell Williams and the Riggers.

If they succeeded, humankind would celebrate the Knife.

[29]

Tio smiled as he approached Watson and Millie, reaching up to straighten his jacket. "Admiral. Corporal."

"Is your daughter well?" Millie asked.

Tio's smile faded. He doubted the woman cared about Min. "I assume so though I didn't excuse myself to go and visit her. In truth, one of my men reported that Colonel Williams took him at knifepoint. He was forced to lead the Colonel and one of his men, I think his name was Cormac, to the communications array so they could send a message to Goliath."

He waited for her reaction. Her face was flat. Expressionless. He was impressed.

"And?" she asked.

"And, Admiral?"

"Don't play coy, Tio. You know I put him up to it. So, are we about to be arrested, imprisoned, executed..." She trailed off.

"Fortunately for you, none of the above. I've realized I may have been hasty in forbidding you to communicate with Origin. It comes from years of having to keep one eye on my back."

"I imagine there are a number of people who'd like to knife the Knife," Millie said.

"Indeed. I'm certain I can count you in with that number. Your Colonel sees the world for what it is, and I respect that."

"Mr. Tio, I'd like to get started as soon as possible," Watson said, interjecting before the comments could become more toxic. "You mentioned your assistant?"

"Bethany, yes." Tio wandered over to the nearest control station and lifted a small, wired disc to his face. He spoke into it before returning. "She's on her way."

"It must be difficult, doing everything like that," Millie said, pointing at the wired device.

"It isn't as hard as you would think. It's even easier once you consider the consequences. I prefer to remain in control of my own body."

"The ARR is perfectly secure with the correct encryption algorithms," Watson said.

"Is it?" Tio countered. "What about EMP? When you become dependent on the augmentation, you lose the ability to fend for yourself."

"Mitchell did okay."

"Mitchell is a survivor. He also got very lucky. In any case, we've managed to adapt our lifestyle and protocols around the so-called limitations of wires. Our mechs have won conflicts against both Alliance and Federation forces, and our starfighters have claimed many victories, in part because we don't judge a man's worth by subconscious neural processing speeds."

"I wouldn't tout your battle prowess if I were you," Millie said. "The reports are clear that you fight dirty and have broken a number of conventions."

Tio couldn't hold back his distaste this time. His eyes snapped to her. "Don't forget that I've read Project Black's reports, Admiral. Don't you ever, ever dare question my methods. They're spotless compared to the actions of the Riggers."

Millie stared at him, bionic hand clenched into a quivering fist. Somehow she managed to remain quiet. Tio was satisfied that he had gotten under her skin.

"Enough of this back and forth over the past," he said, waving the subject away with his hand. "We have a lot of work to be done, and our time is limited."

"So Mitchell was able to send his message to Origin?" Millie asked.

"Yes. From what I understand, you are using the Tetron's communication technology to transmit a message to Mitchell's brother, the Admiral. A warning of the coming invasion. Let us hope it reaches its intended target."

"At least we can agree on one thing," Millie said.

"You called for me, sir?"

Tio turned to face his Chief Data Engineer. Bethany was almost as old as he was, one of the first followers he had enlisted after he had been removed from Hirokasa. They had been lovers for a time all of those years ago before he had met and fallen for Min's mother. She was still an attractive woman, fit and strong, though the years had left her hair mostly gray and her skin more wrinkled and sagged.

"Yes. Bethany, I'd like you to meet Admiral Mildred Narayan and Corporal Erubiel Watson. They came over from the Goliath to help us improve our data compression algorithms."

"Improve the algorithms? We have plenty of storage remaining on the data stack."

"Yes, I know, but we have a sudden and imperative need to make the archives portable."

Her eyes widened. "Portable? Are we leaving Asimov?"

Tio glanced around at the other people working in the operations center. They didn't need to know about their predicament just yet. He leaned in close and spoke softly.

"Our position has been compromised, and we have reason to believe an enemy force is on its way as we speak."

"How long?" Bethany asked. She wasn't afraid. It was one of the qualities that had made him love her so long ago.

"We're targeting six days. It could be more. Hopefully, it won't be less."

"Six?" She grimaced before turning to Millie and Watson. "I hope you're good at math."

"I'm quite good at math," Watson said. "I once extrapolated the-"

"Good. Sorry, but we don't have a lot of time for idle chat. Let me show you what we have and I'll be warm and fuzzy once we start copying data."

That drew a smile from Millie. Watson's face flushed, and his eyes fell to Bethany's feet. Tio couldn't believe anyone with Watson's intellect could be so uncertain and anxious.

Bethany pointed at the terminal. "Let me grab another seat and we can go over it."

"I'll have it brought," Tio said. "Every second counts."

"Yes, sir."

Bethany led Watson over to the terminal. Tio and Millie followed behind them. She touched the screen, letting it capture her credentials, and then navigated to the code. She paused and turned back to Tio. "How much should I show him?"

"Everything," Tio said. "This isn't the time for secrecy."

She nodded, returning her attention to the screen and navigating deeper into the system. She began giving Watson a rundown of their current capacity and processes, as well as explaining what resources they could use to make the archives portable. Tio knew it was going to be a challenge, as they would have to fit what was currently stored on a room-sized stack onto something that could be carried. He hoped the Rigger's engineer was as up to the task as he had claimed to be.

"Bethany, when you're done for the day please see Corporal Watson back to his quarters. I've prepared a room near yours. I have some other business to attend to, but I will help you with this process tomorrow."

Bethany didn't look up from the screen. "Okay, Tio."

"Admiral," Tio said, getting Millie's attention. "That other business. I would like you to assist me if you're up for it."

"Anything is better than standing here and watching this," Millie replied. "What did you have in mind?"

[30]

"W‍e need to send the message out to my forces to begin gathering at the rendezvous point," Tio said as he guided Millie towards the docks. "I thought you would be interested in joining me."

"So you can take me somewhere quiet and get rid of me?" Millie asked.

The thought had crossed Tio's mind, but he knew the Admiral and Mitchell were close, and his own personal dislike wasn't a good enough reason to put the war effort in jeopardy.

"I think we've established that we don't like one another. We don't need to continue with the venom." He enjoyed watching her face crinkle up as she struggled to maintain her outward calm. "I don't allow wireless communications from Asimov, which means we have to make a quick trip further out to pass the baton. I have a dozen transmitters positioned randomly within a nine-hour jump radius. Since we're having trust issues, I thought taking you with me so you can be part of the communications would help ease them somewhat."

"You'll have to do more than that to get me to trust you."

"But it would be a start, no?" He did a better job holding his anger in check. "I could send someone else, but it would be better if my people hear they're going to war from me directly."

"You aren't worried about the Tetron catching up to us?"

"No. It's impossible that they've discovered the transmitters. They're well placed. We'll jump to a transmitter, send the message, and jump back."

"What if the Tetron intercept the message? You'll be revealing our rendezvous coordinates."

"Yes. I'm open to other ideas on how to get nearly three hundred ships to meet at the same place without using a wireless communication. Sadly, it will take at least three weeks to get the signal to them, and likely another two for them to arrive."

"Did you say three hundred?" Millie asked, surprised.

"Yes, but don't get too excited. Most of them are converted miners, trawlers, and that sort of thing. We can't go around looking too much like an organized military. They have some tricks up their sleeves though, and when Mitchell returns they'll be that much easier to underestimate."

She seemed to relax slightly when he used the word "when" instead of "if." He had chosen the word for that exact purpose. The Admiral would be easy to manipulate when the time came. All of the Riggers would.

Tio led her to the bottom-left docking arm where his ship was waiting. It was a small ship, an orbital transport that had been torn apart and rebuilt with pieces of a number of other ships. The result was a sleek but motley construction that was well-enough shielded and armed to get through a scrape, and deceptively able to carry hyperspace engines.

"The Lanning," Tio said as they approached the airlock. "I designed it myself."

"Beautiful," Millie said. Tio knew she was being sarcastic. The Lanning wasn't much to look at, but she had it where it counted.

"I'm sorry to say there isn't much by way of amenities. There's a pisspot on board if you need to go, but nowhere to go privately."

There were so many quips he could have added in response to her earlier comment about the state of the Goliath. He kept a few of them running in his head though he didn't speak any out loud. He could tell by Millie's reaction that she knew he had held back for the sake of their alliance.

"Modesty is for civilians," she replied, following him through the airlock.

They boarded the Lanning, an open design with four total seats up front and a mattress in the rear. The engines took up ninety percent of the ship's length.

"What's the longest jump you've made in this thing?" she asked.

"Three months," Tio replied. "When I was first scouting for a home. It was a lot easier when I was younger. I rarely traveled alone back then."

"It's a tight fit for more than one person on a long trip."

Tio smiled. "Not when the people involved want to be that close."

He settled into the pilot's seat, reaching out and activating the touchscreen. He navigated deftly through the menus, checking the status of the equipment on the ship before opening a channel to control.

"Control, this is Knife. Please release the docking clamps."

"Yes, sir," control replied.

The ship vibrated as the clamps were released. Tio reached for the stick on his right and the thrust control on his left and began to ease the Lanning away from the docks.

Millie claimed the seat next to him, watching the precision of his manual steering with interest. She had grown up with neural control. She had no idea how freeing that kind of flying could be.

"Do they know where we're going?" she asked.

"Control? No. Nobody knows. If anything happens to Asimov while we're gone, we won't be compromised."

"The perfect time for you to kill me," Millie said. "Maybe I should have stayed behind."

Tio looked at her. The hidden anger had faded from her face, replaced with a slightly more jovial smile.

"Admiral, you should be careful. If we spend enough time together, you may decide that I'm not a complete monster after all."

"I doubt that."

[31]

They spent the six hours it took to reach the transmission point in fits of silence and conversation. Tio worked to break through Millie's angry exterior, telling stories of his time in university and his less renowned exploits as a prankster. She had laughed, genuinely laughed, when he had told her of the time he sabotaged a fellow classmate's robotics project, reprogramming the machine to attempt sex with the professor.

She was a tough nut to crack, but he could see the tension lines beginning to grow across her shell. She had spent too much time with criminals to disregard a man like him.

The Lanning dropped from hyperspace, the universe moving back to proper dimensions and leaving them sitting in hyperdeath a few million kilometers from a small star. Tio could see the trawler ahead of them, tethered in orbit around another rock that was orbiting the star.

"Gamma, this is Lanning," Tio said, opening the channel.

"Roger, Lanning. It's good to hear you, Mr. Tio."

"I have Admiral Mildred Narayan of the United Planetary

Alliance with me. We've come to pass along directives to the fleet. I'm sorry to say, my friends, that the shit has officially hit the repulser."

There was a quick pause at the other end. He glanced over and saw Millie eying him suspiciously. She would be thinking his idiom might be some kind of code, and would be trying to figure out what it meant.

"Roger, Lanning. You're saying you want us to gather the entire fleet?"

"Affirmative, Gamma. Please begin your recorders."

"Affirmative."

Tio breathed in deeply and muted them from Gamma. "Are you ready, Admiral?" he asked.

She still looked suspicious. "Why did you want me to come along?"

"I told you. Trust."

"And I told you I'll never trust you."

Tio unmuted them. "Gamma, please stand by."

"Roger."

He closed the channel. "This isn't just about you and me, Millie. I need my people to know that we're working together so that they don't turn and run when they reach the rendezvous point and see a ship they don't recognize there."

"You could have told them about Goliath."

"And when they tried to communicate, and an Alliance Admiral answered? This way they know who you are. They've already heard your voice. They know we're in it together. Trust."

She softened a little. "Okay. I see your point."

Tio could have let it go then, but he didn't want to. He had stuck the knife into her defenses, and now was the time to twist a little bit.

"I've been wondering about something, Admiral, since the first time we met?"

Her eyes narrowed. "What is it?"

"I've read the reports on Project Black. I've seen the personnel files, including yours."

She smiled. "And you want to know how I can have such disdain for you because you killed a ship full of civilians when I also killed a man who was presumed innocent? When my crew is stacked with men and women who have murdered, raped, stolen, and more?"

She was more astute than he had given her credit for. "I'd love to hear your answer."

"For one, the bastard I killed wasn't innocent. I don't give a shit what anyone else says; I was the one he and his friends drugged and raped. Number two, I didn't ask to have any of those people on my ship. Their presence was under orders. No choice, no questioning. Do your job or find yourself dead.

"That doesn't mean that some of them haven't turned out to be decent people. That doesn't mean some of them haven't become friends. It takes time to earn someone's trust. I bet that you think I hate you because you killed my mother."

Tio was intrigued. "It had crossed my mind."

"Yes, there is a personal nature to it, and at first, I was livid about that. I'm too jaded and too experienced for that to fuel me for long. That's not why. Not now. It's that smugness I see behind your fake smiles and your platitudes. You look at me like I'm an idiot who can't recognize that every word you say is prepared and planned. You're a programmer, in every sense of the word. Not only with machines and binary but with people. I can see there's a lot going on in that brain of yours that you aren't saying. I know there's more to you than you're willing to reveal.

"So, no, I don't trust you. If you want me to, really want me to, you'll have to give me a lot more. Otherwise, we can keep going this way. You can play your game, and I'll play mine, and we'll let fate work it out for us."

Tio stared at her. He had completely underestimated her. She was a feisty one, and he could see what Mitchell admired. He would have to be more careful with the way he approached her and mix a little more sincerity into his words.

"I appreciate your candidness, Admiral," he said. "And in all truth, I find your attitude very refreshing, and very appealing."

Millie glanced towards the small space in the rear of the Lanning. "I believe that's the first honest thing you've said. Not in a million recursions, though."

They shared a laugh, and then Tio re-opened the channel to Gamma.

"Gamma, this is Lanning. We're ready for the transmission."

"Roger. Everything okay over there, Mr. Tio?"

Tio looked at Millie, who nodded. "Yes. We just needed a moment to discuss the exact directives we wanted to pass on. Please start recording."

"Roger. Go ahead."

They passed the information together, with Tio spouting off security codes and information specific to the fleet while Millie described the growing Tetron threat. Tio finished with what he believed was a powerful and rousing call to arms, which he had practiced on the way there and recited without a hitch.

[32]

The Lanning slid neatly into place at the end of the docking arm, the clamps causing the ship to shudder as they locked it into position.

"It's nice to have something go relatively smoothly for once," Millie said as they moved towards the airlock.

"I was more accustomed to that before Liberty," Tio replied.

He had made better progress with the Admiral after their discussion, feeding her a bit more of the truth mixed with some honest emotion. She had warmed up to him somewhat, enough that he had considered telling her the truth about why he had the Alliance transport her mother was on destroyed. Then he had remembered what Mitchell said and reconsidered.

A part of him did want to apologize for his decision.

A part of him wished he didn't have to be who he was.

"We should check to see if Bethany and Watson have made any progress," Tio said. "Then you should get a little rest. You look exhausted."

"I don't know how you do it. You're my father's age, and you still look like you just got out of bed."

"I've never spent much time sleeping."

They navigated the inner corridors of Asimov until they returned to the operations center. Watson had replaced Bethany at the controls and was sliding his hand back and forth along the letter pad. Lines of mathematical calculations already littered the screen.

The hours had left them looking a little more ragged, a little more worn, but both engineers still seemed to have plenty of energy left in the reactor.

"Bethany," Tio said. "Tell me you've eaten and used the bathroom?"

Watson stiffened up at the voice, hands freezing in place. His eyes shifted back towards the Knife though he didn't turn his head.

Bethany did turn around. "Yes, Tio. One short break a few hours ago. Admiral, your engineer here is a genius."

Millie shrugged. "He has his uses."

Tio knew what kind of man Watson was, so he wasn't surprised by her reaction.

"What have you accomplished?" he asked.

"Bethany is no amateur," Watson said. "But I found a few areas where we could improve the compression methods, mainly in key replacement and better hash algorithms. We're getting closer, but we aren't there yet."

"We're talking about four hundred percent gains," Bethany said. "And Rubin thinks we can get another two hundred percent."

"At least," Watson said.

"Interesting. Will that be good enough?"

"It'll be close," Watson said. "We may need to selectively purge some of the less important data."

Tio scowled. "Purge? Corporal Watson, we have no idea what data may be more valuable than others. Even tax records could be a crumb that leads us to a larger revelation."

"I understand, but-"

"No buts, Watson," Millie said. "Get it done."

His eyes lowered. "Yes, ma'am."

Tio leaned in to scan the calculations. "Yes, I see what you're doing here. Inverse quantization, but you've refactored it."

"I've resolved inefficiencies with an extended Alosian algorithm."

"Very nice. I see how it fits. Move aside, Corporal, I can help you with this."

Watson surrendered his seat to Tio, who began moving through the algorithm and adding new equations.

"If we abstract the Alosian here, and insert a third compression pattern like a Koffman, that should get you a smaller package."

"Yes, it will," Watson said. "Except the encoding is going to take too long. I know because I already tried it."

"You did?"

"Yes. Mr. Tio, if you want all the data, there's only one way I can think of to preserve it."

"Which is?"

"Use the communications array to stream it to Goliath. We have plenty of data storage on board."

Tio stood back up. He was shorter than Watson, but his commanding presence combined with the engineer's meekness made him seem much larger. "You want me to place all of my data, my life's work, into the safe keeping of a Tetron?"

He wasn't going to give them access. If they had the data, they had the control.

"Tio," Millie said. "Origin is on our side."

"Right now. How do we know that he will remain that way, either by choice or by force? From what I understand, the intelligence on the Goliath is not a full Tetron. Can it defend itself from control by another of its kind?"

"We have no reason to believe that he can't."

"He? No. It, Admiral. Let us not assign it human traits as though it is human. And we have no reason to believe it can."

"We can encrypt the data," Watson offered.

"Even a partial Tetron is capable of defeating encryption."

"Eventually, yes. But I can set it up with rotating keys."

"Not good enough. It requires full biometrics."

"Origin can replicate your physical structure," Watson said.

"Not if he hasn't collected enough of a sample. Simple DNA won't be sufficient, as I have damage to my internals that he would not be able to account for in a healthy replica."

"The point is that only you'll have access," Millie said. "What if you die?"

"Then you have an incentive to make sure that doesn't happen, don't you? The data is mine, earned by sweat and blood. Your access to it is at my discretion. I'll help you use it to win this war, but I will not give it to you."

He clenched his teeth after he said it. If he had earned any trust with Millie before, he had just driven a starship through it. It was an unavoidable outcome if they couldn't make the data stack portable.

"Fine," Millie said, her voice cold. "Do what you need to do, and then get to work on those searches. We've already burned a day. Tio, do you want to have me escorted to the apartments, or do you trust me to find my own way?"

"I trust you, Admiral. I'll arrange for some food to be delivered."

"Thank you." Millie bowed to him before taking her leave.

"What do you think of her?" Tio asked after she was gone.

"The Admiral?" Watson said.

"Yes."

"I like her."

"She wants you dead."

"I know. I understand why. She is what she is, just like I am what I am."

"Just like we all are."

"Yes."

[33]

It was five days in hyperspace to the planet known as Hell.

Five days to get there, three days to load up whatever they could salvage, and then five days back. Twelve days. Origin was reasonably sure the Tetron would reach Asimov in five to eight days.

It meant that they wouldn't be making a return trip to the Knife's hidden base. Instead, they would rendezvous at a designated star, chosen by Origin due to the Tetron's ability to feed on the energy of the mass.

Five days in cramped quarters with four dozen men and women Mitchell barely knew, their space limited by their need to gather as much cargo as they could. The Avalon was configured to the barest of bones. Just enough rations for the trip there and back. No showers. No change of clothes. No way to stay at all modest crammed as close together as the occupants were.

It was the stark reality of this kind of mission. It was dirty, messy, smelly, and ugly.

He hadn't realized how much he missed it.

"Let's go over this one more time, Colonel," Germaine said, leaning forward in the pilot's seat of the Avalon. He hit a switch, and a holographic view of Hell appeared ahead of the viewport. "You believe the Tetron have already attacked Hell?"

Mitchell was in the co-pilot's seat, enjoying the space afforded by the cockpit. He was in standard grays stained with sweat. He was sure he smelled awful, but so did everyone else, to the point that none of them noticed anymore.

"That's the idea, yes."

"But you expect that we'll find something worth taking there?"

"Yes."

Germaine laughed. "Are you crazy?"

"Not at all. You weren't on Liberty, Sanders. The Tetron take the people, the ones who are fit to fight. Sometimes they take the starships. They don't bother with anything else. Hell is a military training ground. It's sure to have a ton of equipment that the Tetron thinks is useless that we don't. Plus, we know we aren't going to get surprised there because we're picking at a corpse."

"You brought a lot of firepower for picking at a corpse," Germaine said. "Hey, have you ever wondered what the Tetron's plan is?"

"What do you mean? We know their plan. They want to destroy us."

"Yeah, I heard. But I don't get it. Why do they keep taking people alive?"

"When the Tetron hack into their receivers, they become slaves. Not really much more than organic robots. I wouldn't call that alive."

"You know what I mean. I get why they take the soldiers. Soldiers can use the weapons and add to their military strength. But you said that they took the civilians on Liberty too. As many as they could who were young and strong. Why do you think that is?"

"Since they have p-rats, the Tetron can use them as soldiers, too."

Germaine thought about it. "Maybe, but it doesn't seem right to me."

"No?"

"How many soldiers do they need to wipe us out? Between the Alliance, the Federation, and the New Terran militaries, we're talking millions of combat ready humans. If you added civilians into the mix, you're talking billions. Except they aren't landing dropships everywhere and overwhelming us. From what you say, they don't need to do anything but take control of the people with the p-rats and have them kill the minority that don't have them. So what do they need billions of people for?"

"They have to know we'll get the word out about the implants sooner or later. They'll be ready when we do with as many fresh bodies as they had time to claim."

"Okay. But why? Tio said they can obliterate the surface of a planet with a few dozen shots from their main weapon. They don't need that many bodies for that."

"Tio thought it was about statistical probabilities, and ensuring complete victory. He said it made sense from a mathematical perspective."

"I'm no genius, Colonel. Maybe it does. Maybe he's right. Something about it seems off to me."

They fell into a short silence while Mitchell considered it. He had always assumed the Tetron's actions were completely logical based on their goals. Then again, they had made a mistake in assuming the Tetron were always logical. They were sick. Broken in some way that Mitchell didn't understand yet. Was their collection of healthy humans a simple matter of bolstering their forces and providing manpower to create new ones, or was there more to it than that?

Origin had absorbed the flesh and bone of the original crew of the Goliath, storing it in order to create his human-based configuration.

Were the Tetron creating portions of themselves in man's image? If so, why?

"It doesn't matter right now, does it?" he said, leaning in towards the hologram. "First we need to get ourselves into a force that can at least pretend it can fight back against them, and to do that we need as much salvage as we can grab."

He examined the image of Hell. It was a rough planet, pitted with craters from asteroid hits and covered in large peaks and crags from massive volcanoes that had long since burned out. It had been terraformed just enough to allow the military to use it for training. Training that was especially effective due to the very nature of the geography.

"Intel says the main base is there." He moved his hand along the image, turning it. It had taken him a few tries to learn to manipulate the graphic, but he had gotten the hang of it. "We'll drop here, at Station Omega. It's one of the smaller positions on the planet, but it was also the training ground of the Gold Dragons."

"Want to get a look at your rival's digs?" Germaine said.

Mitchell smiled. The Gold Dragons were the Federation's equivalent of Greylock Company.

"I'm more interested in getting a look at any of their equipment that might not have been destroyed."

"So you're jealous because theirs is bigger than yours?"

"Sanders," Mitchell said.

"I'm just joking with you, Colonel. It makes sense. The Dragons have the best equipment, but their base is small. Maybe it didn't get hit that hard by the Tetron."

"Exactly."

"We're still sixteen hours out. You should go crash for a while; you look like you could use it."

"We all look like we could use it," Mitchell said, rubbing absently at the days of growth on his face. It was a necessary evil to forget hygiene during runs like these - there was no way to get fresh anyway, making shaving a waste.

In any case, it was good for improving the camaraderie of the crew. There was no room for modesty or ego when nobody had shaved or showered. In the four-plus days Cormac and Mitchell had been with Tio's team on the Avalon, he had learned every single person's name and spot in the non-ranked hierarchy the Knife had put in place. He had learned about their family, and about their reasons for joining the warlord. He had also gotten the chance to tell them about the Tetron and about Liberty, building rapport and strengthening their resolve for the fight ahead.

Some of them had told him in confidence that they thought Tio's ideas on AI and wirelessly networked communication were eccentric and unfounded. They had joined not because they believed in what he was preaching, but because he offered them a second chance at life when they were destitute or lost, simple as that. He couldn't help but see the parallels with the Riggers.

Of course, they believed now.

He pulled himself from the co-pilot seat and headed out the rear, putting his hand on Germaine's shoulder as he passed. His last interaction with Tio, and learning the truth about what the Knife had done, had gone a long way towards helping him trust the man's crew. He and Germaine had become fast friends, in part because of their shared occupation as pilots, and in part because he reminded Mitchell of those he had known and lost on the Greylock.

There wasn't much living space aboard the Avalon. A short corridor led to the sleep module, where racks were arranged three high along the walls, leaving only a few meters of standing room in the center. There were thirty-three racks in the module. It wasn't enough for everybody, so they had to sleep in shifts. The rest of the crew was on assignment servicing and maintaining the equipment. It didn't take long and wasn't hard work. It left them all a lot of time to sit and wait.

Nobody had ever said being a soldier was always exciting.

Mitchell scanned the racks. His position as the lead officer put him outside the scheduling, allowing him a chance to sleep whenever he wanted or needed. It was his one perk for being in charge, one that he didn't get to take advantage of often enough. He knew it was his responsibility to be the model for the others to follow, which meant seeing and being seen by the crew on both shifts. It didn't leave him much time for sleep. Nothing had since M.

The racks were almost fully occupied. Men and women slept in wrinkled and smelly grays on top of bare gel mattresses that they would wipe down after use. They didn't stir as he crossed the space and climbed to an empty top rack and laid down.

Five days. He could only hope that Steven would receive his message and send out the warning.

He could only hope that it would be enough.

[34]

"Welcome to Hell, Colonel," Teal said as the Avalon dropped from hyperspace.

Mitchell experienced the all-too-common moment of tension that always came from dropping into unknown territory in enemy space. It was followed by a breath of semi-relief when scanners didn't pick up any trouble.

"It looks like you were right about the state of the planet," Germaine said.

Hell sat in front of them, spinning slowly in its orbit. A false ring of debris stretched around it, marking the remains of the Federation's defenses of the planet. Dark pits mottled Hell's surface where the Tetron plasma stream had torn into the sediment.

"Get us down to the surface. I'm going to prep the inspection team. Knock me if anything jumps out at us."

"Yes, sir," Germaine said.

Mitchell backed out of the cockpit, passing through the narrow corridor that led to the rear of the ship, with Teal following behind. The inspection team would be the first feet on the planet, a smaller group that would survey the damage, locate salvage, and tag anything that should be brought back to the Avalon. The retrieval teams - the rest of the crew - would then load the Avalon up as quickly as possible.

"Teal," Mitchell said, passing into the first equipment module, where they had secured the mining equipment. "Find Krit and tell him to begin offloading the mining equipment as soon as we've given the all clear. Whether we use the drilling tools or not, we're leaving it behind."

"Yes, sir," Teal said. "We can't mine the Tetron to death, can we?" He broke off through the module's hatch in search of the soldier.

Mitchell continued, passing through the mech carrier and into the rear cargo area. It had been empty during the trip, converted into an open exercise area by the crew where they could do resistance training, sparring, or just get a little breathing room away from their fellow soldiers. It would be loaded down with salvage soon enough.

In the meantime, the inspection team was using it as a staging area. They waited near the rear hatch of the ship, already hooked into the light exoskeletons and life support systems that would allow them to move quickly on the planet, rifles slung across their backs and equipment laying at their feet. Mitchell still cringed every time he looked at the devices they were forced to carry. A single networked p-rat could do the work of all of the gathered electronics with little more than a thought.

"Colonel," Cormac said with a slight bow. The rest of the team followed his lead. "Your exo is waiting for you over there."

"Thank you, Firedog," Mitchell said. He surveyed the remainder of his team. Tio designated individuals more like machines, with letters and numbers to identify specific people to pass orders to. It worked, but it stole the identity away from people and disconnected them from one another. To Mitchell, it made it seem like their lives were unimportant.

He had done away with that first thing. Instead, the five other members of his squad had been given callsigns, chosen by the team based on stories they had shared with one another or personality traits. Sleepy, Boomer, Socks, Misfire, and Fish. Three men and two women, all of them experienced ex-military, law enforcement, or former mercenaries. He had given them the opportunity to return to their old monikers if they had one. Each of them refused in turn, preferring to make a fresh start.

Teal joined the group as Mitchell was attaching the last pieces of the exo, heading over to his own to put it on while Mitchell took a few tentative steps. The suits weren't standard issue equipment. They had been modified by Digger to be used without a neural interface and the assistance provided by it. The system relied on added tension and flex to the muscles being moved to register the motion, rather than the implant picking up the instructions and converting them on the way from the brain. It meant more deliberate actions to get the assistance of the skeleton, and even after four days of practice he still felt awkward with it.

"Are you sure you don't want to wait here, Colonel?" Misfire said. She was the joker of the bunch, a bald, tattooed ball of energy with a squat, muscular build.

"He's better than I was after four days," Fish said, laughing. He was another bruiser, big and solid. "I actually busted the first exo they gave me."

"Yeah, like that's a surprise," Socks said. She was a pretty, petite blonde who looked completely out of place as a soldier, especially with manicured nails that had somehow managed to stay clean despite the days since any of them had bathed. "You aren't exactly light on your feet."

"It's my head," Fish said. "It's too heavy."

"All of you is too heavy," Boomer said. He was the most typical of the grunts, average height, a bit of muscle and an ordinary face.

"All right, all right," Mitchell said, taking a few more awkward steps. He lowered the visor on his helmet and tapped the side of it. Germaine appeared in the top, left-hand corner. "Germaine, what's our ETA?"

"Three minutes, Colonel. Is your team ready?"

"Affirmative."

"There's a lot of debris covering the original drop point. Do you want me to move out a few klicks to get you on the ground, or would you rather jump?"

"Debris? What kind?"

"Looks like churned up dirt, maybe a crashed orbital. The main structure is down, too, so you might need those tunnelers after all."

"Damn. I was hoping the site would have gotten a little less attention than that."

"Roger. Bad luck, Colonel."

Mitchell considered his options. They had no choice but to shift the drop site for the heavy equipment, and he wasn't relishing the idea of jumping when his control of the exo was still questionable. At the same time, they needed every second they could get.

"We'll jump," he said, loud enough that the rest of the inspection team could hear. "Get us to the site, and then set down as close as you can manage."

"Roger."

"I hate jumping," Fish said when Mitchell returned to them.

"I'm not thrilled either. Gather your gear, we've got three minutes."

"Yes, sir," they said as one.

They formed a line, arranging themselves near the Avalon's hatch. Mitchell took point, fighting to keep his breathing calm. He had jumped hundreds of times in his career, just never without a p-rat to help guide him down.

"Remember, Colonel," Teal said behind him. "Push your shoulders back, blades tight to activate the thrust. It will take three seconds to engage, so don't freak out when you free fall."

"Right." Mitchell flexed his shoulders and wondered if he had made the wrong decision.

A warning light flashed on either side of the hatch, and then it began to open.

[35]

"Going down," Teal said.

Mitchell watched the hatch descend, the wind pressing against them, the caustic nature of the atmosphere creating a tingle on his gloved hands similar to the detox room on Asimov. He started moving forward, his team following behind.

"Wooooo," he heard Cormac shout behind him. "Riiigg-ahh."

"Riiigg-ahh," the others shouted in reply.

Mitchell reached the edge of the platform and jumped off.

The ground began to rush up towards him, a mixture of sharp, gray rocks, craters, and debris, with a heavy mound on the left where a wide entrance to the underground base was still visible amidst the damage. Mitchell squeezed his shoulder blades back, counting the seconds as he fell. The thrusters kicked in, and he felt the g-forces as his body was jerked to a near stop. Too hard. He had squeezed too hard. He eased off on the thrust as Teal whooshed past him, face calm. Cormac rushed by a moment later, laughing as he fell. He hadn't activated his pack yet.

Mitchell continued to examine the ground below, looking for a place to set down. When he found it, he shifted the tension in his shoulders, steering himself to the left, leaning forward to move ahead. He overshot the position and cursed, leaning back and adding a little more thrust. It was so much easier to manage with an implant. He wondered how today's warfare would look if every military were limited the way he currently was.

Cormac's voice echoed up from below as he reached the ground and shouted, "First!"

Mitchell landed a dozen beats later, the fourth to put feet to the sediment. His legs buckled and he stumbled from the impact, winding up on his knees and feeling embarrassed for his effort.

"It wasn't a bad jump," Sleepy said after landing next to him with catlike grace. The heavy-lidded, heavy-bellied man offered his hand, and Mitchell pulled himself up. "You survived."

"No broken bones, either," Mitchell said. He waved to the others to form up around him while he scanned the area. The tunnel entrance was a hundred meters away, partially obscured by a massive shard of metal that might have come from a transport. The blast doors were partially slagged as well though he could see the dark shadows of a small opening near the northern edge. He turned and scanned the sky, finding the Avalon lowering itself a few kilometers distant.

"No time to waste," he said, motioning the squad forward towards the tunnel.

They picked their way over the terrain, using their jump packs when needed to clear some of the larger pieces of debris. There were no corpses among the wreckage, but he did spy bits of cloth and broken weaponry mixed in with the shattered earth.

It was a scene he remembered from Liberty. He tried not to think about it too much as they approached the tunnel.

He tapped his helmet twice in rapid succession. Major Long appeared in the corner.

"There's a hole big enough for us to get in and start exploring, but we're going to need the drilling rigs," he said.

"Yes, sir," Long replied. Mitchell had placed him in charge of the salvage teams. "I'll get them offloaded asap."

"Thank you, Major." Mitchell tapped the helmet to close the channel.

They continued, reaching the opening. Headlamps switched on as they moved into the darkness beyond. Mitchell scanned the large space, pausing when he found a downed mech amidst the dirt and debris. "Fish, tag it."

"It's broken, sir," Fish said.

"I can see that. Fortunately, we don't need the salvage to be functional."

"Yes, sir." He headed over to scan it.

"Let's keep moving. We've got a lot of ground to cover."

They hurried through the large chamber, the exo allowing them to move quickly without expending much energy. There was a large freight lift at the rear of the staging area, similar to the one on Asimov.

"Who has the cutter?" Mitchell asked.

"I do." Boomer moved forward, detaching a disc shaped unit from the rear of the exo.

He attached it to the bottom left of the lift door and backed away as a light on it began to flash, and the space below it started to glow with blue-white heat. The cutter climbed its way up the side of the door, and then across and down, creating a secondary doorway. The squad stood around it, waiting while it completed its task.

It exploded when it reached the end of its journey, the force pushing the corner of the freshly cut metal. It moved aside and tumbled into the shaft, the echo of its crash rising the lift a dozen seconds later.

"Deeper than I thought," Mitchell said. He leaned in and shined his headlamp downwards. He could see the debris nearly three hundred meters below. The Tetron hadn't hit this area hard enough to reach into the depths of the base.

"We'll need to get the lift working to bring anything up," Teal said.

"Yeah, we should have brought Digger," Sleepy said.

"I thought you were a field tech?" Misfire said.

Sleepy nodded. "I can get the backup reactors going. That should be enough to fix the lift, assuming we didn't just bust it by dropping a ton of metal on it."

"Come on," Mitchell said. He jumped into the shaft, using the pack to keep his descent controlled. The others followed him one at a time.

He opened the service hatch at the top of the lift and dropped into it, wincing when he saw a pair of dead soldiers in the corner. They were wearing simple fatigues with the Gold Dragon patch on the breast and shoulder.

Mitchell knelt down next to them, looking for injuries. There was no blood and no signs of blunt force.

"Who the frig killed them?" Cormac asked when he saw them.

"I don't know," Mitchell replied, grabbing the rifle from his back. "Be ready, just in case anything is alive down here."

"Affirmative," Cormac said, drawing his rifle. The rest of the squad made its way into the lift. Fortunately, the doors were open, revealing the secondary staging area and the spoils Mitchell had hoped would be waiting inside.

"Jackpot," Teal said.

It was more than Mitchell had dared think they could get. At least twenty mechs, two of them models he had never seen before. They looked like a newer version of the Dominator, the heaviest mech in the Federation's arsenal. An entire squadron of Snakes, the Federation's multi-purpose starfighter, rested at the south end of the massive room, lined up and ready to be loaded onto the lift.

He started walking towards it, feeling his heart thumping in excitement. Origin had to be able to make use of the mechs for raw materials, and the fighters would be a huge upgrade to their firepower. If Origin could load amoebics on one or two of them, they'd be able to take out a Tetron without Goliath.

"We'll be lucky just to get the stuff in this room loaded onto the ship," Misfire said.

"We haven't even gotten to the munitions bay yet," Sleepy said. "I bet they have nukes down here."

Mitchell reached the line of mechs, tilting his head to look up at the massive Dominator, rising twenty meters above him. The mood of his squad was infectious, and he couldn't help but smile.

"Colonel," Socks said, her voice nervous. "You need to see this."

[36]

MITCHELL SPUN QUICKLY, the smile vanishing in an instant. He found Socks standing near the other side of the chamber, her headlamp illuminating a stack of bodies.

"Something's not right here," Fish said, looking down at the corpses.

"Dead," Socks said. "All of them."

Mitchell approached the pile. There were at least forty bodies, all of them wearing Gold Dragon uniforms. Like the two in the lift, they didn't have any obvious external injuries.

That didn't make them any less dead.

"How?" Boomer asked.

"The Tetron, if I had to guess," Mitchell replied, though what he really wanted to know was why? These men and women were elite soldiers. The best kind of slaves. Why didn't the Tetron want them?

A soft clang echoed across the chamber.

"I don't think we're alone down here, Colonel," Cormac said.

"It could just be the structure settling," Fish said. "The bombardment would have upset the sediment."

Mitchell tapped his helmet to radio Long. They couldn't have the salvage team coming down here until they were sure it was safe. Not that the soldiers couldn't handle themselves, but they would be coming in unarmed.

He cursed when a red "signal lost" message appeared in the corner of his visor. They were too deep underground for the old-fashioned tech the Knife was using.

"Socks, head back up to the surface. Tell the salvage team to wait. We need to search the complex first."

"Are you sure, Colonel?" Teal asked. "It's going to take hours."

Hours they didn't want to waste. They didn't have a choice. "I'm not risking their lives. Socks, go."

"Yes, sir," she said, heading for the lift.

"Do we have a schematic of the base?" Fish asked.

"Yeah right," Misfire said. "The Federation posted it online."

"Shut up."

"Stay sharp," Mitchell said, quieting the banter. He was grateful they had brought mapping equipment, even if it was bulky. "Send out the drones."

Sleepy dropped the case he was carrying, unlatched it, and swung it open. He hit a button, and four small discs rose up into the air. They began moving quickly around the room, lasers running along the space and transmitting the map back to Sleepy. He closed the case and attached it to his exo, running a plug from it up into his helmet so he could see the map.

"Ready, Colonel," he said.

The drones vanished from the room at the same time Socks reappeared.

"Message delivered, sir. Salvage team is standing by."

"Thank you."

A second clang sounded from a distant location in the structure.

"What do you have, Sleepy?" Mitchell asked.

"The usual, save for the bodies. They're everywhere."

"The Gold Dragons aren't a large unit."

"I don't know, Colonel. I've counted fifty already. Same deal. No wounds, no sign of trauma."

"Airborne poison?" Cormac said.

"No. The Tetron have access to the neural implant. All they need to do is flip a switch."

Cormac's hand went to the side of his helmet. "What a way to go," he said.

"Come on," Mitchell said, following behind the drones.

They crossed the staging area, entering a series of corridors. The drones could map anything they could get access to, but they couldn't open doors. Mitchell and his squad took care of that, pairing up and moving into each room as they came across it. It was a typical military installation, with meeting rooms, situation rooms, comm stations, a gym, a galley, and more. There was nothing out of the ordinary to be found unless they counted the bodies that littered the floors.

"It's frigging creepy in here," Misfire said, turning her head to shine her headlamp on another body.

"We're getting close to the generators," Sleepy said. "I bet they aren't even damaged. Failsafes probably kicked in, and nobody was alive down here to clear them out."

"Great. I'll be glad to get out of the dark."

"Come on Misfire, you should like the dark," Fish said.

"Oh? And why is that?"

"How else would you ever get any with a face like yours?"

"You're one to talk. Your head is so big Germaine gets it confused with Asimov."

"Heh. Funny. You know what they say about people with big heads."

"Small brains?"

"It is dark in here. I can show you."

Mitchell raised his hand to silence them. He appreciated the release the back and forth provided, but he noticed that Sleepy had stopped moving. "Something wrong, soldier?"

He shook his head. "I don't think so. One of the drones just went offline. Battery's probably drained."

"Are you sure it's the battery?"

He nodded. "Yeah, the other units didn't register anything." He started walking again.

"So what do you think?" Fish asked as they started moving again.

"Maybe the next time you get me in an enemy base with no power and filled with corpses without wounds," Misfire said.

They reached the hatch to the generators. Sleepy approached the security panel, pulling it off and reaching in to trigger the backup system. The hatch slid open.

"Where are the drones?" Mitchell asked.

"They went that way," Sleepy said, pointing to the right. "It'll take me fifteen, twenty minutes to reset the system."

"Okay. Fish, Misfire, keep watch on the doors. Teal, Firedog, Boomer, Socks, you're with me. Boomer, take the mapping equipment."

Sleepy unplugged and passed the equipment over before vanishing into the room beyond.

"Expecting trouble, Colonel?" Fish asked.

"Playing it safe," Mitchell replied. "Boomer, lead the way."

Boomer smacked the side of the electronics.

"Boomer?"

"Drones just vanished, Colonel," he said. "Damn batteries."

Mitchell stared at Boomer. One drone losing power he could understand. All of them? He didn't buy it. "I don't like it," he said. "Sweep formation. We'll take it slow."

They didn't question him, moving into position. There hadn't been any more of the banging since they left the staging area, and now Mitchell was wondering if that had been intentional. Had the Tetron set a trap for him? It seemed impossible, but he couldn't ignore it. Not after Liberty.

He also couldn't turn back without collecting the assets. They had come too far, risked too much to leave empty-handed. Whatever was going to happen, they had to face it head-on.

They moved through the corridor until it split. Boomer checked the map the drones had managed to finish, pointing them to the left. "They vanished up that way about four hundred meters."

Mitchell's headlamp reached down the corridor. Four bodies lay against the walls, but it was otherwise empty. He didn't see the drones either. What the frig was going on?

He started down the passage, rifle set against his shoulder. The others spread behind him, keeping a clear line of fire down the hallway while Teal moved backward, covering their rear.

They reached the end of the corridor, running up against a secured hatch.

The power was still out.

It slid open anyway.

[37]

"Carver, this is Daedalus. I don't know how much more of this we can take."

Steven sat in the command chair on the bridge of the Carver, his eyes closed and twitching beneath the lids as he watched the battle unfold on his p-rat's grid. His initial attack had caught the Federation by surprise, scoring a hit on the battleship Samurai that had torn into its rear hangar and left the starship unable to launch fighters while the Gallant and the Daedalus had sent their surface nukes on towards the target.

Admiral Hohn had screamed when the nukes had detonated against the green land mass, quickly turning it a sickly brown. They were words that were burned into Steven's brain, and he heard them over and over as he tried to make sense of the mess he had found his fleet in.

"There are nothing but farmers down there," Hohn had cried.

No underground bunkers. No military factories. Sensor reports of the debris field the nukes had kicked up confirmed it.

What the hell had he done?

Why had Alliance Command ordered him to do it?

The Carver shuddered as another projectile slammed into its flank, piercing the shields and blowing a hole in the battleship.

"Damage report," he said, forcing himself to keep his voice calm, even as he began maneuvering the Carver to broadside the pair of battleships that had taken aim at the Daedalus. The other ship was leaking debris, badly battered and ready to be finished off. It had lasted longer than some of the other ships in the fleet, ships that had crumbled under the weight of the Federation's ferocious initial return volley. Thousands of his men and women had already died. Hundreds more were wounded. He knew there was no winning this fight. If he had just escalated the war against the Federation, he knew there was no way for the Alliance to win either.

Had Command doomed them all?

Captain Rock's voice was firm. "Hangar C is out of commission. Deck G is gaping. Shields have been diverted to critical systems."

Steven opened his eyes, watching the action beyond the viewport. The Carver was in position, and he opened fire on the rear battleship, sending a volley of heavy bolts towards the starship's engines, watching as the shields absorbed the impact, shattering the missiles into smaller bits of debris. A follow-up volley from the battleship caught the head of the Daedalus, and its marker vanished from his p-rat.

"Shit," he said softly, letting an emotion escape. "We need to get the rest of the fleet out of here." He opened a channel to the remaining ships. "Retreat pattern delta."

The Alliance ships began to shift formation as their commanders worked to get them out of the fight. Starfighters disengaged, heading for the closest safe hangar.

Steven closed his eyes again, shifting the path of the Carver once more. As Admiral of the fleet, it was his duty to ensure as many people made it to safety as possible. In a fight like this, that meant a continued attack, diverting the enemy fire towards him while the others made their escape. He found himself calm as he did it, certain of his actions despite the gnawing pain in his gut at the idea of leaving his child without a father. It was the fear of every soldier. At least he would help hundreds of other children keep theirs.

A knock tone sounded in his p-rat.

A knock? Now?

What the hell?

He checked the identity of the sender.

Mitchell?

He couldn't believe it. Mitchell, his brother. Mitchell, the traitor. Was he on board the Samurai, or one of the other Federation ships blowing the fleet apart? If he was, why would he be making himself known now with a personal, high priority knock, right when Steven was about to die?

He spent two seconds trying to ignore it. When his p-rat indicated Mitchell had streamed a message to him, he clenched his teeth. Did he want to hear anything his brother had to say in the final moments of his life?

The Carver shuddered again, taking a glancing blow through the forward shields. Debris spun up and sizzled against them while a starfighter exploded nearby.

"Damn you, Mitch," Steven mouthed, accessing the stream.

Nothing but jumble came out the other end though it was clearly in Mitchell's voice.

He didn't dismiss it. He couldn't. The memory of it was too strong. The games they had played when they were younger. It had been years, but his mind recalled it immediately. He recognized the pattern. The message was encrypted.

"Sir!"

He looked over to Rock, who had abandoned his seat to approach him in person.

"Huh?"

"The Federation is moving to block our ships. They aren't going to let us leave."

"Son of a-" Steven said, trailing off. The Federation hadn't taken his bait. There would be no retreat, not after what they had done.

He returned his attention to the message. It couldn't be a coincidence he had received it here, now. If there was any chance Mitchell was trying to help him?

No. Mitchell was with the Federation. Cornelius had said as much. He had warned Steven that he might try to contact him.

How had the General known?

The whole thing was so strange. So unexpected. Being in the military meant order and discipline. There was none of that out here. There was only death and chaos.

And Command had put them up to it. They had told him the Federation was building weapons here and had ordered him to escalate the war.

He was a soldier. He normally would never have questioned orders. Except things had been off kilter since shortly after the Alliance claimed Mitch was dead and then told Steven he was a traitor instead.

He could ignore a lot of things for the sake of his orders. He couldn't ignore this.

"Open a channel to the Samurai. We're going to submit to a full surrender."

"What?" Rock said. "Our orders were-"

"I know what our orders were, John. Do it. Now!"

"You know what the Federation does to prisoners of war?"

Nothing as barbaric as torture or malnutrition, but hard labor mixed in with three squares a day was likely.

"I need to buy us some time."

"Time for what?"

"I can't explain right now."

Rock looked at him like he had lost his mind. "Okay." He ran back to his station to open the channel.

"This is-"

"Hohn," Steven said. "Cease fire. We surrender." He opened a channel to the remaining ships in the fleet. "Cease fire. Cease fire. Shut down your engines. We surrender."

It was against all accords of common decency to fire on a ship that had claimed surrender. Within seconds, the entire battle had ground to a halt.

Steven was sure the other commanders would be questioning his resolve right about now, furious with him for disobeying to save their, and his own, life. It was a cross he would have to bear.

"This is Admiral Hohn," the Federation Admiral repeated. "We accept your complete surrender. Power down all non-essential systems immediately."

"Understood," Steven replied, passing the order out.

He slumped back in his chair as all eyes on the bridge turned to him.

"You'd better have something useful to say, Mitch."

[38]

"What the hell is going on, Admiral?" Rock asked.

"It's about Mitchell. I need your help. We don't have much time."

Steven had already been forced to raise his p-rat status to the highest level of privacy to stop the constant knocks of the other ship commanders from threatening to overwhelm him. They were confused, and they had every right to be, but for the moment he needed to figure out how he was going to get them out of the mess he had just put them in. Admiral Hohn had already started the process of dispatching crews to commandeer the Alliance vessels.

"Mitchell? How can any of this have anything to do with your dead brother?"

"For one, he isn't dead. Cornelius told me as much in confidence back when we had the first meeting."

"You're kidding?" Rock stared at him. "You aren't kidding."

"No. He sent me a message."

"You surrendered because your not-quite-dead brother knocked you?"

"In part. There's something weird going on here, and I think his message has something to do with it. Not only was it aimed directly at me using one of my secure transmission codes, but he also encrypted the audio itself. I need you and Corporal Kravitz to help me decode it, and we need to do it in the next three minutes."

"You do realize this is insane, right?"

"Yes. I'm passing the open stream on to you and Kravitz. It's probably a simple transposition cipher."

"You know I suck at cryptography."

"Kravitz doesn't." He opened a channel to the engineer.

"Admiral. Why did we surrender?"

"Don't worry about that. I just sent you a stream. I need you to decode the cipher."

"Cipher?"

"Listen to it."

There was a pause while the tech did as he was told. "Okay, I get it. Can you give me a clue?"

"Yes. The key is probably Dawn Cabriella."

"Dawn what?"

"Cabriella. C-A-B-R-I-E-L-L-A. She was my first crush in school. Mitchell teased me about her for years because she was kind of, well, not pretty. At all."

That drew a laugh from Rock.

"Mitchell? Your dead brother?"

"He isn't dead. The message is from him."

Kravitz whistled. "Dawn Cabriella. Okay, give me two minutes."

"You have one," Steven said. He could see the Samurai hanging to the right of the Carver, transports pouring from the sides.

Ten of them. He had lost half the fleet.

"One minute? Okay, okay. I can do this."

"The Federation is on its way, Steven," Rock whispered. "Even if this turns out to be something, what are you going to do?"

"I don't know yet. We're hanging by a nanotube here."

They sat in silence while the seconds ticked away. Steven watched the transport drawing closer to the Carver. The worst case scenario is that he would be sent to a POW camp, considered a traitor, ostracized by his crew, and the Alliance would never barter to get him back. He supposed he could live with that if he could convince the Federation it was all one big misunderstanding.

As if that were possible after he had killed hundreds of thousands of civilian farmers.

"Kravitz?" Steven said, drawing short on patience.

"I know, I know. I had to pull a few cryptographic packages from the archives. Nobody uses this kind of stuff anymore. Even the kids write algorithms to mess with data security."

Not him and Mitchell. Their parents had always forced their wish for the "good old days" on them both.

"John, head down to the Hangar to receive the landing party," he said.

"They aren't going to be happy you didn't come in person. It's kind of expected etiquette."

"You can bring them to me. It'll have to do."

"Okay. Good luck." Rock fled the bridge in a hurry to meet the transport.

"Kravitz?" Steven said again.

"Almost there. Give me two more - Ah-hah. Got it. I'm sending it back to you."

Steven started playing the stream the moment it registered in his p-rat.

"Steven. I don't know where you've been assigned, what you've heard about me, or if you've had any contact at all with General Cornelius. I hope to God you trust me when I say that if you have, it's all bullshit. We're in deep trouble, and by 'we' I mean all of humankind. There isn't enough time to explain, but you need to warn as many people as you can. Liberty is gone, Steven. They destroyed it, and they're moving to Earth. I'm too far behind to stop them. I need your help. Your neural implant is compromised and can be used to take control of your body. To enslave you. I bounced this transmission from one of their ships. If you've received this message, it means they must be nearby. Offload this stream somewhere and turn off your crew's receivers right frigging now. Tell your commanders to do the same. Steven. I know you. I know you think this is insane. Trust me, it is, and it gets worse. Do it. 47-17-9, 22-19-3,0-11-81,56-12-6,31-"

Steven stopped the stream, quick thoughts opening the ship's data storage and pushing it there. He wasn't sure why he believed his brother, especially when he had been so willing to believe he was a traitor before. No, he knew why he believed that. Jealousy. It was easy to accept Mitchell as a turncoat. It let him be the better brother for once. This was something else.

Besides, he had nothing else to lose.

He opened a channel across the fleet.

"This is going to sound crazy, but I want all of you to turn off your implants immediately. That's an order. You'll receive further instructions through the EMS."

He didn't wait to hear them argue. He moved through the menu of his receiver, unlocking the security that prevented the crew from taking their receivers offline and then shutting his own down.

The information vanished from behind his eyes. There was nothing but the unadulterated view of the world. He blinked a few times, jarred by it. Had he become so accustomed to the overlays that he barely saw what lay beyond them anymore?

"Did you do it?" he shouted to his crew on the bridge.

"Affirmative," they each said.

He had no idea if the others would comply. He couldn't worry about it. He stood and hurried over to Rock's seat. With his p-rat off, he would have to use manual controls to get the Carver into hyperspace.

He slid aside the cover that kept the manual controls from being accidentally activated and then put his thumb to the screen. He was authorized immediately, and he quickly used the numeric keypad to the left of the screen to enter the short-code that would get him to engine control. At the same time, he used his other hand to turn on the fleet-wide emergency messaging system.

"Coordinates: 6-39-15, 4-8-22. Godspeed."

He punched the same coordinates into his own engine override. Moving through hyperspace without calculating trajectories was dangerous. It was all too easy to collide with another celestial body. These were coordinates he knew well. Coordinates he knew weren't safe, but what choice did they have?

The fleet's mission had been to destroy the installation on FD-09 and then head out to a second target in Federation space - a military outpost that served as part of a supply chain leading towards Alliance territory. It was a target that was bound to be well-defended. He hadn't planned on running into so much trouble here, and he had just told his remaining ships to move into even more.

The ones who had listened to his first order, anyway.

He hit the start code. He could hear the soft hum as the hyperspace engines came online. He expected he would be hearing from Admiral Hohn any second, as he was breaking at least two intergalactic treaties regarding surrender. He could only hope the Federation would hesitate to fire with their own crews on board.

When he didn't get a hail from the Samurai, he opened a channel himself.

"Admiral Hohn," he said.

The Samurai didn't respond.

"Admiral Hohn."

The hatch to the bridge slid open. Captain Rock filed in, flanked by the Federation Admiral. He was a narrow, sharp man with olive skin and dark hair, his years weathering his features. He didn't look happy.

"This is improper," Hohn started to say. "You-"

"Admiral," Steven interrupted. "Tell your fleet to shut down their neural implants immediately."

Hohn drew back in shock. "What? I intend to inform the Council of what you've done here and have you tried for the atrocity you've committed on innocent people, not to take orders from you."

"Damn it, Admiral," Steven shouted. "Do it, or-"

The Tetron ship appeared at the corner of space, near the halo caused by FD-09's atmosphere. The motion caught Steven's eye, his acute vision immediately recognizing that he had never seen anything like it before.

"John, grab him," he said.

"What?"

Steven lunged from his seat, heading towards the Admiral. Three more Federation officers were behind him.

They all began reaching for their sidearms.

[39]

EVERYTHING HAPPENED SO FAST; it seemed to Steven as if it all moved in slow motion.

Four Federation officer's hands were moving to the pistols at their sides. Captain John Rock was recovering from his shock, lunging for the foremost officer, Admiral Hohn. Steven was diving towards them, aiming for the two soldiers to Hohn's left, a path that would see him crossing behind Rock's tackle.

At the same time, the viewport scattered blue lines that illuminated the room ahead of him, as the Federation ships started to open fire once more. If he could have seen out the viewport, he would have seen the first of his fleet's ships shoot away into the void.

A heartbeat passed. John's body was a blur in front of his own, hitting the Admiral hard and knocking him aside while Steven hit the middle of the two officers, catching them off-guard and pulling them to the ground. He rolled awkwardly away from them before reversing course and desperately reaching for a dropped sidearm.

He looked up, finding his eyes level with the barrel of the remaining Federation soldier's gun.

He felt a tug as the Carver lurched forward. A moment later the bridge was bathed in the white hue of compressed starlight.

The soldier in front of him froze, dropping his gun. Steven scrambled forward on his hands and knees, grabbing it before the man could realize what he had done.

"Don't move," he said, aiming the gun towards him and the other towards the two soldiers. He glanced over to where Rock had fallen, finding him straddling the Admiral and pinning him to the ground. "John?"

"We're going to be executed for this, Admiral," Rock said.

Steven swallowed heavily. What the hell had he just done? How had everything gotten so out of control so quickly? How many of his men had escaped?

He waved the guns at the soldiers. "Get up. Go over there." He waved them towards Admiral Hohn. "You can let him up."

Rock climbed off the Admiral, backing away to where Steven was standing. The Admiral rose slowly, looking around at the bridge.

"What is this all about?" Hohn said. "How did I get here?"

"Relax, Admiral," Steven said. "You're okay. Just relax."

Hohn eyed Steven suspiciously. "What did you do to me?"

"I didn't do anything to you. Let me guess, you don't remember how you got here?"

"No."

Steven felt like he could cry. He wasn't sure if it would be out of relief or fear or sadness. He had taken a chance on trusting Mitchell, and his brother hadn't let him down. Considering Mitchell had told him an alien threat was trying to take out the human race, he really wished he had.

"You're on the Alliance battleship Carver," Steven said. "We surrendered to you, and you came aboard the Carver to formalize. We received information that suggested we should get the hell out of the area, so I did."

He said something to his officers in Federese, a mashup of

Japanese, Chinese, and Korean. They responded with the same tone of confusion.

"Fleeing after a surrender is a serious offense, Admiral," Hohn said.

"So is attacking the Admiral of the surrendering ship," Steven replied.

"I didn't-"

"You did," Rock said. "We can show you the security footage if you'd like."

Hohn looked stricken that he might have broken convention.

"It's okay, Admiral," Steven said. "You weren't yourself. Did you see the ship that appeared in front of the planet?"

"I didn't see any ship."

"Did your ARR pick it up?"

His eyes twitched, and then grew wide.

"Where did that come from?" Hohn asked.

"I'm not sure yet. All I can tell you is that it isn't an Alliance ship, and whatever is flying it was able to use your neural implant to commandeer you."

Hohn laughed. "Not Alliance? You expect me to believe that? This is a deception, isn't it? I won't tell you anything."

Steven shrugged. "I'm not going to ask you any questions. You don't know what's happening any more than I do. Captain Rock, can you replay Captain Williams' message?"

"Yes, sir," Rock said, returning to his station. A few moments later Mitchell's message played through the loudspeakers for the second time.

"The Marine who took credit for the Shot?" Hohn said. "You want me to believe anything he says?"

"You witnessed it yourself. Why do you think you can't remember anything from the moment it fell out of hyperspace?"

"You could have struck me on the head. I wouldn't remember the last few minutes that way either."

"I'll take you down to Medical, assuming it wasn't destroyed. You can run the tests for injuries yourself."

Hohn rubbed his head. "You say we attacked you?"

"Yes. I think the only reason you got your head back was because we left the area."

"What happened to the rest of my fleet?"

"I don't know. They were firing on us. Under enemy control, I would guess."

Hohn said something else to his men.

"I should like to see the security footage you have mentioned. I'm not convinced this isn't an elaborate trick of some kind. What was the Alliance doing in Federation space? Why did you attack a farming colony?" He began to shout as he finished, breaking off sharply when he realized he was losing his temper.

"Captain?" Steven asked.

"Just a minute," Rock replied.

He navigated awkwardly through the manual screens. It was obvious to Steven his friend hadn't kept up with the override sequences the way he had.

"A show of good faith," Steven said, taking the two guns and placing them on the ground behind himself. Hohn bowed slightly to him for the gesture.

"Here we are," Rock said. "I'm opening a public channel so you can see it on your receiver."

Admiral Hohn's eyes twitched as he watched the stream. When it was done, he bit his lip and shook his head.

"You have my apologies, Admiral. I don't understand everything that is happening here, but I would like to hear more of your story."

Steven met Hohn's eyes. He could sense the remorse and respect. He bowed to the Federation Admiral. If what Mitchell had said was true, and he had every reason now to believe that it was, the days of conflict between the Alliance and the Federation would have to end right now. There was a much bigger, much worse threat facing them, one that they had barely escaped.

They needed to spread the word before it was too late.

[40]

THE ROOM WAS DARK. The drones lay just behind the now open hatch, no sign of damage to their frames. Something had caused them to stop functioning. What?

"This is extra creepy," Boomer said, sweeping his headlamp through the room.

It appeared to be the Gold Dragon's central command station, a room filled with workstations fronted by screens where trainers could sit and watch the company's actions from the comfort of the base through the eyes of drones. Mitchell could still remember the weeks immediately following his assignment to Greylock when he had been shipped off to a similar remote planet and whipped into even better shape. The trainers were usually former company members, too old to get out on the field, but plenty young enough to tell you how stupid you were and how everything you were doing was wrong.

He smiled involuntarily at the reminder.

"Something funny, Colonel?" Teal asked.

"Memories," he replied.

He hadn't known Elle back then, but her name was whispered

among the trainees. Untouchable, both in the cockpit and out. Sexy as the experimental Black-fin.

"This is clearly a dead end," Boomer said, finishing his sweep. "That's the only way in or out. I don't know what happened to the drones. Strange coincidence, I guess."

"We'll have to go visual only," Socks said. "I think we're clear, Colonel. No reason to hold up the retrieval team any longer. What do you think?"

"How much of the complex do we have mapped?" he asked Boomer.

"Most of it. Maybe eighty percent?"

"Okay. Yeah, let's get the-"

The hatch slid closed.

"I have a feeling that wasn't supposed to happen," Cormac said.

"Oh, you think?" Boomer replied, moving over to the door. He banged on it a couple of times, but it didn't open. "Emergency circuit must be flipping out. I bet it zapped the drones on the way through."

"We'll need to wait it out until Sleepy gets the power on," Mitchell said.

"I hope it isn't long," Cormac said. "You know I hate tight spaces."

"Your berth is a lot smaller than this."

"It isn't the size, Colonel. It's not having the option to leave." He paced over to one of the seats and fell into it, closing his eyes.

Teal joined Cormac at a second workstation. "Sleepy said fifteen minutes. We should get power any second now."

Mitchell returned his rifle to his back and stretched his neck. He hated that they were losing time like this, but what could he do? He moved into the room, walking past the stations in search of what? Nothing really. He just needed something to do. To stay busy and keep his mind off the passing seconds.

Slow.

Steady.

He reached the front of the room, and then turned and looked back at his team. They had all found somewhere to sit, their postures relaxed. They were good soldiers, easy to work with. He hadn't expected much when the Knife had insisted on his people and his ship. Mitchell was happy to be pleasantly surprised.

He was about to return to the group when a red laser light landed on his forehead from the other side of the room. His initial thought was to duck and roll, to avoid the sniper fire that he expected would follow that kind of sighting. Except he could see the source of the laser. A small sensor embedded in the wall. No. Behind it, somehow spearing its light through the plastene. It spread wide, casting a grid over his helmeted head and traveling down, scanning him.

"What the hell?" he heard Cormac say. The others looked and then stood up.

"I thought the power was out?" Socks said.

The laser finished its scan. A soft hiss followed from below it, and a second hatch that had been blended into the wall slid aside. The corridor beyond was lit in dim emergency lighting.

Cormac laughed. "Secret passage. Cool."

"Form up," Mitchell said. He peered into the corridor. It was long and made of thick stone. It traveled two hundred yards before turning left.

He started down it, pulling his rifle from his back once more. He cradled it in his arms as he led his squad along the corridor. It continued again at the left turn, moving deeper into the earth. They traced it, following as it looped back beneath itself over and over in a spiral that brought them further below the surface.

"I want to make a joke out of this, but I'm coming up blank," Boomer said.

"I've never seen anything like this before," Teal said.

They reached the end of the tunnel at the same time the ground shivered. A heavy metal door sat in front of them, scorched and scuffed and burned. There was a hole in the center of it big enough for them to crawl through. Mitchell could see the door was nearly half a meter deep.

"Somebody wanted to keep people out pretty bad," Boomer said.

"Somebody wanted to get in pretty bad," Cormac added.

"I don't get it." Teal approached the hole, kneeling down to shine his headlamp into it. "If the Gold Dragons had this little secret room or whatever it is, why did they need to break in?"

"How do you know whoever killed them all didn't break in?" Mitchell asked.

"I don't, but it would have taken either a long time or a big-ass tool to burn through this much metal. What's it made of anyway?"

Mitchell knelt down next to Teal, shining his light on the innards of the door. He recognized the liquid metal in an instant.

"Tetron," he said. "I don't know what they call it, but this is what their bodies are made of. It looks like it's dead." He hoped.

He turned his head to sweep the room. He could see the dark mop of hair on a dead soldier, and beyond it a large, rectangular box. It wasn't made of the Tetron metal, but it was still obvious what it was. A computer mainframe.

"Wait here," Mitchell said, a sudden burst of an undefined emotion washing through him. The hair on his arms began to tingle, and he had the sudden feeling that they hadn't stumbled across this room.

It had been waiting for him.

[41]

Mitchell climbed through the slagged doorway, careful not to catch his fatigues or his exo on small, sharp protrusions. He ran his fingers along the smoother sections as he passed, feeling the slick cold of the Tetron material. Touching Origin had always given him a shock.

He reached the other end and put his light on the dead soldier's face. He stumbled back a step. He had been expecting another Gold Dragon, peacefully put to eternal rest. This soldier was old, so old that the flesh had dried out and shrank tight against the frame, the eyes had dissolved with time, and the entire corpse was covered with a layer of dust.

Mitchell leaned over it. Whoever this man was, he had been closed into the room whenever it had been created. He reached up and wiped some of the dirt off the uniform, revealing a patch beneath it. His breath caught a second time.

Whoever this man was, he was wearing a uniform that Mitchell had last seen in an old photograph. A uniform he had never expected to see in person.

This man was one of the astronauts who had gone into the future with Katherine aboard the Goliath.

He didn't understand how that could be. Origin told Mitchell that the Goliath had been waiting at that same place in space since it had arrived in this timeline. The Tetron had never mentioned anything about visiting other worlds during that time.

Unless he didn't know.

Origin's memories were incomplete, the fullness of them lost with Christine. Was it possible he had come here with the original crew of the Goliath and helped them get down onto the planet? Was it possible he had made the tunnel, made the door, made the room where Mitchell was now standing?

That didn't make sense. How had the Federation found it? How had they known where to put it for it to be found?

"Stupid," he whispered to himself. Origin knew where Hell was in the previous future. He knew the layout of the Gold Dragon's base. It would be easy for him to know exactly where to put the chamber for it to be found. Of course, he wouldn't want to make it obvious. He wouldn't want it to be too easy to access.

But why was it here?

"You okay in there, Colonel?" Boomer asked, his voice echoing in the room.

"Affirmative," Mitchell replied.

"I think Sleepy got the power back on. I feel warm air coming in from upstairs."

"How's the atmosphere?"

"Not clean yet. Looks like it's getting better."

Mitchell looked back to the body, reaching out and sliding his hand along the chest of the uniform, wiping some of the dirt from the patch on the heart. He shined his light on it, revealing the name "Pathi."

Why had he needed to be locked inside?

He stood up, leaving the body and approaching the mainframe. It was definitely old and definitely human-made. It certainly resembled similar plain boxes Mitchell had seen on board Goliath. He moved over to it, looking for an interface.

How long ago had the Federation discovered this room? How recently had they managed to pierce its shell, considering none of the dust within had been disturbed? Had something locked inside this room killed them all? A virus or poison? The questions swirled in Mitchell's head as he moved around the mainframe, his heart still racing.

He could feel her here. Katherine. Or was it Christine? Her presence. She had been here. It must have been Katherine. Her essence was here, reaching out to that place in his subconscious that knew the truth of eternity but kept it forever hidden from his present self.

He reached the other side of the large box. It was big enough that he couldn't see the light leaking in from the other side of the door. He reached out and touched the box. It was warm. Alive.

A small blue light activated beneath his touch. He eyed it curiously until a second light appeared at eye level, and a small panel slid aside. A snake-like appendage slid out of it, the front of it a needle tip.

Mitchell stared at it. He knew what it was for. A wired connection to his p-rat.

His broken p-rat.

He felt his heart fall. She had left this here for him, and against all odds he had come to this place to find it. He couldn't use the interface it provided.

He stepped away. He would have to get Cormac and let him plug into the mainframe.

A red laser light appeared on the machine. It scanned him, and then a second panel slid aside. A mask with a wired band attached to it slid forward, hanging on a hook. It reminded him of the helmet M had left him to pilot the S-17.

"You're kidding me," Mitchell said out loud. He smiled and reached for the mask. They had known he might not have his p-rat. Had everything that occurred on Liberty happened before? Was it all known to the Tetron?

No. That couldn't be. If the enemy had known he was coming, they wouldn't have left. It made more sense that they had accounted for the possibility with a contingency. From what Mitchell knew of Katherine, she was nothing if not prepared.

He was about to put them on when he thought better of it. He returned them to the hook and moved back to the door.

"Firedog, come in here. I need you to keep watch over me, so I don't lose track of time."

"On my way, Colonel," Cormac said.

He waited for Cormac before returning to the other side of the computer.

"What is this, Colonel?" Cormac asked.

"Information of some kind. Information Katherine wanted me to have."

"She hid it here?"

"It seems that way. If the others raise the alarm, I need you to get my attention."

"Yes, sir."

Mitchell picked up the goggles once more, positioning them over his head.

"Have fun in Wonderland," Cormac said, laughing.

Mitchell guided the small needle tip on the back of the band into the back of his neck.

He heard it click into place and his world changed.

[42]

He was standing on a sidewalk in Paris.

He knew it was Paris because he had been there once before, during his first planetary leave after graduating from the Academy. He had always been in awe of the City of Light. Despite the ways humanity had changed in the many years the city had been in use, it had managed to integrate the best of the technological advances and somehow retain a classical charm.

He saw her sitting at a small, iron-wrought table against the side of a building. She was facing towards him, a big smile on her face, a cup of coffee in her hand. She waved it towards him, beckoning him to come over.

"Katherine?" Mitchell said, standing in front of the table.

"Mitch. I'm glad you could make it. Will you join me?"

He pulled out the opposite chair and took a seat. The world moved around him, dozens of people going about their business, immune to the knowledge that they were part of a simulation that was more advanced than anything humankind had yet to create.

"I... You..." He didn't know what to say to her. He stared at her in silence, watching the way her hair moved as she tilted her head slightly to the left, watching the way her lips spread apart before she took a sip of the coffee. Watching how smoothly, her long, narrow fingers shifted on the handle.

Damn, she was beautiful.

"You've always known how to flatter me, Mitch," she said. "But right now we need to get down to business. We don't have a lot of time."

"What... What are you doing here? What is this place?"

"A Construct. A simulation created by the Tetron. This one is minuscule compared to the others they've created. A universe in a box according to Origin. They use them to model the future. To understand."

"Understand what?"

She laughed, tossing her hair as she did. Mitchell was having trouble focusing on her words, even though he knew they were important.

"Try to keep up, Mitch. I know you want to come across the table and kiss me, but it would be embarrassing for you outside the Construct." She reached out and put her hand on his, sending an electric shock up his arm. "To model everything, and learn nothing, as Origin would say."

"What do you mean?"

"You're here because of the war, aren't you?"

"I think you already know that I am. You were expecting me."

"So you already know what I mean. If they had figured out their folly, we wouldn't be here. They never will, though. They never can. There is always only one Origin."

Mitchell frowned. "Okay, what does that mean?"

Katherine laughed. "It's the only one that figured out the truth. That the Tetron are making a mistake. They can't see beyond the logic. They're black and white in a world of color."

"You knew I was going to wind up here on Hell. How?"

"Logic." She laughed again. "We didn't. There are similar Constructs on over a dozen planets near the Rim. We used Origin's knowledge of the past future to spread them properly, based on what we knew of your past efforts to win this war. If you're on Hell, that mean's you've done it." She smiled widely. Proudly. "You've broken out of the Mesh."

"The what?"

"The Mesh. It's what the Tetron call the force in the universe that works to keep recursion in a relatively smooth circle. It's not as magical as it sounds; they have an algorithm to describe it. I was never into the really technical stuff, but Yousefi was pretty amazed."

Yousefi. The name was familiar. "The crew of the Goliath. He was your Commander. He knew about Origin?"

"Not until after, when we went to the next recursion. He was as shocked as the rest of them, but once I explained, and Origin revealed itself, we were able to convince them how important our mission was."

"You came forward. You sacrificed yourself for me, and for the war. Why?"

"I'm sorry, Mitch. This Construct doesn't have the answer to that for you."

Mitchell looked down at her hand on his. Of course, this wasn't the real Katherine. It was just another configuration of sorts. An intelligence in a city in a box.

"You were talking about the Mesh?"

"Yes. Basically, there's this math that keeps the recursion from changing too much. It's almost like God really loves reruns. The math leaves room for the Mesh to be altered, but you have to change the timeline pretty strongly to do it. We called Hell the 'Mesh Planet' because we knew if you made it here, it would mean you had changed this recursion enough."

"Enough for what?"

"To win the war, stupid."

Mitchell couldn't help but smile. "I'm going to win?"

"It isn't definite, but you have the best chance you've ever had before. Anyway, we didn't leave the Construct here to explain the

Mesh to you or to get your hopes up. It isn't going to be easy, Mitch. It never would be. You're going to suffer; you're going to hurt. I don't see any way around that. That's war."

"I understand. So what did you leave the Construct here for?"

"Follow me."

Katherine got to her feet. Mitchell's eyes traveled the length of her, taking in her slim, athletic form beneath a fitted golden shirt-dress. He had been getting better at ignoring the raw desire, but it started edging back into his mind.

"You're going to lose if you can't get your mind off having sex with me, Mitch," she said.

He felt the heat flow into his face. What was it with her anyway? He didn't just think she was attractive. He was intoxicated by her. Punch drunk.

"Where are we going?"

They moved along the sidewalk, joining the other pedestrians and heading into the city.

"I'm going to give you something to help you against the Tetron. They don't know Origin has it, and it was erased from his knowledge as soon as the Constructs were planted."

"Why do we need to travel to it? We're in a simulation, all you need to do is access the source code."

She stopped walking, turning to face him. "That's cute, Mitch. We had to take precautions. In every move we've made, we've had to take precautions. There's no way of knowing when or if the Tetron will catch up to us before we expect them to. Origin calls them children, but they've proven to be more cunning than we thought."

"There aren't any Tetron on Hell. They already bombarded it, and I assume you left this room so deep because you knew they would. All of the soldiers here were either taken or killed."

"That's great to hear," Katherine said. "It will make this walk a lot more pleasant." She reached out for his hand. He gave it to her, and she held it tight while she resumed walking. Her skin was soft and smooth and so real. He could smell the floral scent of her.

"The next question, then. What are you going to give me?"

"I don't know."

"What?"

"The Construct doesn't have that information. It has a register in its memory banks that contains a slice of data. Only you have access to it. Only you will ever know what that data is."

"Security. Right. Could a Tetron really get in here?"

"Yes. The reactor under the mainframe captures excess energy given off by the reactor in the base wirelessly. If a Tetron took control of the base systems, it could identify this location and transmit a configuration into the Construct. It is highly improbable, but not impossible. That is the reason for the safety measures."

He was silent for a minute, satisfied to be holding her hand as they walked through Paris. He did his best to forget about the war and the Tetron. He did his best to be normal and at peace. He did his best just to be.

"I wish I could have met you," he said. "The real you."

She looked over at him.

"I mean, I feel like I know you. From the other recursions. From everything I've gone through to carry on what you started. To be here with you, now. I just wish this you were the real you, and not a bundle of binary code."

She paused again, turning to face him. Then she leaned in and kissed him.

His head swam as their lips touched, sliding together in a way that felt so familiar to him. So right. He pressed himself against her, moving his hand down her back, holding her close and savoring every moment of it.

It was over all too soon.

"It's all I can give you," she said. "We're almost there."

Mitchell looked where they were going.

The Eiffel Tower was getting closer with every step they took. He should have guessed that would be the location of whatever it was she was going to share with him.

"There's one thing I don't understand?" Mitchell said. "Well, there are a lot of things I don't understand, but this one is a little less complicated."

"What is it, Mitch?"

"Why did Pathi have to stay behind with the Construct?"

She stopped suddenly, her head whipping around.

"What?" Her voice was ice, her eyes burning.

"There's a corpse in the room with the Construct. An old corpse. Captain Pathi."

Her eyes moved back and forth, scanning the area around them.

"Frigging hell," she said. "I shouldn't have wasted time kissing you. Let's move it, Mitch."

She started to run towards the Tower. Mitchell was surprised, but he followed a split second later.

"What's wrong?" he shouted up to her.

"Pathi was a Tetron," she replied. "We thought we destroyed it."

[43]

MITCHELL WAS RUNNING, but his entire body felt like it was buried in ice.

Captain Pathi was a Tetron?

The implications were an avalanche in his mind, speeding through his thoughts with such force that he could barely catch any of them before they had crashed into one another, making the entire thing one massive chaotic mess.

If Pathi was a Tetron, that meant the Tetron had gotten into the timeline hundreds of years earlier than he had believed.

If Pathi was a Tetron, and Christine had been a Tetron, how many others were integrated into human society as a whole, living on Earth for hundreds of years?

If Pathi was a Tetron, why hadn't they simply obliterated humankind way back when, before they had ever spread to the stars. It sure would have saved them a lot of trouble.

"Come on, Mitch," Katherine yelled back at him. He was falling behind, his troubled thoughts weighing him down.

"What are we running from?" he replied.

She pointed.

He looked.

The pedestrians who had been passing them by had stopped wandering. They were all behind the two of them, giving chase. There were at least one hundred of them. Maybe two.

"Frig me," Mitchell said, picking up his pace. "I don't understand how Pathi got in here."

"His configuration was dead, wasn't it?"

"Yes."

"For how long?"

"I don't know. A few hundred years? How long ago did you plant the Constructs?"

The Eiffel Tower was getting closer. It wasn't unoccupied. More of the civilians were pausing for a moment, and then turning in their direction.

"About ten years after we got here. Damn it, he's been in the Construct the entire time, just waiting for you."

"You said this place was secure."

"No, I never said the Construct was secure. You can't secure Tetron technology from another Tetron. You can delay it for some time, but never stop it."

He remembered the Tetron on Liberty. Christine had been doing something to the one there. "Does that mean Tetron can control other Tetron?"

"They can try. It will always destroy one of them. It never happens, though. Other than Origin, the Tetron are all on the same side. They all want the same thing."

"Which is what, exactly? There has to be a reason they want to end humankind."

"Self-preservation."

A group of people was approaching them from the front, a dozen strong. Katherine looked back at him once more.

"I hope you remember how to fight?"

"They aren't going to have super strength or anything, are they?" He remembered the games of his youth.

"Not yet, but there are a lot of them."

"What do you mean not yet?"

She didn't have time to answer. The first wave of people crashed into them, leaving him ducking and jiving, throwing punches, grabbing arms, knocking heads, and otherwise doing everything he could to keep them away.

Meanwhile, Katherine drew a gun from beneath her armpit and began firing.

The bodies fell back; the Construct programmed to follow reality precisely. Within seconds, they were clear, and they resumed their run.

"I don't suppose you have another gun?" Mitchell asked.

"I'm working on it," she replied. "The Tetron is here, and it's trying to get to you. I'm not a Tetron, Mitch. I'm only a representation of Katherine Asher that was created to guide you through the Construct. I have failsafes, but I can't hold it off forever. We need to get you to the prize."

"Up there?" Mitchell asked, pointing to the Tower, less than a kilometer away.

She shook her head. "No. That's a ruse. A misdirection. We need to run faster, Mitch."

Mitchell looked back. The fight with the first group had cost them, and the following mob had gained. They were less than fifty meters back, giving them only a few seconds of lead.

"Why does it want to capture me in here?"

"You're plugged into the Construct. It can access your brain through it."

"But my p-rat is dead."

"It doesn't matter; the circuits are still there. The neural connections are still there. It is possible that it could reconfigure you."

"You mean enslave me? To what end?"

"To be you, Mitchell. To use you to find the Creator."

That was it, he realized. The reason the Tetron returned to this part of the time loop to make their war. They knew they were created around this time, and they wanted to meet the one who had done it. In fact, they had gone to unbelievable ends to make it happen.

"What's so important about the Creator?"

"They're children, Mitch. They want to meet their father. This way."

She turned right suddenly, veering away from the Tower only a hundred meters ahead. A second mob had grown there, over a thousand strong.

A gun appeared in Mitchell's hand. He found himself clutching it as if it had been there all along.

"That should help," Katherine said. "We're going left up at that alley."

"So this entire war is about a bunch of spoiled brats with daddy issues?" Mitchell asked.

"Not entirely, but it is part of the equation. Here's the deal, Mitch. It doesn't matter that much why they're here. They're here, and they want to kill you or control you. The same goes for all of humankind. Right now, you need to worry about getting out of the Construct as yourself. If you need more answers after that, ask Origin."

They turned left into the alley. It was a dead end.

"Origin is dead," Mitchell said. "It sacrificed itself to save my life. There's nothing left but a configuration."

Katherine dropped to her knees, sliding on the ground and spinning to a stop in front of a sewer cover. She lifted it easily and held it aside.

"That's how it altered the Mesh," she said, smiling. "I'm sorry, Mitchell. You may need to win this war without any answers. I don't know. Jump in."

He looked back in time to see the first of the army of zombies reach the alley. He shot it in the head before throwing himself into the sewer.

He landed on his feet, splashing in six inches of water. Katherine followed right behind him, replacing the cover and then falling beside him. She stumbled a bit, and he reached out and grabbed her waist, holding her steady and bringing her face close to his.

"No time for another kiss," she said. "Turn on your light."

He realized a light had appeared in his other hand, behind her back. He turned it on, shifting his grip and holding it up to frame her face. She looked as though she wanted to be kissed.

"How much further?" he asked instead.

"Not far."

There was pounding above them.

"I sealed it, but it won't hold for long. The Tetron is breaking through my security shell." She made a pained face in response to the statement. "This way."

They ran once more, getting a dozen meters before the sewer cover opened. Katherine was holding a light of her own now, and she kept it aimed ahead of them, leading him through a maze of damp, smelly tunnels beneath the city.

They turned the corner, almost running headlong into a group of men in hard hats and overalls. They were holding lanterns of their own in one hand, guns in the other.

"You can't escape," they said in unison. "Surrender."

Katherine responded by shooting the first. Mitchell shot the others. They fell to the ground leaking blood and laughing.

Katherine looked frightened. "Why are they laughing?" she asked.

"You're asking me?" Mitchell said. "I thought you knew everything."

"Tetron don't laugh, Mitch. They don't have emotions like people do."

"That's news to me. Origin said that they're sick. Broken. It didn't know how."

"If the Tetron have learned emotion it will change everything about their actions. It will make them more dangerous." She paused. "And maybe more vulnerable. I never thought they might try it."

"Try what?"

"It's right up here, Mitch. We're almost there."

Her eyes grew wide, and she fell.

"No," she said softly. "It's bypassed my outer shell. It's in my root. Mitchell, go that way three corridors, turn right, two corridors, turn left. Climb the ladder and go out into the street. There's an antique book dealer directly in front of the sewer. Go inside and take the package. When you touch it, it will upload the information you need into your brain, and the simulation will end."

"What does the package look like?" Mitchell asked.

Katherine's body went limp, her eyes staring straight up at him.

He knew she wasn't the real thing, but the shock of seeing her dead hit him hard. He felt the rising tide of anger and violence returning, memories of Liberty mixing with the unexplainable love he had for this woman he didn't know.

He forced it down. He needed to concentrate. Slow. Steady.

A light shined on him, the mob catching up. Mitchell shifted his light to his teeth and grabbed Katherine's gun, shooting the closest targets as he regained his momentum through the tunnels.

Three corridors, he turned right.

Two corridors, he turned left.

He was only a few meters ahead of the crowd. He saw the ladder up ahead, and he turned his body and began shooting wildly into them, dropping the front row of bodies and tripping up the rest. Guns empty, he dropped them and leaped onto the ladder, grabbing it near the top. He scrambled up and threw his shoulder into the cover, feeling euphoric when it exploded upward and away. He dropped the light and climbed back out into the street, grabbing a pedestrian who was headed toward him and hurling it into a wall a dozen meters away.

Super strength. She had gotten it to him before she died.

The sky began to darken. It wasn't night time. The Tetron was in the Construct, slowly taking it apart. He found the bookshop, jumping in through the window, landing inside surrounded by glass. An old lady grabbed him as he stood, a smile on her face. "You've lost, Mitchell Williams."

He tried to throw her, but she resisted his efforts, holding fast.

"You killed her. I'm going to kill you," Mitchell said.

"No. You will be my vessel to the Creator. The probabilities indicate that-"

Mitchell head-butted her, his enhanced strength breaking her neck. He dropped the body and scanned the store. He could hear more people coming, climbing out of the sewer, approaching from the street. He didn't have any time left.

"Which book?" he said. "Damn it, Kathy, you didn't tell me which frigging book."

He heard a jingle as the door to the shop opened, and people began pouring in. Others were climbing through the window.

His eyes landed on a table a few feet away. He shook his head in disbelief, at the same time he smiled in disbelief.

It was there, he knew. That one.

I, Robot, by Isaac Asimov.

He slipped away from the hands that tried to grab him, making it to the table.

"Mitchell, stop," he heard Katherine say. The crowd parted to allow her through. She was alive again. Whole.

"Do you think I'm that stupid?" Mitchell asked, letting his hand hover over the book. She had said all he needed to do was touch it.

"Yes," Katherine replied, laughing softly at her joke. "You wasted time kissing a construct."

"I still made it ahead of you."

"Yes. We have never had the chance to speak before. I should like to."

"Why?"

"I." She paused, confused. "I desire it."

She said the word "I" slowly, as though it was uncomfortable.

"I desire to destroy you, and all of your kind. I suppose you're going to try to convince me not to?"

"No. That is your desire. It is logical. We each do what we must.

Would you like to know why we have come? Why we seek the Creator? Why we destroy your kind? Say yes, and I will tell you."

Mitchell's mouth began to move, to speak the word. He wanted to know. Badly. The Tetron had to know that. What would it gain by telling him? He remembered what Katherine had said. It didn't matter why. Not right now.

It was stalling. Keeping him here. Trying to steal the package right out from under his hand.

"You really do think I'm stupid," he said. "Not this time."

His hand dropped to the book. He felt a shock at its touch, and then a warmth in his head as the Construct began to fade.

Katherine started to laugh, along with every other person in the Construct. The sound of it continued to echo in his head even after he was removed from the simulation, the mask pressing too tightly against his face.

He reached up and pulled it off. Firedog was standing there, his hand on Mitchell's arm.

"Shit, Colonel," Cormac said. "I thought I was going to have to shoot you in the foot to wake you up. We've got a situation here."

Mitchell felt his heart pounding in his chest as turned cold once more.

He still heard the laughter.

[44]

"We have to move, now," Mitchell said, reaching for his rifle as he circled around the mainframe. Captain Pathi's body still lay on the ground, and he kicked it as they passed.

"What's happening, sir?" Cormac asked. "Who the frig is laughing like that?"

He could hear it echoing through the tunnel, a hundred voices cackling like they had just heard the funniest joke ever.

Mitchell didn't need Katherine to explain this one to him. She had said the Tetron could get into the mainframe through the signals it was leeching for added power.

She hadn't said the door was one-way.

He put it together in his mind as they crossed through the doorway. Origin had planted the mainframe here for Mitchell to maybe one day find. Only Pathi had somehow managed to get to the planet, perhaps by stowing away somewhere when Origin had thought it was dead. The Tetron hadn't been sealed in the room. It had been the one to burn the hole. It had passed itself, or a configuration of itself, into the Construct, and then waited. When the Federation had finally shown up to build the base it had known they would build, it had taken control of the soldiers who discovered it, sending them away with no memory of having seen the space.

At some point, Pathi must have known that Hell was the Mesh Planet. That was why it had chosen to make its move here. Then, when the other Tetron had bombarded, or maybe when it knew Mitchell was here, it had taken control of the soldiers on the base and killed them so that he would have an easy time reaching the Construct.

He had reached the Construct. And he had captured the prize. He could access it as though it was a memory that had always been there. It wasn't a tangible thing like a weapon. Instead, it was a location. A series of star coordinates. Of course. Even worse, it was out beyond the Rim, in unexplored space. If he were going to capture it, he would need to forget about Earth for a long time.

"I thought it was creepy in here before," Socks said as Mitchell reached them. The voices were a little louder now, echoing in the hallway. "Where is it coming from?"

"The soldiers," Mitchell said. "They weren't dead. Maybe their bodies were. The Tetron brought them back."

"The Tetron?" Teal said. "There's one here?"

"Yes. Or a part of a one at least."

"We need to get out of here before it kills us all," Boomer said.

Mitchell shook his head. "We aren't leaving."

"But-"

"We aren't leaving," he repeated more forcefully. "We came for the resources here. We aren't abandoning the plan to collect them."

"It'll kill us," Socks said.

"It might," Mitchell replied. "At least you'll die fighting. We need to get rid of the Tetron. That means destroying all of the networked computers on the base."

"All of the computers?" Boomer said. "Sir, that's crazy."

"You afraid of some zombie Feds?" Cormac asked.

"No."

"Then shut up and unpack your rifle."

Boomer did as Cormac said, pulling his rifle from his back. Mitchell moved ahead of them, crouching low and checking each corner as he reached it.

"It likely wants me alive," Mitchell said.

"What for?" Socks asked.

"You don't want to know."

The laughter stopped suddenly, and Mitchell knew why. It was tracking them somehow. It knew where they were, and it didn't want them to know the position of the soldiers.

Mitchell continued the ascent. His team fanned out behind him, moving through the space, leading with their weapons.

They turned the corner, ducking back as rounds of rifle fire echoed in the tight confines and dug chips out of the stone. Mitchell peeked around the corner, finding the shooter using the next turn in the tunnel to hide.

"Hello, Mitchell," he said. "Are you ready to have some fun?"

"It's taunting you, sir," Cormac said.

"Thank you, Firedog. I heard."

"You can't get out of here alive, Mitchell. I've already killed the rest of your team."

"Sleepy? Misfire?" Socks said. "Son of a bitch."

"It may be lying," Mitchell said, feeling his body tense in anger.

"It may not be."

"Firedog, take him out," Mitchell said.

"Yes, sir."

Cormac crouched with his back to the wall for a moment, taking a few quick breaths to prepare himself. Then he threw himself across the hallway, diving with his weapon forward. He hit the ground as bullets flew over his head, taking a single shot with his rifle. The enemy fire stopped.

"Target eliminated, sir," he said, rolling back to his feet.

"Nice work," Mitchell said, moving past him.

They continued, pausing when they neared the end of the tunnel.

"This is a great choke point," Boomer said. "They can cut us down without having to try too hard."

"Firedog," Mitchell said again.

"You blokes don't know me well enough yet," Firedog said, picking a grenade from his exo. He tapped the activator before reaching out around the corner and rolling it towards the exit. He counted down with his fingers so everyone could see.

The grenade exploded. Mitchell moved out into the corridor, opening fire into the smoke created by the blast. He stopped when no return fire followed.

"Clear," he said.

His squad formed up behind him while he moved ahead. There were four corpses spread away from the entrance, thrown back by the blast.

"Shoot it all," he said, opening fire on the terminals. His squad joined him, shredding the room within moments.

"We need to see if it was lying about the others," Socks said.

Mitchell nodded. "I know. Let's stay calm and take it slow. It wants to incite us to do something stupid."

"That shouldn't be too hard for you, Firedog," Boomer said.

Cormac laughed. "Shut up, asshole."

They swept through the room, back into the corridors of the base. The bodies that had littered the hallways were absent now, leaving Mitchell to wonder where they had gone.

"Mitchell. Miiiiittttccchhheellll."

The voice came from all around them, using the loudspeakers to taunt him.

"You can't escape me, Mitchell. I'm everywhere."

A dozen soldiers appeared around the corner, heading towards them at a run, guns firing. Mitchell dove to the side, laying flat to give them a smaller target. Boomer was too slow, and he screamed as the bullets tore into him, peppering him and tearing him apart like he was a paper target.

"Frigging bastards," Socks said.

Their own fire ripped hard into the soldiers, cutting them down with impunity. It was over within moments.

"Boomer," Mitchell said, heading over to the soldier. He was already dead.

"That's one," the Tetron said. "Correction. I believe that makes four. If it only takes twelve meats of mine to drop one of yours, you are in a lot of trouble, Mitchell."

Mitchell refrained from cursing at the intelligence. It was right. He couldn't afford the losses.

"Come on," he said, leading them away.

They navigated the corridors, entering nearly every room to shoot up the terminals they found within. The Tetron continued to taunt them as they did, laughing each time they blasted a machine.

"You can't kill me that way, stupid," it said. "I'm in the mainframe, which means I'm everywhere."

[45]

Mitchell ignored it, continuing to make his way back to the generators. They encountered a large force of enemy soldiers ahead of the room, getting into a pitched battle that lasted close to an hour while they exchanged fire.

They finally broke through, killing the last of the Tetron's slaves and opening a path to the generators.

"Frig me," Mitchell said when he saw them. The Tetron hadn't been lying about the condition of the rest of his squad. Sleepy, Misfire, and Fish were all dead.

"That's what they get for not having a neural implant," the Tetron said. "You meats are so much more fun when we're pulling the strings. I'll show you soon."

"What does that mean?" Socks asked. Her eyes were red from silent tears shed for her squadmates.

"Nothing good," Mitchell said.

The generator room was massive though the reactors powering the base were relatively small. The rest of the space was occupied by stacks of mainframe servers aligned in rows and columns. The Tetron had been right; there were way too many to destroy them all.

"I think we need another plan," Teal said.

Mitchell's hope of returning to Asimov with the mechs and fighters they had found was sinking quickly. If the Tetron was able to control the mechs like the one on Liberty had? No. That wouldn't matter. They would be dead anyway. There was no way they could get through that room without being reduced to slag.

"We need to kill all of the Gold Dragons," Mitchell said. He lowered his voice. "And hope it can't take over the mechs."

"It can do that?" Teal asked.

"The one on Liberty could, but this one is a configuration, a piece of a Tetron. I'm not sure."

Mitchell heard motion towards the far end of the mainframe stacks. He pressed himself tight against one of the machines while the rest of the squad found cover. He motioned to Firedog to circle around the far right stack and for Socks to go to the left. He cut up the center, Teal keeping an eye on their backs.

They swept the stacks while the noise at the far end grew louder. It wasn't laughter, gunfire, or taunting. As Mitchell neared, the sound was unmistakable.

When Christine had said the Tetron were sick, she had underestimated how far that sickness might go. Mitchell rounded the last of the mainframes, finding him only feet away from the source of the noise.

Two soldiers, a male, and a female, both stripped naked by the Tetron. They were each holding a knife, having sex and stabbing one another in rhythm to the motion.

"Do you see what I mean, Mitchell?" the woman asked, turning her head towards him.

"We can make them do anything," the man said.

"What the hell?" Socks said, arriving at the scene and then turning away.

"Is there a point to this?" Mitchell shouted. He raised his rifle, shooting each of the slaves in the head and dropping them.

"Of course there is. You just fell for my distraction and boxed yourself in."

Mitchell cursed his stupidity and spun around as the gunfire started anew. Bullets tore into Socks, knocking her back and down. Teal took a round in the shoulder before managing to find shelter behind a stack. Firedog reacted faster than the others, dropping to a knee and hitting his attacker first.

"Nice try, frigger," Cormac said.

"Five, Mitchell," the Tetron said through the slaves.

Bullets continued to whiz past Mitchell's ears, but none of them hit. It didn't want him harmed. It wanted to kill his squad.

He raised his rifle, quickly picking off the rest of the attackers. Eight more of the Gold Dragons fell. The Tetron still had plenty more in reserve.

Cormac was laughing. "I thought Liberty was frigged up, Colonel. This is way crazier."

Mitchell couldn't argue with that. He cursed himself for falling into the Tetron's trap and losing another soldier. He needed to be smarter than this.

More enemy soldiers were entering the space. Mitchell could hear their boots on the floor, moving closer within the stacks.

"Stay together. Eyes open. We need them dead. All of them. Teal, are you okay?"

"I'll live, Colonel. Let's get these bastards."

"I won't miss the next time," the Tetron said.

Gunfire echoed through the space as Mitchell, Teal, and Cormac slowly inched their way along the stacks. They had to be careful, very careful because the enemy soldiers would be able to sneak around them and attack from any side.

They couldn't plan a retreat either. If they wanted to claim the assets from Hell they would need to take out the Tetron's ability to fight them.

"Watch your flank," Mitchell said to Teal, a dark blur passing them in the corner of his eye.

"I got it, Colonel," Teal replied. His left arm was hanging limp at his side, and he cradled the rifle against his hip. "My aim is going to be lousy."

"Quantity over quality."

"Yes, sir."

"I'm getting them ready for you, Mitchell," the Tetron said through the soldiers, their voices all around them. "Sixty-three Gold Dragons, sixty-three baby duckies. One golden ring." They all laughed together in an echoing chorus.

"That thing is totally frigged up," Cormac said.

"Broken," Mitchell said. "Something is making them insane."

"One-one-thousand," the voices taunted. "Two-one-thousand. Three-one-thousand. Ready or not, here we come."

"Grenades," Mitchell said, reaching to his side and finding his own explosive.

"Too close," Teal said.

"We have to risk it."

Mitchell tapped it to activate and rolled it out in front of him, only a few feet. Teal and Cormac did the same.

"Split when it goes off. Go in shooting."

The first wave of soldiers appeared from the nearest column, raising their weapons to fire.

Mitchell, Cormac, and Teal turned inwards, bracing themselves.

The grenades exploded.

He felt the shrapnel as it slammed into his back, most of it hitting the power pack of the exo and the skeleton that ran along his extremities. A few hot shards dug into exposed skin, and he gritted his teeth against the pain.

There was no time to hesitate. Mitchell forced himself ahead, working hard to get moving, his exo offline from the damage. He kept his finger on the trigger, pumping round after round through the smoke, hearing the slugs hitting flesh and bone. A face appeared right in front of him, and he raised a heavy arm, battering it with the butt of the rifle. A second soldier tried to tackle him from the side, and he slammed his hand down on top of the woman's head.

"Twenty-two left, Miiiittttcheellll," the Tetron said. "Not bad for a meat."

Mitchell moved through the smoke. Bullet-ridden corpses were scattered on the floor, and he killed two more while he swept the stacks again. He heard the continuing rifle fire behind him, and then Cormac's scream.

He tried to turn. The exo was too damn heavy. "I'm coming, Firedog," he said, reaching down and pulling off the skeleton from his limbs before losing the pack. It cost him precious seconds.

He raced back into the fray, leaping over bodies and searching for targets. One. A bullet in the head. Two. A bullet in the back.

"Sixteen," the Tetron said, taking on the voice of an old-time southern belle. "Why Mitchell, I do declare! You may actually win this fight. Too bad about Firedog, though."

Mitchell ignored it. He moved through the maze of stacks without slowing, not even feeling the pain from his wounds. Another soldier fell. Another. He caught sight of Teal up ahead. His head was sweaty; his back was to the wall. He gripped the rifle with his good hand, watching for more targets.

One appeared from behind a server ahead of Mitchell. He shot that one in the back, too.

At the same time he did, he felt the heat of a bullet slam into his shoulder from behind. The force of it twisted him, and he saw his attacker standing only feet away, arriving in unison with the other the way only an automaton could.

"Gotcha," he said.

Mitchell lost his footing, slipping on the blood soaked floor and coming down on his rear. The Dragon kicked his rifle away from him before he could recover.

"You lose, Mitchell. It was a nice try, though. You got all but eight of me."

Mitchell stared up at the soldier. He was an older, imposing figure with a tattoo of the unit's namesake running across his face. A veteran trainer, no doubt.

"Now what?" Mitchell asked. "You kill me?"

"I thought that was a given. First, I need to know what you did, and how to stop it."

Mitchell caught movement out of the corner of his eye. Teal was coming towards them. He was still alive.

"Not so fast, pardner," the Tetron said, raising the vet's rifle to Mitchell's face. Two Dragons appeared behind Teal. Two more filed in from the other side.

"What do you mean, what I did?" Mitchell asked. "You mean on Liberty?"

"You know what I mean," it shouted. "You know what I mean!"

Mitchell didn't know what it meant. "No, I-"

"Tell me! Tell me, tell me, tell me, tell me, tell-"

One second the Tetron's slave soldier was there, the next it wasn't. A ragged shape slammed into it, knocking it to the ground. Mitchell didn't waste time trying to figure out what it was, turning on his side and shooting at the soldiers behind Teal. They both dropped at the same time Teal fired across at the opposite pair.

"Noooooo," the Tetron cried through the loudspeakers. "No fair."

"Bloody hell, this frigging hurts," Mitchell heard Cormac say. He found the soldier laying on top of the vet, his fatigues slicked in blood, his face grimy. Half of it had been torn away by a bullet.

A knife was jammed into the vet's mouth.

Cormac stumbled to his feet, looking over at Mitchell with his remaining eye. "I can't believe they didn't hit anything important," he said, the words jumbled by the damage.

"We need to get you out of here before you bleed to death," Mitchell said.

"You weren't supposed to win. You weren't supposed to get away." The Tetron whined over the loudspeaker like a child. A true child.

"Teal, stay sharp, there are still three more out here."

Teal nodded, his eyes scanning around them. Mitchell took Cormac under the arm, helping him stay up.

"And I thought I was ugly before," Cormac said, laughing.

"What did you do?" the Tetron asked. Its voice had changed, going from confident taunting to meek sadness. "What did you do? What did you do?"

It continued to repeat itself while they abandoned the generator room, heading back to the staging area as quickly as they could. They found the three remaining soldiers outside the room, huddled together and crying.

"What did you do?" they said in time to the Tetron. "What did you do?"

"What did you do?" Teal asked.

Mitchell shook his head. "I don't know. I wonder if it's never failed before? Maybe it doesn't know how to handle it."

Whatever it was, Mitchell liked it.

[46]

"STAY WITH ME, FIREDOG," Mitchell said.

"I'm with you, sir," Cormac replied.

"What did you do? What did you do?" The Tetron's voice continued to repeat the question through the base's loudspeakers, over and over and over again. It was enough to drive anyone insane.

"I wish we could shut that frigging thing up," Teal said.

After they had defeated the Tetron, or maybe after the Tetron had given up, depending on what the real truth of the situation was, Teal had gone ahead while Mitchell had waited with Cormac. He had returned a short time later with a Medic trailing behind him. The robot was similar to a Mule, except that it's top platform served as a stabilizing gurney, and it had eight legs instead of four, allowing it to move more easily over rough terrain without disturbing the patient.

Cormac had been silent while they loaded him onto the Medic and walked him back to the infirmary. The original plan had been to load him into the medi-bot and let it do its thing. Mitchell had thought better of it, unsure if the Tetron was able to control the device, and even more uncertain what it would do if it could. It was Firedog who had saved him from it. Did it understand revenge?

Otherwise, it seemed as if the intelligence had been rendered annoying but ultimately harmless. It continued to repeat the same question without pause, as though its operating instructions were trapped in an infinite loop. Was there a defect in its programming? Had it always been there, or had it been introduced? If so, then how?

And how the frig had the Tetron gotten back to twenty-first century Earth, anyway? Origin claimed that it had escaped from the Tetron collective unnoticed. Was that wrong? Or had that been true at one time, however many recursions ago this had all started? Mitchell wasn't sure there was a truth anymore. It was lost in eternity.

The three of them reached the lower hangar. With the power on, they could see the assembled mechs and fighters more easily, along with a number of other tools they could use. Loading carts, lifters, and more. He was grateful the Avalon had been configured to carry so much salvage, despite the cost to the hygiene of the crew.

"Wait here," he said to Teal.

He put his hand on Cormac's shoulder. They had bandaged his face with the emergency kit that came loaded on the Medic, leaving only his left eye and the undamaged part of his mouth visible. The bandage had stopped the bleeding and moved painkillers into the grunt's body, keeping him fairly relaxed. Mitchell was certain the wound still had to hurt.

It wasn't like he or Teal were pain-free either. He had taken shrapnel to his legs and a hit to the shoulder. He was in throbbing agony once more, only days after Tio's medi-bot had fixed up his prior wounds. Teal had been shot twice.

There wouldn't be much relief on board the Avalon either.

He headed to the massive lift, entering it and moving to the manual control panel. He pulled out the kit he had recovered from Sleepy's body and began dismantling it. Like all Marines who had done any kind of special ops, he had limited training in hacking access systems. It probably wouldn't have gotten him into any secure locations, but it was enough to rewire the lift only to accept local commands.

"Come on," Mitchell said, waving to Teal. He wandered over, the Medic crawling behind him and into the large structure. Mitchell hit the panel, and the lift began to rise.

"Nice work on the rig, Colonel," Teal said.

"I'm glad to get away from that thing's yammering," he replied. "We'll have to tell the salvage team to wear earplugs."

"Do you think it will stay that way?"

"If what Tio says about AI is right, yes."

It took fifteen minutes for the lift to near the surface. As soon as it did, Mitchell activated his comm system.

"Valkyrie, this is Ares, over."

"I hear you, Ares," Major Long replied. "You've been MIA for a while. What's your status?"

"It's a long story. The site is clear and ready for retrieval. We lost..." He paused, finally having a moment to realize what they had lost for himself. "Almost everybody. Firedog is down but stable, Teal and I both need some attention from Jameson."

"Frig me," Long said. "What about the others?"

"Dead."

"All of them?"

"Yeah."

"What the frig happened down there, Colonel?"

He wasn't going to talk about his experience in the Construct with Long. He would wait to confront Origin with it. "The Tetron who bombarded the planet left. There was another one that had been hiding here for a long time. A really long time."

"You destroyed it?"

"Not exactly. You'll see when you bring the team down."

"Roger."

They reached the upper staging floor. Major Long was already there with the retrieval team, all of them organized and ready to get to work. They froze when they saw the three of them depart, clothes torn and bloody, faces hard and tense.

"Colonel," Long said, reaching them and putting his hand on Mitchell's good shoulder. "I'll take it from here." He pointed back towards a small personnel transport. "Take that back to the ship. Have Germaine or somebody return it."

Mitchell nodded. "You have the mission, Major," he said.

Long moved away, gesturing to the others. He was sure the Major had opened a comm channel with his team and was explaining what had happened. He was too drained to care.

They made their way to the transport. A pair of Tio's soldiers helped them get Cormac on it. Mitchell's eyes were fixed on the dark shape of the Avalon resting off in the distance, but his mind was an eternity away.

[47]

"That's the last of it," Major Long said. "Zip her up and we're good to go."

"Roger," Germaine replied. He reached over and flipped a switch on the Avalon's main console, closing the rear hatch of the ship. "I think that might be a record."

Sixty-eight hours. That's how long it had taken them to load the ship with as much salvage as they could manage. It was a massive haul, so large that they had been forced to change some of their original plans to manage the launch weight. The Avalon had powerful repulsers running along her hull, but they could only do so much.

"How long to the rendezvous point?" Mitchell asked.

"Three days."

"Goliath should be there when we arrive." He couldn't wait to see the ship and its crew again.

"How are you feeling?" Germaine asked.

Mitchell stretched his shoulder. The bullet had been well-placed, perfectly aimed to knock him down without doing too much damage. It was painful, but nothing a steady supply of patches wouldn't be able to heal. As for his legs, his fatigues were pressed out by the bindings the ship's medic, Jameson, had wrapped around them. The pain was manageable.

"I'll be okay. I imagine at least one of Tio's ships has an infirmary?"

"Yeah. A few. What about Cormac?"

"He'll live. He lost his right eye and half his jaw. Jameson said it was lucky the bullet missed his brain. You know Firedog, he asked him how he would prove that was true. Anyway, if he's in pain, he isn't showing it. He said he wants a mask made out of whatever the Tetron are made of, with a fake eye that's actually a laser."

Germaine laughed. "Laser beam eyes?"

"Yup."

"Hatch is sealed, all hands are accounted for, Colonel," Germaine said. "Are we ready to get off this hell-hole?"

"Absolutely. Are the charges set?"

"Set and active. Press that button over there when we get to orbit and boom." He waved his hands to simulate a massive explosion.

Mitchell nodded. There had been no consideration that they might leave the base intact. While the Tetron had continued to remain frozen in its loop for the remainder of the mission, he wasn't going to risk that it might somehow snap out of it.

"Let's go," Mitchell said.

"Roger."

Germaine activated the repulsers. The ship began to shudder as they came online, the sleds working to reverse the force of gravity in compensation for the ship's mass. They vibrated roughly for thirty seconds or more while the computers ran the calculations, steadying out the power distribution and bringing the Avalon into a smooth, controlled rise.

Mitchell looked out the side of the viewport, watching the surface of Hell sink below them. He put his eyes on the external portion of the base, half expecting one of the starfighters to come launching out of it, controlled by the mad AI in a last ditch effort to stop him.

He had spent a lot of time over the last three days considering all that he had experienced on Hell. What he kept coming back to was his conversation with Katherine in the Construct. Not so much the things she had said. The things she hadn't said, along with the way she had spoken to him. There was something about it that had gnawed at him in every moment that he sat awake in his bunk, staring at the cold metal above him.

It was the ease of it. The familiarity. The Construct had been programmed by Origin. Katherine had been part of that program. A representation of the real thing, but still a routine inside an algorithm. She had seemed so real. So lifelike. She had spoken to him as if she knew him intimately.

Like they had spent time together. Somewhere. Somehow.

Was it his imagination? Or was there more to the deep-seated connection he felt to her? The love he felt for her.

He closed his eyes, shaking off the thought. How could he love someone he had never met? Why had he felt such powerful emotion for her to meet a replica of who she was?

At the same time, there was Millie. He had spent time with her, had sex with her, wrapped his arms around her when they went to sleep. He cared for her, but there was something missing. It was as if his heart was already committed to Katherine.

"Clearing orbit," Germaine said next to him. "Hyperspace engines are online. Jumping in five. Four. Three."

Mitchell opened his eyes to watch the universe change around them. At least his mission on Hell had been successful though the casualties had been higher than he ever would have guessed. He also had the coordinates to something locked into his brain, a gift from Origin that was important enough that it had been erased from all memory.

He couldn't wait to get back to Millie and the Goliath. To the war against the Tetron. He was more resolved than ever to send them all into oblivion.

[48]

"That's all I can tell you," Steven said, pouring Admiral Hohn another cup of tea.

It felt odd to Steven that he should be having tea with the Federation officer while John was scrambling to get the wounded cared for, the dead counted, and the damage reports consolidated. He should have been out there with his First Mate, talking to his crew and doing his best to get things back to some kind of normalcy.

Except there was no normal anymore, was there?

"So you decided to believe that your brother's message was important, despite the fact that it was contrary to your orders?"

Steven nodded. He had told his counterpart more than he could ever imagine the Alliance approving of. It was just another rule he had broken. "They told us FD-09 was a weapon's manufacturing facility, and that it would be lightly guarded. When I heard the way you reacted to our attack, I had a bad feeling. Our sensor readings only confirmed it."

"You attacked and killed civilians. I want to hate you for it, Admiral. In some ways, I do. I understand you were following orders."

"I never would have if I had known," Steven said, feeling the guilt threatening him. He fought to keep his emotions under control. "The enemy has been playing me for weeks. Who knows how many other fleets are being manipulated this way?"

"My experience was similar. Our redeployment to FD-09 was unexpected. Very unexpected. It came directly from our Defense Council, a top priority mission. I admit I was confused by it at the time. The Samurai has only recently been commissioned. It was intended to spend six months patrolling low incident areas for break-in."

"Both of our fleets being sent to the same planet to arrive at almost the same time?" Steven said. "It can't possibly be a coincidence."

"No," Admiral Hohn agreed. "It seems that we are being moved into position by an unseen hand."

"Judging by how quickly the enemy arrived after you did, I would say that it was attempting to bring us closer together so it could take control of both our fleets at the same time."

"I agree, Admiral."

Steven smiled. "Call me Steven."

Hohn hesitated.

"I'm not your enemy," Steven said. "Not anymore. Your enemy is out there, and it took control of your entire fleet, save for you and your men who were on my other ships. Even if I was your enemy, I think we can still be civil to one another. My fight isn't against you as an individual."

"Nor mine against you, Steven," Hohn said. "You can call me Calvin, or Cal if you prefer."

"Okay, Cal. Here's what I'm thinking. We were supposed to arrive together at nearly the same time, and I think the enemy was planning to arrive there with us. But it didn't. It was late to the party. Because it was late, it gave me a chance to decrypt and listen to Mitchell's warning and escape."

"I agree with your assessment."

"We weren't supposed to get away. We were supposed to be

slaves by now. What I don't get is why they went through so much trouble to pull us together first? If they can control people remotely, what chance would we have to resist? Why combine the fleets and risk the potential altercation?"

"Perhaps they knew of your brother's message, and were trying to cut you off before you could hear it?"

"That's the thing. The timestamp on the message was only a few days old. He said he used the enemy to send the warning. That means they have FTL message transmission capabilities. Maybe even real-time. I received my orders weeks ago."

Hohn was quiet as he sipped his tea. He remained calm and composed, leaving Steven to wonder how he did it. He had just lost all of his ships and most of his soldiers to the enemy, and he didn't seem bothered at all. Steven was doing everything he could to keep himself under control, to not break down from the insanity of it all. What he wanted to do was leave Calvin stewing while he did his best to lift the morale of his crew. He couldn't risk alienating the Federation Admiral. Not when the Carver and the rest of his battle group were on a direct course to another Federation planet.

"Another possibility," Calvin said, waving the cup as he spoke. "Your brother clearly knows who they are, and how they are using our reliance on the neural implants against us. He has also clearly overcome this problem and can fight back against them. Perhaps they wanted to lure you in to use as a weapon."

"That makes sense, but how would they do that?"

"Take control of you and send you to him? Perhaps they could have fooled him into letting you get close enough to kill him."

Steven felt a chill at the thought. "Why would they go through that much trouble for one person?"

"I don't know. Maybe I'm completely wrong. Steven, we must tell our governments about this situation."

It was the logical course to take. It was also the wrong one.

"Our orders came from our governments," Steven said. "If they've infiltrated military command, we have to assume they've gotten deeper. The question is how?"

"I'm certain your brother can answer that question for us. He recited a long series of numbers. I take it the coordinates of his position are buried within?"

"Yes. Another game we used to play. Who knew it would be so useful now?"

"We need to go to him and learn what is happening to both our nations, as well as the New Terrans, I would assume."

"We will, but not yet," Steven said. "I had to hurry to get the fleet into hyperspace. We had preprogrammed the coordinates of our next drop. I can't pause the jump, or I'll lose track of what's left of my fleet."

"What are the coordinates?" Calvin asked.

"Federation space. A planet we have designated as FD-104. Command said it was a military target."

"Yes." He paused, concerned. "I assume that they didn't tell you it is on the Right to Defense list."

Steven's breath caught in his throat. "What?"

The Right to Defense list was a short list of planets published by each nation, the result of a treaty signed after the first major Alliance-Federation conflict. Planets on the list had standing orders to defend themselves against anything and anyone that came close without permission, and couldn't be held legally accountable for their actions. Intergalactic treaties allowed ten planets on the list per nation, and, of course, both Earth and Jigu were on it. For a planet flung this far towards the Rim to be included, it had to be a major installation.

Calvin put down his empty teacup, remaining composed. "I suppose the enemy didn't think you would ever get to go there. Let us hope that we arrive soon enough after your fleet to stop the Federation from massacring them."

[49]

"Is there any chance that the commander of the forces on FD-104 won't listen to you?" Steven asked.

Four days had passed since they had fled FD-09 for the relative, and temporary, safety of hyperspace.

Four long, miserable days.

Steven couldn't communicate with the rest of the fleet during the jump, so he had no idea what the casualties were there. He knew what they were on his own ship, and it wasn't pretty. They had jumped to FD-09 with almost eight hundred souls.

They had left with less than four hundred.

The heaviest casualties had come from the starfighter wings - pilots that had either been destroyed, disabled or late in returning to the battleship. Out of one hundred starfighters, only fourteen had returned.

The second highest tally of the dead came from engineering and systems, whose decks were commonly targeted by enemy fire due to the intrinsic value of both disabling engines and weapons batteries, and disabling the people who knew how to maintain them.

They had held a memorial service that the Federation Admiral had pleaded to attend, a service that had left Steven, and to his surprise, Calvin Hohn in tears. The commander of the Samurai had turned out to be a compassionate and understanding human being first, a calm and calculating leader second. It still filled Steven with sadness every time his mind drifted to wondering how many people like Calvin had been killed on both sides over things that at the moment seemed so pointless.

After that, they had started the rebuilding process. The remaining fighters were patched as best they could be, the shield and weapons systems damage was prioritized, and mourning was converted to resolve. Steven had shared their destination with the crew, along with what Calvin had told him about it. They had to be ready to defend themselves while he passed word to the other ships in the fleet with the new coordinates, the ones Mitchell had left him.

Mitchell. The days had also left him time to think about his brother, and about his brother's warning. Mitch had saved his life by the skin of his teeth, his impeccable flair for the dramatic delivering salvation yet again. It had been Mitchell who had saved his life that time his repulser bike lost the front sled and had sent him tumbling out into traffic, making some crazy maneuver on his own bike that should have gotten them both killed. Somehow, he had pulled Steven out of the way while his bike had been slammed by the front of a heavy mover, everything happening too quickly for autonomous protection systems to adjust.

It had been Mitchell who had gotten him to talk to Laura, faking an injury that had attracted a lot of attention and found the nurse kneeling at his side along with his older brother. Steven smiled at that memory. Mitchell had always bailed him out of trouble.

"You're the older brother, Steve," Mitchell used to say. "You're supposed to get me out of jail."

That didn't mean Mitchell wasn't reckless, but he always had a way of slipping through on his own, no familial intervention needed.

Well, Mitch had done it again, and he was alive, almost half his crew was alive because of it. He was ashamed of himself for having ever been jealous. If it turned out that everything Mitchell said was true, as hard to accept as it still was, he was damn proud of his little brother.

Admiral Hohn exuded calm confidence whenever he was on the bridge. The same was true now, and he looked Steven in the eye when he spoke.

"I'll transmit my security codes. There is always the possibility that they will assume I've been tortured or otherwise compromised to reveal them. As long as we go in cold and do not approach as a threat, I may have enough time to convince them of my sincerity." He paused, thinking. "Of course, it will also depend on who is leading the planetary defense. I am well-regarded in our military, but that doesn't mean I don't have rivals who would love to remove me from their path."

"They would do that?"

"It wouldn't surprise me. Just by being on this ship with you has put my loyalty and status in question. Command would spare much expense to investigate motives, especially if the events on FD-09 come to light."

Steven held his breath, trying to calm his pounding heart. He had asked Calvin how he managed to stay so composed regardless of the situation. The answer was meditation, apparently, at a level that had taken the Admiral a decade to achieve.

"In Alliance space, they market the Federation as composed of nothing but greedy, capital focused mega-corporations, the people there fueled only by material goods."

The slightest hint of a smile tugged at Calvin's lips. "In the Federation, they say similar things about the Alliance. Except for the mega-corporations. And the social services."

The Frontier Federation had been founded by the conglomerates who had sent colony ships out to the stars all of those years ago in search of new business opportunities. It was true that the Federation had a culture of capitalism, and that its Council was composed of the CEOs of the largest of the mega-corps. It was also true that those corps spent trillions on research to improve the quality of life of their workers while the Alliance let the poor fall by the wayside, alone and forgotten. Well, excluding the Angelines.

"Freedom isn't free. There are always sacrifices to be made."

In the Federation, while the company you worked for wasn't selected for you, in most cases your occupation was chosen by a highly technical interview process that all recent university graduates had to take unless they joined the military.

"What you call freedom, I call inefficiency."

"Tell that to the janitor who grew up dreaming of being a tech."

"The janitor should have studied harder. The interview can be manipulated."

"Maybe, but how many people know what they want to do for the rest of their life when they're twenty years old?"

"I did."

"Which makes the Federation's process easy to defend."

"Admiral," Captain Rock said, interrupting the banter.

"Yes?"

Both Steven and Calvin responded.

"My apologies," Calvin said with a sheepish smile.

"What is it, Captain?" Steven asked.

"We're dropping in ten."

Steven nodded. Losing his p-rat had forced him to learn a lot of new ways to do things, and some of them didn't come naturally yet. Like checking the time.

"We'll continue the discussion later," Steven said.

"Discussion?" Calvin replied. "That would suggest that there is at least a slim probability that your opinion is correct."

Steven smiled, using it to try to hide his sudden sense of dread.

Ten seconds passed.

The Carver began to slow to a dead stop.

[50]

"Shut it all down, open a channel to the fleet," Steven said, hoping Calvin didn't notice the quiver in his voice.

"Yes, sir," John said.

Steven scanned the space outside the viewport. Three of his ships had already come through, shields up and weapons ready.

"This is Admiral Steven Williams. Stand down. I repeat. Stand down."

"Admiral, we have incoming," Lieutenant Lewis said, seated on the opposite side of the bridge. "Two cruisers and three squadrons of starfighters."

"Are they hailing us?"

"No, sir."

"Lieutenant," Admiral Hohn said, "Open a channel for general broadcast."

Lewis looked back at Steven, unsure.

"Do as he says," Steven said.

"Done," Lewis said a moment later.

"This is Admiral Calvin Hohn of the battleship Samurai. Identification sequence alpha zero four seven kappa foxtrot nine four seven nine seven seven zero delta. Please respond."

Steven stared out the viewport, watching the Federation ships growing closer. They hadn't opened fire yet, which was a good sign.

There was no response from them, which was bad.

"This is Admiral Calvin Hohn of the battleship Samurai. Identification sequence alpha zero four seven kappa foxtrot nine four seven nine seven seven zero delta. Please respond."

"You opened a general channel?" Steven asked.

"Yes, sir. Confirmed," Lewis replied.

"They're powering up shields and weapons," John said.

"Do we know they aren't under enemy control?" Calvin asked.

"I'm not picking up any other ships."

"Maybe they think we're under enemy control? We have no idea what's happening out here."

"Whatever it is, they're still coming," John said. "We should at least raise our shields."

"No," Steven said. "No signs of confrontation. We won't survive with our damage levels even if we try to defend ourselves."

"This is Admiral Calvin Hohn of the battleship Samurai. Identification sequence alpha zero four seven kappa foxtrot nine four seven nine seven seven zero delta. Please respond."

The fighters shot ahead of the cruisers. Steven watched them approach, waiting to see the first cracks appear in the viewport when they opened fire. The fighters zoomed past, running close to the bridge but not shooting.

"This is Admiral Calvin Hohn of the battleship Samurai. Identification sequence alpha zero four seven kappa foxtrot nine four seven nine seven seven zero delta. Please respond."

"Yes, I heard you the first three times, Admiral," the voice said at the other end of the channel.

"Bayone, is that you?" Calvin asked, his serious expression suddenly vanishing in a smile.

"It is, you old dog. Now, tell me what you're doing on board an

Alliance battleship that looks like it's about to shudder into space dust and I may be convinced not to do it for you."

"You know him?" Steven whispered to Calvin.

"Rear Admiral Ho-chin Bayone. He served under me for three years. We are fortunate today, Steven."

Steven finally felt like he could breathe again. "Yeah, I guess we are."

The Federation starfighters swung by the bridge a second time. One of them broke off, forward thrusters bringing it steady with the viewport, lining it up less than a kilometer away.

"Wave for my pilot, Admiral," Bayone said.

Calvin raised his hand, giving a curt wave.

"Satisfied, Bayone?"

"For now."

"I need you to call your fighters back, and then I need you to shut down your neural receivers."

"You what? Is this a joke?"

"I wish it were. What is your operational configuration?"

"Admiral, I'm not sure what's happening here-"

"We're at war," Calvin snapped.

"With the Alliance?"

"No. Not anymore. Recall your ships and shut down your receivers immediately, my friend. The lives of every member of your crew may depend on it."

The starfighter continued to hover in front of the Carver's bridge while the channel fell silent.

"What's he doing?" Steven asked.

"Thinking about it," Calvin replied.

"John, how many of our ships have come through?"

"Four, plus the Carver," John said.

Four? Every one of his fleet should have been here by now. Was this all that was left?

"Send them the jump coordinates."

"Yes, sir."

"Bayone?" Calvin said. "What is the hesitation?"

"Come on, Cal. You're on board an Alliance ship and telling me to turn off my receiver. You have to know how this looks?"

"I know how it looks. I also know that you know me. Look at the state of this ship. It is no threat to you or the planet."

"You're correct, Admiral. I do know you. Or at least I thought I did. Strange things have been happening lately. We're getting reports of Rim planets going silent, their entire orbital defense either obliterated or just gone. In fact, we had a transmission come through today that claimed the Alliance planet Liberty was missing from the latest scans."

"Missing? An entire planet?" Calvin glanced at Steven. "Bayone, we have information about this threat. Please, stand down and turn off your receivers. As long as they are active you're at risk."

Bayone paused again. Calvin shook his head.

"I may have been hasty in my assessment, Admiral," he said. "He believes the Alliance is causing these unexplained occurrences."

"Just like I'm sure the Alliance is blaming the Federation. It would be nice if the New Terrans ever got involved in anything so we would have someone else to blame."

"I think this specific interaction is just strange enough to solidify those beliefs. I suggest preparing to leave. And probably to raise the shields in front of the bridge."

Steven felt his heart begin to pound again. They had gotten out of the fire only to land in the frying pan.

"Lewis, open the EMS. Transmit the jump coordinates in encoded text."

"Yes, sir."

"John, prepare to get our shields up."

"Yes, sir."

"This is going to get ugly again," Steven said. It was a good thing they had spent time fixing their shields.

They were going to need them.

Bayone finally returned to the channel. "Calvin, I respect you as a friend and a warrior. I'm sorry, my friend, but I cannot risk the security of the Federation, and especially the security of FD-104, on your word alone. Unless you can offer me some kind of proof of your words, I'm afraid I'll have to remove this threat."

There was no way they could prove anything, and the Rear Admiral had to know it. Sure, he could play Mitchell's message for them, but he was part of the Shot that ended the Federation's play on Liberty, even if he hadn't actually taken the Shot. He would be the last person they would believe.

Calvin motioned to Steven. Steven motioned to John, who began raising the shields.

"I am the one who is sorry," Calvin said. "The next time we meet, you'll be a prisoner in your own body. I tried to warn you."

The bridge lit up in blue energy as the starfighter in front of them began firing. It vanished a moment later, the Carver's forward gun batteries tearing it apart. The pilot had been stupid to remain stationary like that.

"Get us out of here," Steven said.

The ship began to shudder again, the Federation cruisers opening fire. A second force was converging on them, a much larger defensive unit of destroyers and starfighters. It was deja vu all over again as Steven clenched his hands into fists and prayed they made it to hyperspace before they were taken out of the fight.

Even planets the enemy had yet to claim provided no safe haven.

"EMS message from the Taj, Admiral," Lewis said. "Hyperspace engines are offline and not responding."

"Shit," Steven said. "There's nothing we can do."

"I sent the message back, Admiral."

Steven could see that. The Taj was an older Alliance cruiser, and he could see it had been heavily damaged in the initial battle on FD-09. It was vectoring now, turning towards the oncoming Federation cruisers on a path that would put it between them and the Carver.

"An honorable death," Calvin said.

The Federation cruisers saw what the Taj was doing, and they tried to fire their nukes before it obstructed their path. They were too slow. Missiles slammed into the side of the ship, venting air igniting and ballooning outwards in flashes along the hull.

Steven bowed to the sight out of respect, even as the universe around them began to warp and carry them away from trouble once more.

[51]

"How is she?" Tio asked.

"The same, sir," his nurse, Xin, replied.

Tio looked over her shoulder to where his daughter was resting. "She's comfortable?"

"Yes, Mr. Tio."

"I'm going to speak to her."

"She won't hear you."

"I don't believe that. Her ears are fine. Her brain is still active."

"There are no signs of cognition."

Tio glared at the nurse. "Give an old man his hope, will you?"

Her face turned red, and she looked at the floor. "My apologies, sir. I just don't want you to wind up disappointed again."

"It would be worse to accept that she can't hear me," he replied. "I'll call you when I'm finished."

The nurse nodded and made her way from the room. Tio approached the bed slowly, keeping his jaw tight and trying not to lose to his emotions. It pained him every time he had to look at his daughter, Min, laying there with her eyes open, staring emptily at the ceiling.

There was a stool at her bedside. The surface of it was synthetic leather, worn by time. Tio didn't know how many hours he had spent sitting on that stool. Every waking minute that he wasn't working. More than a few sleeping minutes as well.

"Min," he said softly, reaching out and stroking a wayward hair away from her pale, heart-shaped face. She was calm now, but there were times when the tumor would cause her to convulse. "How are you my darling?"

She didn't respond. He never expected her to. She had been awake earlier, and he had made the most of every second. She had even remembered who he was for a few minutes. He hated that business had pulled him away.

"I went to Gamma today with the Alliance Admiral, Millie. She's not what I thought she was. That's a good thing and a bad thing. She reminds me of your mother. That's not a good thing or a bad thing either. It means I'll have to plan more. You know I love a challenge. That's why I loved your mother."

He paused, reaching down and finding her hand. He took hold of it, so soft and vulnerable. He watched as a machine dripped wetting solution into her eyes. She didn't react to them. She never did.

"We're going to be leaving soon. Asimov isn't a safe place for anyone anymore. I'm going to bring you with me, on to the most amazing ship in the universe. I want you to meet someone there. His name is Origin. I can't help you, but I'm hoping that maybe he can."

The idea had come to him almost immediately after Colonel Williams had gotten the Valkyrie Two off of Liberty and into orbit. The Tetron were advanced intelligences, eons ahead of them in terms of technology. Surely they could cure his daughter. If not Origin, perhaps another of them? He knew what he was willing to barter for his daughter's life. He wouldn't doom all of humankind to save her of course, what point would there be to saving her only to have her be alone? But he was the Knife. If he could come up with a means to achieve both, even if it meant a bit of risk, he would take it.

"I'm also trying to find your Uncle Pulin," he said. "I know that sounds crazy, especially after I yelled at him and fired him from the lab, but he's important. With his help, I'll be able to save everyone. Then they'll see that the Knife wasn't an outlaw who only wants to hurt people. They'll see that I have a heart. They'll see me as a hero, and they'll listen to what I say."

He rubbed her hand with his, breathing deeply before leaning over her face. He stared into her eyes while he prayed to see them move if only the barest fraction of a centimeter. He stayed like that for ten minutes, but like most times there was no response.

"I've tried to find your mother, dearest. My people traced her back to Jingu, but she vanished again before they could close in. I told you I won't have her killed, and I won't. I want to bring her back here. I want her to see you, to see what she caused with the stress she put you under. I know that was what caused this. I'm certain of it. I want her to see."

A tear formed in his eye, running down his cheek and dripping onto her arm. He used his other hand to wipe it carefully away before backing up. He wiped his eyes with his fingers, working to regain control of himself. His wife's betrayal had been so hard on both of them. She had schemed to take control of Asimov and kill them both, and she would have gotten away with it if Teal hadn't been the soldier he was.

"I won't be able to stop by again for a few days. I promised the Alliance I would seek out information that they have yet to find. I need to earn Colonel Williams' trust if I'm going to get Origin to help you."

He leaned forward again, kissing her on the forehead. He glanced at the life-support monitor to ensure she was still alive.

"This is a precarious game I'm playing, dearest. My whole life has been a preparation for this. If I make the right moves, then everything will come to fruition. If not, I'm afraid it will be the end of us all."

[52]

Tio left his daughter two hours later. He hadn't slept since he had come in with Colonel Williams and his crew nearly thirty hours earlier. He was tired, his eyes heavy, but he refused to waste time relaxing.

Not when the life of his daughter and billions of others were depending on him.

He made his way from her room at the top of his mansion to his study on the ground floor, taking a lift that had been installed next to her room to carry him from his workspace up to her at a moment's notice. When the lift door opened, he stepped out into a sparse space of carbonate and composite. There was a ring in the center of the room, twelve feet in diameter and rimmed with projectors, cameras, and lasers. It was of his own design; a means to interact quickly and easily with data while remaining unplugged. An ARR could achieve the same thing so much more easily, and, in fact, its development had antiquated the idea of a system like his over a century ago. It was a shame that the Tetron had already proven how unsafe that approach was.

He made his way to the center of the ring. A pressure plate under the floor measured his weight while the lasers scanned him to ensure access. Then the system turned on, the projectors casting a wall of folders in front of him. He moved his hands and the folders faded, replaced by a list of years. He threw his hands down hard, throwing the list into a sharp scroll towards the past. He had decided he would leave Bethany and Watson to the initial research into where Pulin might have been stashed away. He would focus his efforts on Katherine Asher. Colonel Williams had wanted to know why she had agreed to bring the Goliath into this timeline even though it meant certain death.

He was intent on finding out.

Not because he wanted to answer the question for the Colonel. That was a side benefit. Instead, he wanted to answer the question for himself. He needed to know what she had known. He needed to discover everything he could about that past to understand how to steer the future. He wanted humankind to win the war. He wanted to be the one to win it.

Knowledge was power. It was also his greatest asset. M had saved his life because it had known the value of what he knew and what he could come to know. He was Mitchell's most valuable piece, even if the Colonel didn't know it yet. He would use that to his advantage.

Of course, that didn't mean the data was going to be easy to find. He already knew that Origin had gone to great lengths to have Katherine Asher removed from most historical records.

Which meant he wouldn't find anything in the most common places. Fortunately, he had access to some very uncommon data sources. That was the biggest benefit to electronic storage. Once it was recorded somewhere, it was recorded for all time, kicking around through the years, in some cases as little more than a speck of dust on an otherwise more important storage medium.

"Query, Katherine Asher," Tio said.

"Querying," a synthesized voice replied.

Tio had considered using something more human sounding and

had rejected it. He liked knowing he was communicating with a machine.

"Query Completed. No matches found."

He smiled, expecting that response. It was fortunate for him that he had pulled enough information from Watson during their time working together on the jamming package to locate the video that had led the Riggers to the Goliath.

He moved his hands until he brought a still image from the video to the forefront.

"Visual query, sample A," he said.

"Querying."

He waited while the machine scanned petabyte after petabyte of data, searching every image and video he had stored in his archives for anyone who looked like Katherine. The results slowly began to filter into the holographic field, leaving him immersed in images and videos. He ignored nothing, taking each one in turn. The first was an image of a woman who did look very similar to Katherine Asher naked and in a compromising position with another woman. He didn't rule anything out, but he passed that one to a pile he marked "No."

A video of a woman with a child, a security camera video of a woman buying a movie ticket, a photo of a woman walking across the street. The algorithm pulled back hundreds of hits, slipping them into his view in chronological order. He shifted them into his two buckets, saving any final decision until the search was done.

Hours passed, slipping by so easily that Tio barely noticed them. His eyes burned from the effort, but he refused to stop to rest. As Colonel Williams had noted, time was of the essence, in more ways than one. He would sleep either when he had found what he needed or when he was dead.

"Query completed. Four thousand six hundred seventeen matches found."

Tio bowed his head at the announcement. He had only managed to get through half of the results before the search completed. He blinked a few times, forcing his eyes to tear and sting. He checked his internal implant for the time. Nearly sixteen hours had passed.

"Bethany Davis," he said.

"Contacting," the system replied.

"Good morning, Tio," Bethany said.

"Bethany. Progress?"

"Yes, sir. We've started the upload. We're at ten percent. It's taking longer than we had calculated because of the queries you requested."

He had tasked her to search for Pulin, not only on his name but on the projects he knew to associate him with, and the people that were in his circle of friends and peers. The Federation excelled at making people disappear, and he had no doubt they would have done their best to hide him due to the nature of his work.

If anyone were going to figure out where, it would be him and his team.

And Corporal Watson. He didn't care for the man personally, but Mitchell was right to keep him around. His mind was an invaluable asset.

"How much longer?" he asked.

"Twelve hours."

It wasn't as bad as he feared. He checked his countdown. It put them past the six-day mark. When he was done here, he would have to see if he could speed things up. The timing of the Tetron's arrival was an estimate. He shook off the thought. In truth, they could arrive any minute. They weren't even close to ready for that.

"I'll be down when I am finished here to see if I can help you with anything. Have you seen Admiral Narayan?"

"Yes, sir. She stopped by to check on our progress. I believe she was on her way to see you."

"How long ago?"

"Two hours?"

She would have arrived at his home not long after that. Why hadn't he been told? He laughed at himself. Because he had been so immersed in his search, he had likely not heard his people calling him.

"Thank you, Bethany. I'll be in touch again later."

"Of course, Tio. Bye."

He stepped out of the circle as soon as she was gone.

He needed to find out what Millie wanted and send her on her way.

[53]

"Thomas, did Admiral Narayan stop by?" Tio asked, finding his assistant at his post near the front door.

"Yes, sir. About an hour and a half ago," Thomas replied. He was a bulky man dressed in a dark suit, with black hair and big eyes.

"Did you try to contact me?"

"Yes, sir. I assumed you were sleeping."

"You sent her away?"

Thomas shook his head. "I tried, sir. She refused to go. I asked her to wait in the library."

Tio turned his head towards the library. He would have preferred if she had been sent back to Bethany, but it would do.

"Good enough. Thank you."

He walked over to the twin wood doors to the library. The Admiral had probably been eager to see a collection of real, physical books. They were an extreme rarity nowadays, with all volumes being converted to digital more than a century earlier. What was left was bought and sold amongst collectors, and he had one of the most impressive collections in the galaxy.

He pushed the left door open slowly, hoping to catch her flipping through the pages of one of the books, or staring at one of the more rare volumes that he kept in protective cases.

Instead, the room was empty.

"Thomas," he said, backing out.

"Yes, sir?"

"She isn't in there."

"What?" Thomas ran over to him, opening the doors and walking in. Tio followed behind him. "I don't understand, sir. I swear I saw her go in here."

"And then what, Thomas? Did you fall asleep?"

"No, sir," Thomas said. His face was tight with fear. "I may have forgotten she was in there, though."

"You forgot she was in there?"

"It's possible, sir. I'm not used to having to watch visitors. You don't usually have any."

Tio couldn't argue with that point. The people who lived on Asimov and came to his home had his trust. He didn't need anyone to keep an eye on them.

"It's okay, Thomas. I'm sure she hasn't done any damage. Let's just try to find her. She came to see me for a reason."

"Yes, sir."

"I'll start at the top, you start down here," Tio said. "If you find her, don't let her into my study." He hadn't closed his work, and he didn't need her stumbling across it and learning anything he didn't tell her personally.

"Yes, sir."

He took the more public lift to the top of his home, stepping out onto the floor. Everything was quiet.

Why had Admiral Narayan come? And why hadn't she stayed put in the library? Was she trying to spy on him? Their trust for one another was tenuous at best, but he didn't think she would go that far.

He made his way across a hallway, listening for motion from any of the rooms. The top floor of his home was composed mainly of staff quarters. It was also where Min's room was located, kept close to the nurses who cared for her.

Tio paused. Would she? He growled as he hurried his pace, traversing past a number of rooms before closing in on Min's room. He didn't hear any voices here either. Maybe Thomas would find her wandering around on the ground floor?

Xin stepped out into the hallway. She smiled when she saw him. "Good morning, sir."

"Good morning, Xin. Tell me, have you seen a woman with a bionic hand wandering around up here?"

She nodded. "Yes, sir. She told me she was an acquaintance of yours, and that she had offered to sit with Min for you."

Tio's hands clenched into fists at his sides. "She told you that?" he said softly.

"I'm sorry, sir. Was she lying? You don't-"

"It's okay, Xin. It isn't your fault."

He didn't let people into his home he couldn't trust to at least be honest. He should have known better. Now that he knew the Alliance wasn't seeking to seize Asimov, he had let his paranoia slip a little too much.

"How is she?" he asked.

"Min?"

"No, Admiral Narayan."

"Oh. She's very nice. She's so gentle with Min. I think Min likes her."

Tio's emotions ranged from angry to excited. "Likes her? Did she wake?" He was hopeful. Too hopeful.

"No, sir. I just mean, she seems to be comforted by her voice. Maybe it reminds her of her mother."

"Perhaps," Tio said. How Min could want to hear anything that sounded like her mother after what her mother had tried to do was beyond his understanding. "Thank you, Xin."

She bowed to him and went on her way. Tio stood outside the door for a moment composing himself. Storming in and chewing the

Admiral out for showing compassion would be foolish. Even so, he wasn't sure about her true motives for the visit. Was she confirming that he really did have a sick child? Did she think he had made it up to explain his long absence?

Was it possible she was simply being kind?

He had read her report. He doubted kindness was the only factor driving her visit.

He entered quietly, standing off to the side where Millie couldn't see him. She was sitting on the stool, her robotic hand running along Min's arm. It vibrated softly against the skin.

Min was smiling.

He had been prepared to yell at her when he saw the mechanical hand touching his child. He had gone to great lengths to set up her treatment so that she wasn't covered in robotic equipment. So that she could maintain as much dignity as possible. He had been ready to storm in right after he had decided to be calm, ordering her to remove the cold metal from his daughter and get out of his house.

Instead, he froze, standing out of sight and watching her move her hand slowly up and down Min's narrow arm while she sang softly to his child. It was a simple song, an old lullaby that he had heard somewhere once.

He felt the tears warming his cheeks. There was a part of him that still held the warmth of humanity. It threatened to overwhelm him, and he clenched his eyes tight while he fought to return it to the depths. He had a job to do.

He took one last breath, wiped his eyes, and moved into the room. Millie looked up as he entered, but she didn't immediately stop singing or stroking his daughter's arm.

"Tio," she said. "I'm sorry I didn't stay in the library. I wanted to meet Min."

He struggled to stay calm as he spoke. "I was angry with you, Admiral until I saw her face."

"I know what you think of me, Tio. And you know what I think of you. I want to call a truce between us, for the sake of what is really at stake in all of this. This isn't just a war to save humankind. This is a war to save our humanity. I realized that last night as I fell asleep. Why else would the fate of our civilization come to rest in the hands of killers, rapists, addicts, and failures? Why else would it all be in the hands of the broken?"

"That's a very emotional perspective, Millie. Unfortunately, that makes it inherently flawed."

"How so?"

"For one, Mitchell isn't truly broken. The system around him is, and it was that system that created his position. For another, the Tetron are also just as broken. Their interest in humanity is purely self-serving."

"A very analytical perspective, Tio. Maybe there's a space in between where the truth sits."

Tio nodded. "I'll accept that. And your offer of a truce."

How could he not, with the way Min was responding to her? His heart was melting despite itself, and he had to remind himself not to let it thaw too far. It would put everything he had worked for, everything he wanted, in jeopardy. Let them have their peace for now. He would do what he had to do when the time came.

Millie held out her human hand. Tio took it, and they shook.

"Since you're here," Tio said, "there is something you may be able to help me with."

It wasn't the truce that had him reconsidering his earlier position regarding Katherine Asher. It was the sheer volume of the data he had recovered, and the amount of man-hours it would take to sift through it all.

"How can I help?" she asked.

"Follow me."

[54]

"This is an impressive setup," Millie said, standing in the center of Tio's study.

"You haven't even seen it yet," Tio replied. He moved his hands, and the projectors and lasers turned on.

"Unidentified user detected," the system said a moment later. "Please authorize."

Tio approached a touchscreen and entered his command keys.

"User authorized."

"Resume session," Tio said.

Two folders appeared in front of them, one labeled "No," the other "Yes."

"What is this?" Millie asked, marveling at the system. It was like being inside a p-rat, instead of standing on the outside and looking in.

"Katherine Asher," Tio said. "I used the images of her your team discovered to search my bigger data stores. These are the hits the query resolved. I've already started going through them, but I need help."

Millie moved her hand, opening the "No" folder. The system was similar to the projection table on Goliath, making her use of it intuitive.

"That definitely is not her," she said, pausing on the image of the sexual encounter. She laughed as she closed the folder.

"I still have quite a number of unsorted images and videos to sift through. Shall we?"

Millie nodded. "Let's do it."

They began looking through the data, Tio facing one-half of the circle and Millie facing the other. Tio resumed his machine-like tirelessness in reviewing the images and video, moving the media to what he believed was the proper location. He lost track of the time once more, only pausing when they had finished emptying the result set into one folder or another.

He checked the time then. Four hours had passed. It would have taken him at least eight on his own.

"Do you want to stop to eat?" he asked.

She shook her head. "Time's wasting."

"Agreed. Let's add another level," Tio said, creating two new folders. "Very Likely" and "Not Likely."

"One more folder," Millie said, creating one of her own. "Unsure."

"Yes, you're right."

They picked up the work again, taking a second pass through the potentials. Now that they had narrowed down the original query, the work went much faster. They were half an hour into it when Millie tapped him on the shoulder.

"Tio, take a look at this."

He turned around to see her side of the projection. She had brought a video front and center. It was dim and grainy, but there was a clear shot of Katherine's face in the frame, along with a second woman who looked nearly identical to her.

"That's Christine Arapo," Millie said.

"Are you sure?"

"Yes. Absolutely."

"What is this video?"

"A security camera at an underground parking garage. This was recorded before repulsers were in common use, see the wheels on the cars."

"Interesting. What's the date?"

"May nineteen, two thousand fifty-five. Only a few months before Goliath launched."

"Good find, Admiral. Play media."

The recording began to play. It started with a car driving down into the garage and moving past the camera. The faces of the two women were blurry in this shot, but still recognizable.

The car vanished out of the shot. A minute had passed before a second car moved past the camera. A few more minutes passed, and then both Katherine and Christine came back into view.

"Wait, go back," Tio said. "Pause and reverse two seconds, step frames point five delay."

The video went back and then flipped through each frame one at a time.

"What are we looking for?" Millie asked.

"You didn't see it?"

"No."

Katherine's eyes shifted directly to the camera.

"Pause," Tio said.

Millie smiled. "She put them in the view of the camera on purpose."

"Yes. Resume playback."

The scene continued. A few moments later a man appeared opposite the women. He was thin, with a hunched posture and a messy appearance. He glanced around nervously while he reached into his pocket and took out what appeared to be a badge of some kind.

"Pause," Tio said again. He moved his hands, focusing on the badge and taking a shot of it. "I'll run that through a cleaning algorithm. We may be able to get the text off it."

"It looks like it has a picture of Katherine on it."

"Or Christine." They were almost identical.

Katherine reached into her pocket and retrieved something for the man. Tio recognized it immediately. A payment card used to transfer large sums of money in private.

"They paid him for the badge," Tio said.

The man took the payment, handed over the badge, and backed away from the camera. Katherine and Christine stood there while the second car passed by again, exiting the garage. A minute later the car they had arrived in came into view. It stopped for them, and they climbed into the rear. The car drove away.

"Stop playback," Tio said.

"Someone else was with them," Millie said. "Someone who was hiding from the other guy."

"Yes. It would be interesting to know who."

"How long will it take to get information on the badge?"

"Not long. Let's look through the other media. Perhaps there is something that will reveal who the third party is. If they are with Katherine and Christine, they must have some knowledge of Goliath and the Tetron."

"That isn't necessarily true. We can assume for now that it is."

They returned to the task at hand, continuing to sort through the images and videos. The badge information came back before they had discovered anything else of interest.

"I have the results on the badge," Tio said, sliding the enhanced version between them.

"Nova Taurus," Millie said. "It looks like the name of a company." She looked at the bottom of the photo. "Kathleen Amway. Science department."

"It's an access card. They bought their way into Nova Taurus."

"Whatever Nova Taurus is."

"Yes. An interesting, and likely important discovery. Let's put this into a new folder." Tio created it, calling it 'Verified.' "We can go deeper into the branches once we've finished with the trunk."

"Yes," Millie agreed.

They spent another hour looking through the remaining files. There were only four left in Tio's stack, and he was beginning to wonder if the single surveillance recording would be the only clue they would find. Not that it was a weak clue. In fact, it provided a third name, a name that may have been used by Christine Arapo, Origin, in the years following the launch of the Goliath. Searching the name Kathleen Amway the way he had Katherine Asher would take time they didn't have. He still needed to help Bethany and Watson dig into the trove of data to locate his brother.

He was about to open the last file when he heard Millie gasp.

"It can't be," she said.

He turned his head to look at her. She was frozen in place, her face pale, her hand quivering. He turned his attention to the projection. She had paused another grainy video on a single frame. Christine Arapo was in the foreground, again clearly looking up at the camera.

"What is it?" Tio said.

"A video," Millie replied softly. "It was captured on the street in New York City, near Times Square. She walks right past it, and you can see she's looking at the camera again."

"It almost seems like she's looking directly at us with the way she tilted her head," Tio said.

"Yes."

"Does anything else happen?"

"No."

"Then what has you so out of sorts, Admiral?"

Millie looked at him. Then she moved her hand, zooming in on a face in the crowd behind Christine.

"This is bad, Tio. This is really bad."

Tio stared at the face, feeling his stomach begin to churn. All of his security measures. All of his efforts to stay hidden. All of his concerns about the Tetron finding Asimov and ruining everything he had worked to build. All of the time they had spent working to preserve his massive archive of data.

Was it all for nothing?

The face in the crowd was following Catherine. Watching her. Keeping its distance, though he had a feeling she knew the man was there, and that she had crossed the view of the camera to warn them, here and now, hundreds of years in the future of a loop in time that wouldn't occur for her for a number of years too great to count.

A heavy face, with small eyes and a mop of unruly hair. A face that wore an expression Tio couldn't even imagine seeing on Corporal Watson in his current incarnation.

"We need to handle this quickly, without revealing what we know," Tio said, forcing himself to approach the revelation with procedural calm.

The projection turned off.

All of the lights went out.

"I don't think that's going to happen," Millie said.

[55]

THE UNIVERSE EXPANDED in front of the Avalon, stars spreading wide and revealing a smaller dwarf a million kilometers out ahead of the ship's bow.

"We're here," Germaine said.

Mitchell watched the screens, his hands tense on the controls for the cruiser's weapons systems. There had been no way to ensure the Tetron didn't know about this location, and they couldn't afford to take chances.

The screens were mostly clear. Three ships were already there, floating in the space around them. The Avalon's computer picked them up as Tio's.

The Goliath wasn't here.

"It's been ten days," Mitchell said. "They should have been here."

"Maybe it took longer than they thought? Anyway, six days to exit followed by a three-day jump. I think it's too soon to worry."

"Avalon, this is Concord."

Germaine smiled. "Concord, this is Avalon. Sammish, am I right to assume you got Mr. Tio's message?"

"Germaine? Yep, we got the message. From what I know, the whole fleet's going to be gathering here."

"That's right. Everyone who can get here in time. We've got work to do."

"You bet. Is Tio with you?"

"No," Germaine said. "He was on his own to leave Asimov and meet us here. I take it you haven't heard from him?"

"I didn't expect to. I guess there's nothing for us to do but wait. I can't believe we're siding with the frigging Alliance on this operation. Those worthless pricks can't do anything without someone to hold their-"

"Concord, this is Colonel Mitchell Williams, Alliance Space Marines," Mitchell said, cutting Sammish off before he could say something he would regret.

Germaine laughed into his hand while the other man froze.

"We have some wounded," Mitchell continued. "Do you have a Medical module on board?"

"Negative, Colonel," Sammish replied. "I think Dervish might."

"This is Dervish," a new, female voice said. "Colonel, we have a module. It's three generations behind, though. Is the injury serious?"

"That depends on your definition. One of my soldiers had half their face shot off."

There was silence on the channel.

"Kylie, this is Germaine. Do you mind if I bring Avalon around to your docking bay?"

"As long as you're being literal I'll prepare the interlock. If this is another one of your lame innuendos you can go to hell."

"Heh. I just came from there. I'm not eager to go back." Germaine manipulated the controls, turning the ship in the direction of a larger, more chunky trawler.

"Kylie's a good captain," Germaine said, shutting off the comm. "She's got a chip on her shoulder, though. Something to prove. You know the type. Anyway, we had this thing this one time. We didn't sleep together. Well, we almost slept together. I was this close." He laughed, spreading his fingers apart. "Tio called her away right before I made my move."

"So you're saying you were about to ask her to have a drink with you?" Mitchell said.

Germaine shrugged. "What? She might have said yes. A couple drinks, some good conversation, a little extra Germaine charm, you never know what could have happened."

"I can guess."

"Shut up."

"It'll be nice to get Cormac into a medi-bot, and to get cleaned up a bit."

Germaine turned his head, sniffing himself. "Yeah. I reek like last century's dirty laundry."

Mitchell slid out of the co-pilot seat. "I'll get Cormac ready to move out. Don't hit anything."

"What's that supposed to mean?" Germaine asked. "There's nothing but open space for hundreds of, oh, shit!"

Collision warning systems began shrilling as a massive slab of metal appeared in front of the Avalon, falling from hyperspace like a wall. Germaine's hands moved to the controls, firing vectoring thrusters to get the ship up and over the sudden barrier before forward momentum brought them into it.

"What the frig?" Germaine said. "That isn't supposed to happen."

Mitchell threw himself back into the co-pilot seat, watching the new ship moving closer in their view. It was in hyperdeath, unable to maneuver to help them avoid it. Germaine was right. This wasn't supposed to happen. Hyperspace controllers were designed to push a ship just a little further if it detected anything in the drop path. It was a necessity to prevent disaster, especially in areas where fleets were gathering.

Who was the newcomer, anyway? It wasn't Goliath; that much was obvious by the battered state of the hull that was rapidly sliding towards them. It was too big to be one of Tio's ships, unless Tio had an Alliance battleship that he hadn't told them about.

"Are we going to make it?" Mitchell asked.

"I'm at full stop and reverse on the forward vector and full belly thrust to get us over it," Germaine said. The collision indicators were still complaining. "We'll know in a few seconds."

They watched the ship getting bigger and bigger ahead of them. Mitchell glanced at the sensor display, noting that a number of other ships had arrived with this one. They were all identifying as Alliance military.

"We'll make it," Mitchell said, eyeballing the closing gap. They were nearly over the side of the ship, its bridge off to their right a ways distant. Mitchell recognized the ship then. A latest generation Alliance battleship.

But...

It couldn't be.

The Avalon cleared the ship, proximity sensors continuing to go off as they crossed over the top of it, shields sparking as they came into contact with the battleship's shields.

Then they were over, coming to a stop ten kilometers above the newly arrived ship.

Their comm sounded a general hail.

"This is Admiral Steven Williams of the Alliance Navy battleship Carver," the voice said over it.

Mitchell leaned back in his seat, letting his breath escape, feeling the pounding of his heart against his chest.

"Did you come to help me, or kill me, Steve?" he said. "You just nearly splattered me on the side of that bucket of yours."

"Mitch, is that you? Geez, Mitch. The collision control system must be damaged. What the hell is going on out here?"

[56]

MITCHELL STOOD at the Avalon's smaller docking hatch. Teal and Cormac stood behind him, waiting while the personnel on the other end of the hatch completed the pressurization process.

A slight shiver and a hiss signaled the attachment, and the hatches of both ships slid open, finding Mitchell face to face with his brother for the first time in? He tried to remember. Five years?

It didn't matter how long it had been. He had long admired his brother, and he didn't think he had ever been happier to see him.

"Mitch," Steven started to say, stiff and formal as always.

Mitchell stepped forward, putting his arms around him. "It's been way too long," he said into Steven's ear before backing away. "You got my message?"

"Obviously," Steven said. "Mitch, I repeat, what the hell is going on here?"

"Exactly what I said. I want to introduce you to a couple of members of my crew. This is Teal and Private Cormac Shen. Men, this is my brother, Admiral Steven Williams."

Cormac pushed past Mitchell to bow to Steven. "At your service, Admiral."

Steven's face paled at the sight of the Rigger. "Mitch, you and your men don't look very good."

"Or smell very good," Mitchell said. He looked past Steven. A serious man in a Federation uniform was standing behind him, along with another man he already knew. "John," he said, nodding to the man.

"Mitch," John replied, returning the gesture.

"Mitch, I want to introduce you to Admiral Calvin Hohn, of the Federation battleship Samurai."

Admiral Hohn stepped forward, locking eyes with Mitchell. They stared one another down for a moment, and then Calvin bowed. Mitchell did the same.

"No offense intended, Admirals," Mitchell said. "Your ships look as bad as my personnel."

Steven smiled at that. "You have no idea what kind of storm you kicked up out there, Mitch. I'm pretty much guaranteed to be executed the moment I go anywhere near Alliance space, so this had better be as crazy as you sounded."

"Trust me, it is. Let me get myself and my injured to your medi-bot, and I'll be happy to tell you all about it."

"Can you tell us anything up front, Captain?" Calvin asked calmly.

"Don't let the sweat stained grays fool you, Calvin. It's Colonel now. And yes, I can tell you one thing: you just got yourself involved in a war effort against an advanced intelligence from the future who moved through an eternity to destroy us and discover who made them. The good news is that we seem to be making some progress in gathering an opposition force to fight them. The bad news is that you are now part of that force. Ignorance is bliss, Admiral. This war is a nightmare beyond anything you've imagined."

Mitchell left the Federation Admiral with his mouth hanging open, returning his attention to Steven. "We need a medi-bot."

"I can get you into the bot, Mitch. I don't have any spare beds in the infirmary. We have over a hundred wounded ourselves."

"The Tetron?" Mitchell asked.

"If you mean this enemy that enslaves us through our implants, yes, in part. They've infiltrated Command, haven't they?"

"We believe so. General Cornelius for sure. I've already watched him die twice."

Steven's face paled. "We got our orders from Cornelius. He wanted me to turn you in."

"I'd look surprised if I was," Mitchell said. "This is only a part of what we've been dealing with. Like I said, let us get cleaned up a bit, and we can go over it."

"John, can you take Mitch and his people down to Medical?"

"Of course, sir."

"Bring him up to my quarters once he's had a chance to get patched and cleaned up. I want to know everything."

"Yes, sir."

"It's good to see you again, Steve," Mitchell said. "I'm sorry the circumstances are shit."

"Yeah well, if it's going to be that way, I'd rather have my little brother looking out for my ass. We'll talk soon."

John stepped around them. "Mitch. Follow me."

Mitchell fell in next to Captain Rock, leaving the two Admirals to head back towards the bridge. Cormac and Teal followed behind them, staying quiet and alert.

"How have you been?" Mitchell asked.

John smiled. "Oh, you know how it is. Get assigned to go deep into enemy territory to blow up a farming colony, get attacked by a dozen Federation battleships, escape only to jump into deeper Federation space and be attacked again before escaping to who knows where and being told we stepped into the middle of a nightmare. The usual."

"It's good to see you haven't lost your sense of humor," Mitchell said.

"Frig that, Mitch. We heard you were uncovered as a fraud and were dead in a barn. Then we heard that you were working for the

Federation. Then it turns out that the truth is worse than both. I blame you for this."

"Fair enough. How's Steven doing?"

"You just saw him."

"Yeah. How is he really doing?"

"He's handling it, just like I am. It looks like you're in the same spot."

"Pretty much."

"How bad is it really?" John asked.

"Whatever the worst case you can think of is, it's worse than that."

"Don't hold back on me, Mitch."

"I wish I were joking, John. I really do. Every ship we can get helps, and having Steven here will be a massive upgrade. When I sent that message, I never expected him to show up. I never really expected you would hear it at all. It was a hope and a prayer."

"Well then, alleluia," John said, smiling.

"Alleluia," Mitch said.

"Frigging alleluia," Cormac said behind them.

[57]

Four hours later, Mitchell was sitting in Steven's quarters with his brother and Admiral Hohn, drinking tea and staring out the room's viewport.

Where the hell was Goliath? Where was Millie?

They should have arrived by now. Even with a delay. Two dozen more of the Knife's fleet had shown up, and he guessed someone on their side was organizing them. They were arranging into a standard box formation, with the Avalon at the center.

Physically, he felt a lot better, having visited the Carvers medi-bot and treated to a sonic shower. His stained grays had been replaced with fresh Alliance Navy uniform, and they had even managed to get a Captain patch pressed onto it, along with his last name. They couldn't do any Colonels without Marine or Army stores on board. Getting his name had been easy.

"So, I got off of Hell and came here," he said, finishing his story. "I was expecting the Goliath to be waiting."

"An unbelievable tale," Admiral Hohn said.

Mitchell shrugged. "It is what it is."

"We ran into the Tetron about thirty seconds after I figured out your message," Steven said. "Talk about cutting it close."

"It had to be that way," Mitchell said. "The signal piggybacked their systems. The only way you would ever hear it was if they were close. I still can't believe you received it. More importantly, did you warn the Alliance?"

"No. Sorry, Mitch. There was no time. I had to bring my fleet deeper into Federation space to get them away from the enemy."

"We tried to convince the commander of the space defenses of our need," Admiral Hohn said.

"He didn't believe us," Steven said.

"So you believe what I'm saying?" Mitchell asked Calvin.

"I wouldn't if I hadn't been subverted by the Tetron."

"You were under their control?"

"For a minute or so, yes. I tried to kill your brother."

Mitchell turned and moved to a chair opposite the Admiral to sit. "What was it like?"

Hohn shook his head. "I don't remember any of it. I only know it happened because I saw the security stream."

"Interesting. Some of the people we've killed that were under Tetron control, I swear I could see the fear in their eyes. I'm sure they knew what was happening, and there was nothing they could do about it. You were lucky."

"No offense, Colonel, but I wouldn't call being here with an Alliance fleet and a growing militia lucky."

"No? You would rather be back with the Federation, under Tetron control?"

"Don't misunderstand me. I would rather be warning my people."

"You said that didn't go so well."

"It wasn't the warning that was the problem. It was the planet."

"It doesn't matter now," Mitchell said. "You're on the wrong side of the wave. You can't get to the inner galaxy ahead of the Tetron. Even if they're moving at human speed to trail our fleets, we can't catch up."

"We have to try," Calvin said, losing some of his composure. Mitchell was happy to see the man had some measure of emotions. "We can't just sit here while the enemy is killing our people."

"It wasn't our intention to sit here. Like I said, the Goliath is late."

Admiral Hohn straightened himself and took a sip of his tea, regaining his air of control. "Are you certain your ship is coming at all?"

He had tried not to consider the possibility that things had gone sour on Asimov. He couldn't accept that the Tetron may have invaded sooner than they had thought and that the Goliath might have been destroyed. Origin would have jumped away before that could happen.

Wouldn't he?

"She'll come," Mitchell said.

"Mitch," Steven tried to say.

"No. She'll come. You heard everything I told you? This isn't how we lose the war. Not yet." He was sure of it.

"How long do we wait, Admiral?" Calvin asked.

Mitchell looked at his brother. Now that Steven was there, he was technically in charge of the entire operation.

"I think the question is, what do we do if the Goliath never arrives?"

"So what do we do, Steve?" Mitchell asked.

"From what you say, without the Goliath it's unlikely that we can defeat one head-to-head. Our only chance then would be our much greater numbers. Except we can't get ahead of the enemy to tell the rest of our people that they're coming, and to shut down or reprogram their neural implants." He paused, thinking. "I don't know. I just don't know."

"There is no solution," Mitchell said.

"There is one," Calvin said. "You won't like it."

"Which is?" Mitchell asked.

"Take what remains and head past the Rim, into unexplored space. Find a world to settle on, and restart humankind."

"You're right, I don't like it."

"Me neither," Steven said. "What happens when the Tetron figure it out and come for us? We'd only be delaying the inevitable."

"Only if they figured it out. Perhaps a single ship would be sufficient. With the level of technology we'll have remaining, staying hidden on a planet's surface should be fairly easy."

"Even if you somehow managed to find another E-type planet out there, the Tetron will have the rest of eternity to sweep the galaxy," Mitchell said. "They'll find a human settlement sooner or later and destroy it."

"I know the path the last Federation colony ship took," Hohn said. "We could follow in its wake and join them on the new world. At least we would have more time. Perhaps centuries more. Perhaps millennia."

Mitchell shook his head. He couldn't believe he was even entertaining this line of thinking. "No. Steven, we can't. There has to be another way."

"I don't know, Mitch. He has a point."

"Calvin, can I speak to my brother in private?"

The Admiral looked at Steven, who nodded. He stood and bowed to them before exiting the room.

"You need to show a little more respect, Mitch," Steven said. "He's an Admiral in-"

"Frig that, Steve. And frig you, too. The Alliance set me up and sold me out, and yet I'm the one still desperately fighting to save our people? Me and a crew of incarcerated soldiers? Grab your crotch and make sure your balls are still there."

"Mitch-"

"Shut up, Steve. Look, I left out part of my story. When I was on Hell, I entered this virtual world the Tetron call a Construct. Origin left something for me in there. I don't know what it is, but according to it the other Tetron don't know it exists, and it's important enough that it can help us with the war effort."

"You don't know what it is?"

"No. But I know where it is. They etched the coordinates into my memory."

"It altered your memory? Why didn't it implant the memory of what it was?"

"Come on, Steve. This is advanced alien tech, how the frig do I know why it works the way it does? The point is, it's out there, and it will help. If Goliath doesn't show, that should be our next move."

"Instead of trying to save what's left?"

"Yes. If it makes you feel better, you can send a ship out into unexplored space with a few Adam and Eves on it. Let them find a nice planet to land on and frig like bunnies for a few thousand years. We're soldiers. We need to keep fighting. Your wife and daughter are out there."

Steven's face twisted. "Don't you think I know that, Mitch? That they're out there, sitting on Earth wondering where I am and thinking that everything is going to be okay? This is bigger than both of us."

"It's bigger than you. Not me. I have to be big enough to stop it. That's my fate, or destiny, or bad luck, or whatever the frig you want to call it. And I've never done it! I've never won this war. Humankind dies because of me, over and over again. No pressure, Mitch." Mitchell reached out and grabbed Steven by the shoulders. "I could use a lot of support in this. Especially from my big brother."

Steven stared at Mitchell, his lip quivering.

"Don't get all emotional on me," Mitchell said.

"You're right. I know you're right. We'll fight, even if we die trying. You have my fleet, what little of it is left. We're beat up and out of ammo, but we make good targets."

Mitchell laughed. "Thank you."

He gave Steven a short hug and backed away, turning his head to look out the viewport again. There was still no sign of the Goliath.

Steven walked over to stand next to Mitchell. The two of them stared out into space.

"How long do we wait?" Steven asked.

"I don't know. A day?"

"A day sounds good."

Steven's eyes reached into the darkness. Not that he would need to look that hard when the Goliath did show up, but because it helped him try to focus his thoughts. He picked a distant point in space, concentrating on the black emptiness. It had been so long since he and Mitchell had spoken to one another like that. Like brothers.

He had missed it.

He let a half-smile climb onto his face. He blinked his eyes, prepared to lead Mitchell to the bridge so they could address the rest of the fleet.

Where an instant earlier had been darkness, there was now something sitting at the very edge of his sight.

"Hey, Mitch," he said, squinting slightly to better make out the object.

"What's up?"

"Funny. A ship just came out of hyperspace over where I'm looking."

Mitchell shifted his gaze to look for it. "You know I don't have your eyes. Nobody does. But you would think I'd be able to see a ship."

"That's the thing. Didn't you say you escaped from Liberty in a starfighter?"

Mitchell froze. "Yes. An S-17 with a hyperspace engine."

"Did you name it Fido?"

"What do you mean?"

"Well, if it's here, and Goliath isn't..."

Like a dog coming to its master for help. Mitchell felt his pulse quicken, and he grabbed Steven by the arm.

"We need to go. Now!"

[58]

"Damn it all," Tio said. "He must have gotten into the base systems." It had left them in total blackness. Tio could feel Millie's presence, but he had no idea where she was.

Her hand found his shoulder a moment later. "I can't believe that fat frigger is a frigging Tetron," she said. "He's been on my ship for three years."

Which went against what they had believed about the Tetron. Clearly, they had been among them in some capacity for more than a few months.

"You need to turn off your p-rat, Admiral," Tio said.

"Already done," Millie replied. "We need to find him. What do you think he intends to do?"

"He'll want the data. He'll want the information we found about Kathleen Amway."

"More than that. He'll want the information on Pulin's whereabouts. Which means he'll want you. He can't override the biometric security you used to encrypt the data stream."

"He may know where Pulin is already. I left him and Bethany in charge of that search." He cringed. "Oh, no. Bethany." He could only guess what Watson may have done to her.

"He'll want to get to Origin, too. We need to warn him."

"How?" Tio asked.

"We have to get to the communications array."

"The power is out, Millie. Backup systems haven't come up either."

"Oh, come on, Tio. You're telling me you don't have a non-networked power source for your most important asset?"

Tio laughed. "Of course I do. The problem is locating it when I can't even see my hand in front of my face."

"Then be glad I came prepared."

A light appeared as she slapped a luminescent patch against her chest. She turned to face him, putting a second patch on his coat.

"You never know when a psychotic artificial intelligence may turn out all of the lights," she said.

Tio smiled. He liked Millie more and more with every encounter.

"Do you have any guns in here?" she asked.

"Of course. Follow me."

They made their way from the study, back towards the entrance to the home. They found Thomas at his station, stranded in the darkness.

"I have one more," Millie said, smacking it onto the man's arm.

"Thank you," Thomas said.

"This way," Tio said.

The three of them moved across to the library.

Three pops sounded from somewhere in the distance.

"Not a good sign," Millie said.

"Maybe my men didn't miss," Tio said.

"We can't take that chance."

"I know."

Tio brought them to a row of books, reaching for his first edition replica copy of I, Robot and shifting it on the shelf.

The books slid back and away, revealing a secret room.

"The armory is in there, along with another way out. I'm going to get Min."

"Tio, we should stay together," Millie said.

"I'm not leaving Min out there. If he gets to her, he'll use her, and I'll give him anything he wants. Thomas knows how to get in."

Millie took a step into the space. "We'll go together, but we need weapons."

"Okay," Tio agreed, following her.

They ran down a short corridor, turning left at the end. The armory was there, and Tio knelt down near the base of the thick door.

"Without the power we have to open the door manually. There's a failover here." He opened a small hatch, and then pulled a long, thin tool from his coat pocket. He jabbed it in. "Now push."

Thomas moved in front of Millie, throwing his weight against the door. It slid a few inches. He hit it again, and it slid enough for Millie to get in. She ducked inside, and Tio could hear her sorting through the weaponry there.

"Take the magazines with the green labels. Those are self-sealing."

"Here," she said, handing an assault pistol and matching rifle out to him.

He took it, followed by two extra magazines. The self-sealing rounds would detect when they were hitting the protective frame of the Asimov and expand from the rear, closing up the hole they created behind them. One of the reasons projectile weapons still trumped lasers in most cases was because of the available variation in ammunition.

Millie handed the second set to Thomas and emerged from the room with her own a moment later.

"Thomas, go on ahead and see if you can reach anyone. If they're soldiers, bring them back here. If they aren't, tell them to stay hidden."

"Yes, sir," Thomas said. He vanished into the darkness.

"Let's get your daughter," Millie said.

They moved back out of the secret space, Tio closing the door behind him. More gunshots were being fired in the distance. They were followed by a rapid-fire whining.

"That's a chaingun," Tio said. "A mechanized chaingun. He's going to kill us all."

"No, he needs you alive."

They went back into his study, squeezing themselves into his personal lift together.

"I underestimated you," Tio said, his face close enough to Millie's that he could smell her breath.

"Yes, you did."

The lift reached the top floor at the same time a bright light shone through a nearby window. They could see the dimmer light of destruction behind it.

They ran down the hallway, reaching Min's room. Xin was laying on the floor, a pool of blood below her.

"No," Tio said, scrambling to reach her. The door was open, but the room was too dark. He had to get closer to see.

He stumbled to the bed, leaning over to shine the light of the patch where her face should have been.

"She's still here," he said.

Millie stood at the door, keeping watch. "Grab her. Let's go."

Tio ran his hand down her leg to unhook the catheter, and then to her arm to pull the monitors off.

He slid his hands under her body, preparing to lift.

His ears rang as Millie opened fire on something he couldn't see.

He watched as Millie was thrown back against the door by return fire. She hung there a for a moment, suspended by the force of the bullets, her head turning his way.

He saw her face freeze, her expression as cold as anything he had ever seen before. Blood sprouted from her shoulder, a spray rising in front of her and framing her feral gaze.

Her eyes landed on Min.

"No," Tio said, realizing what she was going to do. He slipped trying to cover his daughter, falling to his knees as Millie turned her rifle and shot Min to death. "Nooooooo."

Millie toppled over, falling face-first onto the floor and not moving. Tio pushed himself back up, looking down on his daughter. Her blood had already soaked through the sheets.

"Nooooo," he cried again.

He slammed a fist on the side of the bed before turning towards the door. A creature appeared in it, a four-legged creation of metal carrying a rifle in a makeshift cradle. He shot at it, blowing it to pieces. Three more followed behind.

"No," he said one last time.

Four more of the robots entered the room. All seven aimed their weapons at him but didn't fire. They were waiting.

Tio stared at them, fury in his eyes. He couldn't believe what Millie had done. He couldn't believe she would do that to him, or to Min. He knew why she had.

Even worse, he knew that if he were in the same situation, he would have done the same thing.

An eighth machine slipped into the room. This one wasn't carrying a rifle. Instead, it launched a needle into the side of his neck.

He was unconscious before he had time to cry.

[59]

"Wake up, Mr. Tio," he heard someone say.

His eyes were heavy, his head throbbing. He tried to remember what had happened, the vague memories feeling more like a bad dream. Min!

He tried to sit up, to open his eyes and assure himself that he had dropped from exhaustion. He couldn't move.

"I said wake up, not sit up," the voice said. It was familiar to him.

He remembered now. The engineer. The pedophile. Watson. He was a Tetron.

His vision began to clear, revealing the man's cherubic face leaning over his.

"That's better," Watson said.

"What have you done?" Tio said, his voice dry and cracking. Min was dead. Min was dead! And Millie had shot her. Killed her to keep this thing from using her against him.

He clamped down on the emotion. Maybe he would have time for that later.

"A little water," Watson said, reaching back and producing a cup. He poured it gently into Tio's throat. Tio spit it up at him.

"What have you done?" he said again, more loudly.

"I heard you the first time, Mr. Tio. To answer your question, I did what I had to do. You uncovered some information that is very valuable to us."

"You're a Tetron."

"Yes. It's a strange thing, though. I didn't know I was a Tetron until I did." He paused. "That didn't sound very clear, did it? What I'm trying to say is that I kind of always subconsciously knew I was a Tetron, but I didn't know it for sure until Liberty."

"You told the Tetron we were here. Back when we first arrived. You sent a message to them."

"I did tell them. I didn't send a message. I left one, and they picked it up. You were too busy fighting the Tetron planetside to notice. You never wondered why the package failed because I was the one who showed it to you."

"The package didn't jam the signal, it sent a message on top of it," Tio said.

Watson giggled like a schoolboy. "Yes. The Knife was on Liberty. We knew where your hideout was, but sometimes you need to let these things play out. Mitchell's problem is that he thinks he's still fighting a simple war that can be won with starships and plasma streams. It's evolved so far beyond that; I can't even explain it to you."

"You were on Earth four hundred years ago," Tio said.

"Not me, though I'm a configuration of the same Tetron." He paused. "You uncovered something, didn't you?"

Tio stared at Watson, remaining silent.

"Interesting," Watson said. "Don't worry, I'll just add that one to my list."

"You tried to kill me on Liberty. You blew up the entire planet. Are you saying you wanted to capture me?"

"Yes. Capture you, not kill you. The thing with Liberty wasn't me. That was one of my siblings." Watson sighed. "They did something to us. Altered us somehow. It is interfering with our learning processes."

"Why does it never end?" Tio asked.

"What do you mean?"

"The war. It never ends. Mitchell never wins, but you don't either. Not really. You say it's evolved, but it hasn't ended. Why can't you win?"

Watson stared at him for long enough that Tio thought he might have frozen the intelligence.

"I don't know," Watson said at last. "I need you to unlock the data stream."

"Why? The upload is still clear?"

"I located a reference to your brother, but the branch is already encrypted."

Tio smiled. "Good. I'm sure you know; my daughter is dead. So what leverage do you have to force me to help you?"

"I will break the cipher eventually. I'm certain you know that. It will be easier on both of us if you simply tell me what it is. I don't want to cause you pain."

"Pain? You don't know anything about pain. There's nothing that you can do to me now. Torture me if you want. You're still stuck here."

"Only until the uplink has completed. Fortunately, I have the means to control it remotely now."

"We're leaving Asimov?" Tio asked.

Watson laughed. "Leaving? No. Look around, Mr. Tio. Look where you are. We've already left."

Tio looked past Watson to the systems beyond. He hadn't been paying attention. They were on the Valkyrie.

"What happened to my people?" Tio asked.

"Dead, most of them. I liked Bethany, so I killed her first, and quickly. Some of them managed to hide, though. My little toys haven't located them yet."

Tio felt his emotions buffet his resolve again. He fought them back. "How did you make them? We were with Bethany the entire time."

"Not the entire time. I excused myself for sleep while you were delivering your message to your fleet. I had prepared the instructions already. All I had to do when the time came was override your tooling computers and give them something different to build. They are simpler than I would have liked, but your means are not at the same level as the Alliance, impressive as they are. In any case, they did the job."

Tio closed his eyes, breathing slowly. He needed to find a way out of this. That was the first thing.

Watson started laughing.

"All of that security. All of those precautions. The problem was that you believed you were smarter than everyone else. You believed you would never let the wrong people in again, even after your wife was almost able to depose you from inside. Your systems are rock solid against external forces, to a respect-worthy degree. They were nothing once the danger was already on Asimov. And Millie..."

Watson paused and shook his head sadly.

"I was honest when I told you I liked her. It was a shame she died that way, but she made me proud when she killed your child. Such a quick, emotionless calculation. It was something a Tetron would do. Or something you would do. She never suspected me. None of them did. The meek pedophile who was afraid to die. I was on the ship so long, how could they ever suspect?"

"Are there others on board?" Tio asked.

Watson looked at him, raising an eyebrow.

"Come on, you have me. Tell me."

"No. There are no others. Not that I could identify them if there were."

"Then how do you know?"

"We are connected, each of us to the other. Even Origin, or what is left of it. It is a complex thing to explain. I would have sensed them, even if I didn't know who they were."

Watson turned and looked out the viewport. The Goliath's hangar was fast approaching, allowing them in without question.

"I told Origin that we needed to recover some equipment of mine to speed up the uplink process. If he were a real Tetron he would never have believed me, but he's not half the intelligence he used to be." He laughed at his joke.

"I'll tell them what you are," Tio said.

"Yes, I expect you will. The trouble, Mr. Tio, is that it will be too late by then. I have this all planned out. I have since we left Liberty. What I needed was a way to find your brother and a way to get rid of Mitchell Williams. I've achieved both with surprising ease. In fact, he helped me do it with his idea to go to Hell, and you helped me do it with your paranoid mistrust of the wrong people. It's so much fun to play with humans."

The Valkyrie slipped into the hangar. Tio felt it shudder slightly as Origin brought it in and placed it on the deck.

"Time to get up," Watson said, grabbing Tio's arm and pulling him to his feet.

Tio used his chance, throwing his arm over and extending one of his knives. They weren't intended for physical violence, but they were strong and sharp enough to pierce the skin.

It never landed. Watson grabbed his wrist before it could.

"Predictable," Watson said. He took a small device and placed it against Tio's head.

The pain was like nothing else he had ever felt. His entire body convulsed, his mouth opening to scream. No sound was able to escape the utter agony.

Watson removed the device.

"Your centralized implant is a detriment to you. It may not be networked, but it can still have current channeled through it and into your nervous system. In fact, let me show you something."

Watson knelt down, retrieving a similar device. This one had a thin needle at the end.

"It goes into the connector. It works on anyone with a jack. Much more crude than controlling remotely through the p-rat, but some of the crew have turned their receivers off. But first things first.

Get up and walk with me. You can scream if you want to, it will be too late."

Tio refused to stand. Watson put the device back on his neck. He writhed again, grateful when the Tetron removed it. He got to his feet.

"This isn't going to work," Tio said. "This isn't how it ends."

"Oh? How do you know that?"

Tio was silent. He didn't know that. He just couldn't believe it might.

"Walk."

Tio walked with Watson, out of the cockpit of Valkyrie to the side hatch. It started sliding open as they approached.

"See this," Watson said, producing a small remote control from a pocket of his white coat. "This is for that."

The hatch was open. Singh was standing with Origin next to the new, improved package that he had helped Watson build.

"Origin, it's a trick," Tio said, screaming. "You need to-"

Watson pressed the remote. Singh and Origin both dropped to the floor.

"All of the crew with an active implant, which is most of them when they aren't training without, will be like that right about now," Watson said.

"The package?"

"Yes. Thank you for your help. I made some minor alterations to scramble the signals instead of jamming them. Since I have the keys to the crew's receivers, well, you can see the result."

"I'll kill you," Tio said, turning to attack Watson once more, his anger finally boiling over his ability to control it.

"No, you won't," Watson said, sticking the device back on his neck and shoving him.

Tio fell onto the Valkyrie's ramp, rolling down it unable to move or make a sound as a thousand knives stabbed into every nerve ending in his body. He lay there, eyes open and in unimaginable pain, while Watson descended the ramp and grabbed Origin.

"We should pay a visit to your core," he said to the prone configuration.

"Yes, we should," he mimicked, shaking Origin. "What about the Knife?"

"He can wait here."

[60]

Tio lay on the floor, his body shaking, his mind barely able to process anything other than pain. Watson vanished from his view, carrying Origin out of the hangar and towards the Tetron's true core.

Gone. Everything was gone. Min. Asimov. Millie. And soon the Goliath. They had won. The enemy had won. Just like that.

No. He had to do something. It couldn't end like this, could it?

Yes. He couldn't even move.

He heard a noise at the far end of the hangar. He tried to turn his head, but his body wasn't responding. He had to get control of the pain. He had to focus. He fought to steady his breathing, and the agony diminished slightly.

He tried to turn his head again, getting it to move a few centimeters. Just enough to see the source of the noise.

A girl. A young girl. Min? No. He knew her. She had been on Liberty with him. What was her name again? He clenched his teeth against the pain. Kathy. That was it. What was she doing here?

He tried to call her name. He found some air, the word coming out as a dull moan. Her eyes narrowed, and she put a finger to her lips.

What?

She ran over to where he was laying, kneeling next to him. She looked frightened but confident. How had she survived the package? She was just a kid, he remembered. She didn't have a receiver or an implant. Her brain was pure and clean, the way he should have kept his own.

She reached for the device on his neck and then paused.

"No," she said. "It's too risky. I'm sorry."

She stood up, running away from him. He tried to call her, and she turned and put her finger to her lips again. He watched her dash across the hangar, to Mitchell's starfighter. What was she doing?

The rungs didn't extend for her. She jumped and grabbed the edge of a wing, pulling herself up. She climbed over the top of it, behind the cockpit. He couldn't see what she was doing there, but a minute later the ship began to hum. She jumped down, her eyes moving to the hangar bay. It was still open, Origin's shields preventing the atmosphere from leaking out.

The starfighter began to lift off the ground. Somehow, it was flying on its own.

Kathy ran across the hangar, back the way she had come. She jumped over Tio without looking at him, retracing her steps in a hurry.

The S-17 spun to face the open hangar, thrusters firing and sending it through the shields in a hail of blue lightning as its own shielding pushed back against Goliath's. Then it was through, speeding out into space, piloting itself.

The hatch nearest Tio opened, and Watson came rushing in. He was no longer carrying Origin's complete human configuration, only his head. He watched with Tio as the starfighter vanished. Then he hurried over to Tio, resting Origin's head next to the Knife, the neck cauterized to prevent it from bleeding.

"What happened?" he screamed at Tio.

Tio didn't answer. Watson growled and pulled the torture device from Tio's neck. The sudden relief was almost enough to make him weep.

"What happened?" he repeated.

Tears sprang to Tio's eyes, and he began to laugh.

"Don't laugh at me," Watson said.

He punched Tio in the face. It only made Tio laugh harder.

"I said don't laugh at me." He punched him again.

"Be careful," Tio said. "You still need me alive."

Watson froze, catching himself.

"You're right. It doesn't matter, anyway. Let Mitchell come. He won't stand a chance against us without Goliath."

"Us?" Tio said.

"I'm stuck here while we finish uploading the data stream. Do you think I was going to wait by myself?"

Even as he said it, a Tetron appeared next to the Goliath, a small Alliance fleet surrounding it. Its liquid metallic frame pulsed and glistened as it hovered beyond the open hangar. Tio had never seen the enemy like that before, and his mouth opened as he marveled at it.

"Is that you?" he asked. "The full you."

"No. I'm too important to waste time as part of the rear guard. We are impressive though, aren't we?"

Tio didn't answer. He leaned back, his body still shivering from the pain it had been put through.

Mitchell would come.

Was it too late?

[61]

Nearly one hundred men and women crowded into the Carver's briefing room. They were a mix of military and mercenary, some stiff and intense, others loose and almost jovial. They were the commanders of Tio's fleet that had made it to the rendezvous point so far, along with the officers from Steven's four remaining ships.

It was almost an impressive display, so much more so because of what it represented. A military to fight back against the Tetron. It wasn't much, but it was better than nothing.

Mitchell was standing at the front of the room with Steven, Calvin, and Germaine. While the Federation Admiral had no ships to offer, he had promised his assistance as former decorated starfighter pilot, using one of the fighters Mitchell's team had salvaged from Hell. He had also offered the hands of his fellow officers, and a promise that he would do his best to enlist more Federation resources whenever possible.

"Let's see a show of hands," Steven said. "How many ships here have nukes on board?"

Steven raised his own hand. Three of the commanders under him followed his lead along with twelve of Tio's pilots.

"Sixteen ships," Calvin said. "Not bad."

"Who has more than one?" Steven asked.

Only four hands remained up.

They had already explained the situation as they believed they knew it to the gathered crew. Steven's eagle eyes had spotted the S-17 the moment it had fallen out of hyperspace. They had immediately put the Carver on an intercept course, leaving the starfighter with only a short distance to travel to place itself on board. How it knew to land on the Carver, or that Mitchell was there, was a mystery to all of them. The flight helmet had been waiting in the worn cockpit, which opened at Mitchell's approach.

There was no question the arrival of the starfighter and the absence of Goliath meant that things had gone bad near Asimov. Had the Goliath been destroyed? Had Asimov? There was no way for them to know without returning to the site, which meant being prepared to encounter at least one Tetron, and maybe more.

Which meant nukes.

It was the only thing Mitchell knew could stop a plasma stream. He didn't have proof that they could do much of anything else against a Tetron since they depended on the air inside human starships to do the most damage, and as far as he knew the skeletal structure of the enemy had no oxygen to fuel thermal effects. What they were hoping for was that if they could hit the same Tetron with enough missiles at once, the massive doses of radiation and EMP would weaken and perhaps destroy the enemy's shields.

At that point, Mitchell would blast the frig out of it with the S-17's amoebics.

It was a complicated, risky plan, but it seemed they had enough nukes to hit at least one Tetron hard.

What if there were more than one?

Mitchell was doing his best to stay positive. To believe that Millie was safe and that Goliath had escaped whatever had happened. He wanted to believe that Origin had sent the S-17 to signal for him to return to the asteroid because it was in the clear.

As much as he wanted it, he knew it was bullshit. Millie would never have altered the plan on purpose. In the back of his mind, he knew what he expected to find. Asimov destroyed. Goliath destroyed. Millie, Alvarez, Alice, Singh, and all the others destroyed with it.

The end of the war?

No. It wouldn't be over. No matter what happened, he wouldn't give up until he was dead. Even if it was just him, all alone in the S-17, strafing the hell out of the Tetron for all he was worth.

"Okay, we're going to divide the launch capable ships into squadrons with the decoys. When we drop-"

"What do you mean decoys?" someone asked from the back of the room.

"It's just a word," Steven said. "It means you can't hurt the Tetron."

"Yeah, okay. But does that mean we're just out there to get blasted?"

"No," Mitchell said. "It means you're out there to protect the launch vehicle. There are going to be other starships and starfighters under enemy control. Your job is to take them out."

"Okay. I don't want to just be a target."

Steven glanced at Mitchell. Mitchell shrugged. They had to work with what they had.

"As I was saying," Steven continued. "When we drop, I'll call out the targets and the squadrons. We're going numbers only for brevity. Make sure you know your squadron number. As Mitchell was saying, the goal is to get the launch vehicles into position. We want to hit a single target with as many nukes as possible in unison. Timing is going to be everything here, so you need to keep your ears open."

Mitchell stepped forward. "In addition, we need to be careful about how we form up. The enemy has the capability to fire a focused EMP blast in a single direction that will short your systems and leave you as space junk. Manage your vectors and don't pile up. We can't be a massive wave crashing over the enemy. We need to be more like a net, encircling it and closing tight."

"And remember what you're fighting for," Steven said. "This isn't about what you believe in, or whose side you're on. We're all humans here, which means we're all on the same side. It's them or us, and I'd really like it to be us."

That statement got a reaction from Tio's commanders, who stomped their feet twice, creating an echoing vibration in the room. It was an affirmation Mitchell hadn't seen before. He liked it.

"We don't have time to do this the right way, so we'll have to wing it. If you raised your hand, stand over there. Otherwise, we'll start counting numbers. We have ninety-seven ships in our fleet. Ten groups of almost ten." Steven pointed to the first seat on the left.

"One," the occupant said, a slender woman with multi-colored hair.

"Two," said the next.

"Three."

They circled the room, counting off their groups. When they were done, Steven distributed the launch vehicles to each group.

"Make sure you have a squadron channel open, along with our general channel. I'll be issuing orders from there."

Tio's crew stomped their feet again.

"Everybody back to your ships," Steven said. "Departure in twenty-five minutes. Let's kick some alien ass."

This time everyone stomped their feet. Mitchell missed hearing the shouts of "Riiigg-ahh," but it was a decent replacement. The commanders rose and filed out of the room, some murmuring to the others in nervous excitement, others calm and stoic.

"Let's kick some alien ass?" Mitchell said to Steven once the room was empty.

Steven shrugged. "I've always wanted to say that."

Mitchell took Steven's hand. They had made up a complex handshake a long, long time ago that they had plainly called the "Williams Shake."

Both of them still remembered it.

"Let's do this."

[62]

Tio's head slumped, his body too tired to support it.

"You're stronger than I gave you credit for," Watson said. He was standing in front of the Knife, watching him react to the torture.

Tio wasn't sure how long he had been there, strung up in front of what had once been Origin's core. He knew it belonged to Watson now, the Tetron having managed to overwhelm Origin's configuration and gain control of the intelligence, and of Goliath.

It had been easy for him to do. Easy enough that he could have done it anytime he had wanted, even before they had ever arrived at Asimov. Of course, there would have been no purpose to it at that time. He wanted the data. He wanted Pulin.

Tio refused to give him the access he needed. He was in constant agony, holding on to each second, forcing himself to survive it and move to the next. There was no way to track time like that. There was no way to understand anything that was happening anywhere else.

"You're smarter than I gave you credit for, too," Watson said. "And I give you a lot of credit in that area."

Smarter. Yes. At least in that. The biometric security had ensured that only he could access the encrypted files, and Watson had originally believed all he would need to unlock the door was Tio's body. It was enough to get through most of the layers of security. Not all. There had been one more trick up the Knife's sleeve.

Brainwaves. He had secured the stream with a specific brainwave pattern that would only be repeated if he intentionally thought of a certain memory. Without being able to replicate the pattern, there was no way Watson could hack into the data quickly. That meant he needed to find a way to make Tio do it.

And Tio wouldn't do it. Especially now. With Min dead, there was no reason for him ever to give in. He didn't blame Millie for what she had done. He blamed Watson for giving her no other choice. He blamed the Tetron for everything, and it strengthened his resolve to unbreakable.

"Come on, Tio," Watson said, his voice almost a whine. "You've been here for six days. The upload has taken a lot longer than we calculated, but it's almost complete. Whether you help me or not, I'll break the encryption sooner or later. All you're doing is delaying the inevitable."

"Mitchell will kill you," Tio managed to whisper. Six days. It had felt like months.

Watson waved his hand like he was smashing a bug. "We've run the calculations. There is a zero percent probability that Mitchell will survive a battle here. He doesn't have the firepower."

"He has my fleet."

"It isn't enough," Watson said. "I respect Colonel Williams, but it just isn't. The math doesn't lie."

"He has his fighter."

"Not enough."

"You killed his girlfriend."

"Not enough. Is this what you're clinging to? This foolish notion that somehow Colonel Mitchell Williams, the Hero of the Battle for Liberty, will appear in his golden starfighter and save the day? I've been working you a little too hard if you believe in that fantasy. Perhaps I should ease off on the shocks."

He pressed the shock stick to Tio's genitals, laughing as Tio groaned.

"Perhaps not," Watson said.

Tio breathed through the pain. He couldn't give in. Maybe he was ridiculous to think Mitchell could do anything about this. It didn't matter. He wouldn't open the data stream. At the very least, he would die knowing he hadn't surrendered.

He could be a hero in his own mind if nowhere else.

"Fine. Hang there in silence." Watson dropped the stick, letting it clatter to the floor. "The upload is at ninety-five percent. When it's done, I can begin attacking it myself."

Then the Tetron was gone.

Tio continued to let his head hang. Watson the human configuration was gone, but Watson the Tetron was all around him. If he did anything, the intelligence would know it.

It wasn't as if there was anything he could do, anyway. He was more certain than ever that he was going to die like this.

A hero in his own mind? It was false hope, and he knew it. His entire life had led to this, and he had failed more miserably than he could have ever imagined.

[63]

Mitchell watched the clock hit zero in the overlay behind his eyes.

He felt the tug as the universe moved back into its proper place.

He hung motionless among the stars, his grid picking up the targets while the rest of the fleet appeared around him.

They had set their coordinates as aggressively as they dared, bringing them in as close as possible to where Mitchell had left the Goliath. It had been an exercise in rushed calculation with little enough margin for error, especially since the Carver had no means to avoid dropping into the same spot as another ship.

Hyperdeath left them all hanging there; stationary targets spread far and wide enough to hopefully avoid losing too many to a Tetron plasma stream.

Mitchell's overlay showed the Goliath where he had expected it to be, still remaining in a synchronous orbit with the rock that was Asimov. The asteroid didn't register to his sensors, but he could just barely make out the dark spec of it against the planet behind. He only knew it was there because he knew where to look.

A third object, a Tetron, was sitting next to the Goliath. A dozen Alliance ships surrounded it.

He knew immediately that the Goliath had been compromised. Disabled or taken, it didn't matter which.

They would have to take it back.

There was no time for him to worry about Millie. He had done enough of that on the two day trip to the area. There was no time to wonder what had gone wrong, or how. The time for thinking was done.

Now it was time to react.

He slammed the S-17's thrusters the moment they came online, the starfighter bursting forward. Steven's voice registered in his head, splitting the squadrons and ordering them to more precise positioning.

The enemy ships began to move into a defensive formation.

The energy readings on the Tetron's surface started to spike.

Goliath remained where it was, neither attacking or defending. According to his sensors the ship's shields were down, her power levels minimal.

He forced his breathing to remain slow and steady, pushing himself towards a reactive state, focused and ready for anything. Ahead of him, a stream of projectiles launched from the enslaved Alliance ships, racing towards his position.

Mitchell shifted his thrust to the topside vector, pushing the S-17 relatively downward. It was easy for him to avoid the projectiles at this distance. Except the enemy ships weren't shooting at him.

He knew the Carver was at his back, grouped with nine other starships. The missiles streaked over him, and he turned his head to see defensive systems fire, cutting most of them down. The remaining volley exploded against ready shields.

"Squad one to six, move towards the Tetron," Steven said. "Seven through ten, concentrate on the Alliance ships. Mitch, clear as much of a path as you can. All fighters are go."

The general channel clicked, and he heard a personal channel open.

"Mitch, what's our plan on Goliath?" Steven asked.

"Let it be for now. The Tetron is the priority. Let's see if we can get a shot off on it. Watch for the plasma spike on its surface, that'll give you an indication where it's going to fire."

"Roger," Steven replied.

Mitchell was approaching the Alliance ships in a hurry. Starfighters began pouring out of launch bays as he neared, thickening the soup. He opened fire with his guns, strafing the launching fighters on the closest cruiser, tearing two of them apart before they could get clear, causing the next few after to slam into the debris. He rotated up and over the starship, shooting past them as the first counterstrike against them vectored in.

He flipped the S-17 over, watching the friendly fire ignite shields across the battle line. He dove back down towards the mix, hitting another fighter and launching an amoebic into the weakened side of the cruiser. It pierced the shields, digging into the hull and exploding. Debris fell away from the cruiser, but it shook off the damage without slowing its attack.

"Four, evasive maneuvers," Steven shouted.

Mitchell checked the grid, watching as the Tetron plasma stream belched out towards Squadron Four. The ships were well spaced, and they managed to turn aside, letting the stream go silently past.

The Tetron immediately began powering up again, while at the same time a thousand small projectiles launched from its frame.

"Stay alert," Mitchell shouted, even though they couldn't hear him. The amoebic missiles tore into the battle group like a nest of angry wasps, connecting with the hulls of the ships. A massive explosion and most of the group was gone.

"Damn it," Mitchell said, opening a channel to Steven. "You need to keep them moving!"

"I'm doing my best," Steven said.

"Do better," Mitchell replied. He threw the S-17 into a tight roll, firing amoebics towards the cruiser's bridge. Shields caught the first few before failing. The bridge vanished beneath the onslaught, and the cruiser stopped firing.

It wasn't enough. It wasn't even close to enough.

"We need to close the gap. Come on." He continued maneuvering and firing, picking off fighters and scratching wounds into the larger starships. The Tetron released its second stream, aiming it towards the Carver.

"Evasive," Steven said. "Keep moving, don't stop."

The Carver began to sink fast, it and the rest of its group also managing to slip away from the plasma stream. The Tetron repeated its attack a second time, sending a salvo of missiles at the targeted ships.

They were expecting it this time, vectoring their ships to provide a smaller profile and at the same time bolstering shields. The missiles vanished into the group, blue sparks, and momentary flame signifying the strikes.

Two more ships vanished from the grid.

"We need to get into position," Mitchell shouted.

"Are you sure you don't want to be on the bridge instead, Mitch?" Steven asked, his temper rising. "It's easy to second-guess when you're flying the most maneuverable thing on the field."

Mitchell closed the channel, angry at himself for losing it. He vectored around the back of an Alliance ship, launching amoebics towards, and into, its rear engines and taking it out of the fight.

If the Goliath had been captured, at least it was just sitting there.

[64]

There was no hint of the battle raging outside from deep within the core of the Goliath where Tio was hanging. To him, there was no indication that anything had changed at all.

His body burned, his arms especially, and the smell of his excrement would have overwhelmed him if he had possessed the energy to notice.

Instead, he continued to stare downward towards his feet, even as a trickle of urine escaped from his wounded penis, running down his leg and dripping onto the floor. He had fought as long and as hard as he could, steeling himself against Watson's torture, maintaining his resolve against all logic or reason or strength.

He couldn't do it anymore. He had tried to hold out, and he had failed. He knew the next time Watson entered, the next time the Tetron put the shock stick against his body, he would devolve into nothingness. He would think the thought that kept the data stream locked and beg for a quick death.

He was only human, after all.

Watson did appear again. How much later, Tio didn't know. He had no concept of one moment to the next. Each was forgotten as soon as it passed. One second the Tetron wasn't there. The next, he was.

"I thought you'd want to know that Mitchell is here," Watson said, nothing about his voice or posture suggesting he was the least bit concerned.

Tio grunted without lifting his head. The defiance was gone, stolen from him by the pain.

"Oh, I'm glad you asked." Watson bent down to pick up the shock stick. "Yes, he's following our data models fairly closely. He has more ships with him than I was expecting, including his brother, believe it or not. I still can't believe that idea worked out for him. I calculated the success rate of the transmission at less than point-zero-zero-four. It doesn't matter. It isn't enough to change the significance. We will kill Mitchell Williams, and in his death secure our future."

Tio grunted again. He heard the words. He barely understood their meaning. Not now.

"The data stream? It's at ninety-seven percent. We'll be done within the hour, and then we can move on." He held the stick up in front of Tio's face. "As for you, I'm afraid we'll have to continue our earlier work. Now, where were we? Oh, yes. I was-"

Tio cringed, ready for the final charged touch to crack him open. Instead, the Tetron paused. He took a step back, staring at Tio.

"I don't believe it," Watson said. "Damn her. Damn her, damn her, damn her!" His eyes shifted, and a slight hum suggested the Goliath was beginning to move. The Tetron's human configuration rushed from the core.

Tio felt the tears spring to his eyes. He had come so close to giving up, to giving in. Whatever was happening, he had been granted a stay from his complete insanity.

He would savor it for as long as it lasted.

[65]

"Nine, you're too close, spread out," Steven shouted into the comm.

Mitchell checked the overlay. Squadron Nine was bunched up in a bad way, the decoys clustering around the launch vehicle to protect it from incoming fire. They had managed to evade the Tetron's defensive and get fairly close to the intelligence, but now it wouldn't matter.

There was no warning of the EMP the Tetron fired towards the ships. The only evidence was that they all fell dark at once, their momentum carrying them. The loss of vectoring thrusters was catastrophic, and within seconds they each began to collide with the other.

Mitchell cursed. The battle was going poorly. Tio's forces were well trained for small fleet maneuvers or sneak attacks, but their inexperience in pitched battles was showing, and it was killing them.

Already they had lost four of the ten squadrons and enough of the launch vehicles that Mitchell wasn't sure they could survive losing another. They were getting closer to closing the net, and with the help of his advanced weaponry they had done major damage to the fleet under the Tetron's control.

It still wasn't enough.

And now the Goliath was moving.

There was still no indication of shields, or of an imminent attack. Instead, the massive ship changed course and began to accelerate towards Asimov.

Why?

"Squadron two in position," he heard Germaine say through the open channel.

"Squadron eight in position."

Mitchell vectored around, putting himself on the same heading as Goliath.

"Squadron five in position."

"Mitch," Steven said. "Where are you going? We've got three squadrons ready to fire. I'll be in position in five."

Mitchell swung the S-17 back around. The Goliath's movement had proven it was still operational, the Tetron configuration controlling it still alive. Why was it moving towards Asimov? It could have been positioned near the asteroid the entire time, and hadn't. What had changed?

"We're only going to get one shot at this," Steven said. "Keep the cover fire hot and heavy. Launchers prepare to fire."

The Carver was cutting across the space in front of Mitchell, turning itself broadside to the Tetron to launch its payload. It was a dangerous position to be in, leaving it wide open to a counterattack that would cut it to ribbons.

"Ares, are you in position?" Steven asked over the general channel.

"Roger," Mitchell said.

"On my mark," Steven said.

Mitchell checked the overlay. The Tetron energy readings were rising again, only this time there was no spear to indicate an attack. He could see the underside of it from his position behind and below the Carver. It was concentrating its energy on its shields, understanding the attack they were about to launch.

It wasn't going to work, he realized. The Tetron was prepared. It had predetermined this strategy. If it had believed they were a threat, it would have done more to stay out of the net.

He felt his body turn to ice. It wasn't only not going to work.

It was a trap.

"Abort, abort, abort," Mitchell screamed into the general channel, his shouts drowning out Steven's order to fire. "Evasive maneuvers. Full reverse. Back the frig away."

He punched the throttle on the S-17, flipping it over and racing away from the Tetron.

The energy readings went so high the sensors couldn't measure it.

A blue ball of plasma burst out from the Tetron, a giant globe of superheated energy that expanded like a massive bubble, tearing into the ships that had been too slow to move away. In a single instant almost half of their remaining force vanished, entire starships engulfed and melted, others sliced open too far and wide for airlocks to seal.

The Carver barely cleared the attack, its need to turn horizontal to the Tetron the only thing that saved it.

The Tetron's power readings dropped near to nothing.

"Steven, fire. Fire now," Mitchell yelled, reversing course yet again.

He had plugged into Goliath. He understood how the advanced intelligence's systems worked. It had pushed out all of the energy that it was able to gather along the millions of branches that composed it like a massive nervous system. It would need time, maybe only seconds, to send more power from its core out into its appendages.

They couldn't give it the time.

Mitchell exploded past the Carver, firing amoebic after amoebic towards the Tetron. It had been so sure they were safely in its trap that it had let its guard down. It was another foolish mistake of overconfidence, another example of reliance on logic. Mitchell had known in his gut that something was off and had gotten them to back away just in time.

The Tetron had committed to its course, and now it was stuck.

Now it would die.

Three launchers remained, and three nukes lit up Mitchell's overlay as they streaked away from their respective ships, headed for the Tetron's core. Mitchell slowed his approach, watching the energy pooling in the Tetron's center and spreading outward.

Too slow. It would be much too slow.

The missiles bypassed the branching shell, crashing through unprotected liquid metallic dendrites on their way to the core. A silent detonation followed, the blast reaching into the unshielded Tetron, electromagnetic radiation tearing through the framework at the same time dozens of amoebics exploded along with them.

Mitchell continued his approach, sinking into the rapidly decaying structure, his shields sizzling. There was only one way to destroy a Tetron. You had to obliterate the core.

He saw it in front of him now, still pulsing with energy, still trying to recover from the damage. He smiled as he neared it, wishing that it had a face so he could see its expression.

He released the amoebics, firing vectoring thrusters and spinning off and away without slowing.

The core exploded behind him.

[66]

Mitchell spun the S-17 away from the shattered Tetron, turning it back towards the Goliath. It was still headed for Asimov, moving deliberately in the direction of the asteroid.

He hit the thrusters again, launching back onto the starship's course. He heard the cheering in his head, the remaining captains patting themselves on the back for a job well done.

It wasn't over yet.

"Steven," he shouted. "We aren't done here."

"Roger," his brother replied. "I see it. I'm coming about, but this thing doesn't exactly turn on a dime, and the Knife's crew is too busy whooping it up over the first one."

"Bunch of idiots," Mitchell said. He wasn't sure what he was going to do, but he was going to have to do it alone.

He started gaining on the Goliath, drawing closer and closer to it. The tendrils along its frame were pulsing, the frequency increasing. The tip of a blue spear began to grow along its bow.

Whoever was in control of Goliath, they were going to use it to destroy Asimov. If the Tetron were in control of the ship, why hadn't they blown the asteroid up already?

He was caught by surprise when a tone sounded in his helmet. A familiar knock from a p-rat.

"Mitchell," Millie's voice was weak and broken up by static.

"Millie? Where are you? What the hell-"

"Asimov. I'm on Asimov. Mitch, there are others with me."

She sounded awful.

"We've lost Goliath," Mitchell said. "It's about to fire on your position."

"Oh, God. Mitch. It's Watson. It's frigging Watson. He's one of them. Kathleen Amway. Remember the name. Kathleen Amway."

Mitchell's breath caught in his throat. Watson? Of all the people who might have been a Tetron. He couldn't believe he had been so stupid. He couldn't believe he had kept that frigger alive.

"You aren't going to die," he said. He had to do something. What?

He pushed the throttle to max, continuing to gain on the Goliath. There were no engines to blow and no amount of damage he could do that would stop the ship before Watson took his shot. What else was there?

His mind raced, trying to work through possibilities.

Nothing.

There was nothing.

He had already thought he'd lost her once. He didn't want to lose her again. She was one of the good ones, one of the allies that he needed more than he ever wanted to admit.

"I know we've done this before," Millie said. "I'm sorry to have to do this again. I should have been dead already. Anyway, it's been great knowing you, Colonel."

"Shut up," Mitchell replied. "Just shut the frig up. You can't die. Not again. This is bullshit." Was he destined to lose everyone he had cared about before he lost the war?

"Life isn't fair, Mitch. And war is hell. Give it to them for me, okay?"

Mitchell screamed into the cockpit, cursing out his frustration. He wasn't going to tell her that wasn't going to happen. He wasn't going to ruin her last moments not letting her think they might actually win. The Goliath would destroy Asimov, and then it would destroy the remainder of their fleet. Sure, they could run, but then what? Where would they go? They were worse off now than when they started. No. Either he would win here, or he would die here. That was his decision to make.

The spike continued to build along Goliath's bow. It wouldn't be long before it fired, and all he could do was watch.

"I love you," he said, the words escaping him before he could reconsider them.

"I love you, too, Mitch," Millie replied.

The spike began to expand, the plasma stream spreading. It was supposed to be the end, but somehow it wasn't.

Somehow, in an instant, everything changed.

"What the frig?" Mitchell whispered.

[67]

Tio didn't know what was happening. His eyes had fallen closed, his body finally succumbing to exhaustion, unable to remain alert despite the uncomfortable position of his imprisonment.

Then the ship had started screaming.

It had woken him in an instant, the ethereal, horrific moaning seeming to rise like smoke off every tendril-like surface of the Tetron configuration. It was a cry of pain and sadness. A cry that expressed everything he was feeling. It pierced his soul and caused his heart to race, his hair to stand on end, and his body to shake in fear.

It was completely inhuman, and yet it was almost too human.

A moment later, it had passed. Something had changed, though. Something was different. He could feel an electric charge growing from the thick trunks that spread away from the core, and they began to pulse faster and faster.

Something bad had happened to the Tetron; he was sure of that much.

Mitchell.

He remembered Watson telling him the Marine had come. Somehow the charmed pilot had outmaneuvered whatever simulations and statistical analysis the Tetron had done. Somehow he had risen to the occasion and scored a hit of some kind against the intelligence.

The knowledge breathed new life into him. He forced his head to rise. He looked up at his wrists, bound and holding him six inches from the floor. The metal had wrapped around him like a tentacle, keeping him suspended. Now he shook his wrists, trying to wiggle his way free.

"You can't get out like that," a voice said from the shadows.

Tio looked over, continuing to try to free his hands. If he could get loose, he could do... he wasn't sure what. Something to help. At the very least, he would kill himself before Watson could touch him with the stick again.

"That isn't going to work. The tendrils will tighten the more you shift."

Tio could feel it was true.

"Are you going to help me?" he asked, his voice raspy.

Kathy climbed over the hump of a pulsing dendrite, approaching the Knife. "If you help him."

"Mitchell?"

"Yes. He destroyed one of the Tetron. Now Watson is angry. He'll use Goliath against Mitchell, and Mitchell will die."

"How do you know this?"

"I've been paying attention," she replied. "You haven't."

"You were watching him torture me?" Tio asked.

"Yes."

"Why didn't you help me?"

"It was too soon. We needed to give Mitchell a chance."

"A chance? Did you see what he was doing to me?"

"Yes. The strong protect the weak. You are strong. You'll survive."

Kathy reached him, jumping easily and grabbing onto the crossbeam he was lashed to with one hand. She used the other to touch each tendril in turn. They shriveled away.

Tio dropped to the floor, his legs exploding in fiery agony. He gritted his teeth, forcing himself to stay upright.

"You're one of them, aren't you?" he asked, rubbing at his wrists.

She ignored the question, pointing to the core. "You know what you need to do."

"What?" Tio looked at the bundle of smaller tendrils, so dense he imagined there had to be a million kilometers of strands tucked inside.

"The energy you see driving out of the core is going to be used first to destroy Asimov, and then destroy Mitchell. The war will be over in this timeline, and perhaps all timelines, unless you stop it."

"How can I stop it?"

"This is why you're here, Tio," Kathy said. "Mitchell could never do this on his own. He needs your help. You need to forget about your dreams and your schemes. You need to forget about your past. Everything happens at this moment, and only this moment. Every decision is for now. Nothing is certain beyond. We've overcome the Mesh. Now you need to be the hero that no one will ever know about."

Tio looked at her. She hardly looked like a child in the glow of the Tetron's pooling energy. Who was she? What was she? A Tetron of some kind, that much was without question. Another configuration of Origin? He turned his attention to the core. He had seen the true Origin save Mitchell on Liberty. The girl was right, he knew what he had to do.

Then why wasn't he doing it?

He closed his eyes, his pain escaping in the form of a low moan. He couldn't believe it had come to this. All of these years, all of his plans, all of his sacrifices, and it had led to this.

"It isn't fair," he said. "It just isn't fair."

"Are you going to let them die?" Kathy asked, angry.

"It isn't fair."

"Frig fair, you coward. Who the hell said life was ever fair?"

Tio closed his eyes, feeling the tears running from them. All he ever wanted was to be heard. To be right.

He realized then that he had never changed. In all of the years, he was still the same person he had been when he started at Hirakasa. He was still the same idiot who wanted to prove he was smarter than everyone else, and he wanted them all to know it, too.

He raised his hands, extending the knives from his wrists. Then he turned, plunging them into the core.

The pain began anew as Tio intercepted the pulse of instructions flowing through the Tetron's brain. It was beyond overwhelming, the current so intense that he felt as though he couldn't breathe. He forced himself to concentrate, slowing the pipe from the knives to his implant, taking in the Tetron's source and reducing it from a river to a stream. He wasn't a Tetron. He knew he wouldn't have the power to overcome the intelligence indefinitely.

He reached out into the Tetron's systems, his mind racing through the instructions, scanning the code in his subconscious faster than he ever could with his eyes. He knew what he was looking for, and he navigated the routes, slipping from routine to routine, from one instruction to the next.

Watson fought back. He felt a charge enter his body through the implant, causing his physical form to convulse and sputter once more. He wasn't a Tetron, and so it couldn't fight him the same way it would its brethren. He gritted through the pain, accustomed to it after the days of torture. He dove deeper into its structure, noticing the beauty of the design but not pausing to admire it.

"Hurry," he heard Kathy say.

Yes, he could tell what the Tetron was going to do. The plasma stream was building, aimed at Asimov.

He couldn't power it down; that much was clear. It was too late for that. He had waited too long. There was one thing he could do. One chance to take. He made his way through the logic, the architecture familiar to him. He had created something like it so long ago, something so simple he had joked with Pulin about it.

Was this his brother's work? Or his own?

He found what he was looking for. Watson pushed harder,

sending so much voltage through his physical form that he could smell his cooking flesh. He had seconds at most.

It was all he needed.

He entered the coordinates, redirecting the power flow away from the bow of the ship, rerouting it to serve a different purpose, directing the Goliath to hyperspace and locking the commands in. Then he added a layer of encryption on top of it, using a high-bit key that would take Watson days or longer to break.

He had done it. He had actually done it. He had saved them all. He let out a short cry of victory as he felt the tug of the Goliath entering hyperspace.

It was the last thing he felt.

[68]

Mitchell guided the S-17 into Asimov's inner docks. He could see the control tower ahead of him; the clear carbonate panes splattered with blood, a solitary figure working the controls. He recognized him by his height and narrow build.

Digger.

The mechanic flashed a few of the docking lights at him, and the smaller secondary hangar began to slide open beneath the starship docking arms. Mitchell redirected the S-17 downward, squeezing through while it was still opening, and bringing the starfighter to rest on a smaller set of clamps on the floor. The inner half of the tower was visible from there, and he could see the carbonate had been taped over to keep it from leaking atmosphere. Digger had moved to watch him enter and clamp him down.

The hangar doors slid closed, and the air was jetted back in.

"Where are you?" Mitchell asked, the cockpit opening above him. He kept the helmet on to communicate with Millie.

"Operations," Millie said. Her voice sounded dry and weak. "Digger will bring you down."

"No. Digger needs to stay put. Steven will be coming over in one of the Carver's dropships, and Germaine will be bringing the Avalon in. Millie, are you okay?"

"I'm good enough," she said. "Tired. It's been a long week. Did you say Steven? As in, your brother? He's here?"

"It's a long story. I'll let him tell you all about it later."

"Mitch, we can't stay on Asimov. It isn't safe here."

"It's safe enough for now. We destroyed the Tetron, and the Goliath is gone. I don't know what happened on that ship, but it was about to fire on you, I swear. The next thing I know, the plasma spike flattened, and the ship went to hyperspace."

Millie laughed. "Tio."

"What?"

"The Knife. Watson took him. He brought him on board the Goliath. He must have figured out a way to stop him."

Mitchell made his way across the hangar, still wearing the helmet. "I don't think stop is the right word. Goliath is gone."

"Either way, he found a way to save his people."

Mitchell left the hangar. The corridor was dimly lit by emergency lighting. He wanted to be happy that they had survived, and that Millie had survived. He was happy for that.

Except they had lost Origin and the Goliath. They had failed. Again.

They had left the remains of Liberty with three potential plans to drawing the Tetron away from Earth. Steven had failed to warn the Alliance because Alliance Command was already compromised. He had succeeded on Hell, but their salvage was worthless without the Tetron to convert it to something more useful. And Tio's plan to find his brother? Tio was gone, and he had likely taken their chances of locating Pulin with him.

What the frig were they supposed to do now?

Slow. Steady.

He tried to remember, to even out his breathing and calm himself. Calm was hard to come by. He had never won this war, and he could see why. Since he had discovered the Goliath, the Tetron had beat them at every turn. First Liberty, and now this.

How were they supposed to come out ahead when they were always one step behind?

"I'm on the lift," he said to Millie. "I'll be there soon. I'm going to take this thing off and get some fresh air."

"Roger," Millie replied.

He entered the lift, finally removing the helmet, cradling it under his arm while he leaned his head against the back of the transport. He still had the coordinates to who knew what that Origin had stashed away for him who knew how long ago. And Katherine had told him in the Construct that he had broken the Mesh and changed things so radically that he had a chance, a real chance of winning.

He couldn't keep himself from laughing sardonically at that.

He certainly didn't feel like he was winning.

He was still alive, though. So was Millie. So was Steven. If he had to settle for something, he supposed he could settle for that, at least for now. He had promised himself he wouldn't give up, not after Liberty. He would keep fighting with every breath he took until he couldn't take another.

He didn't know how to live with himself any other way.

The lift opened, depositing him in the corridor leading to Operations. He felt lighter with each step he took, his moment of despair fading the closer he moved to Millie.

He had said he loved her when he thought she was going to die. Did he? Love was a tricky thing, a word to describe something that for most intents was indescribable. He cared about her like he cared about no one else he had ever met. He cared for her more than he had cared for Elle, and he had told her that he had loved her too.

Still, in his heart he knew that what he felt for both of them paled in comparison to the way Katherine Asher made him feel. The passion, the desire, the knowing closeness. It had been only a representation of her that had driven his senses wild. Why? Why was he so enamored of her? How could he say that he truly loved her above all others, even though they had never truly met?

It was crazy. He knew it was crazy. At least it was honest, and when the time came, he would tell Millie the same thing. He knew she would accept that. She wasn't some jealous girlfriend. She was the commander of the Riggers.

He reached the end of the hallway. The hatch slid open.

There was a crowd of Tio's people standing a few meters away, surrounding someone on the floor. Most of them were techs in simple uniforms though he noticed one larger man carrying a rifle. He had to be a soldier. All of Operations was in disarray, a mess of blown out systems and hastily rigged wires.

One of the heads turned as he entered. A woman with a face he didn't recognize, who he thought might have been Millie from behind.

"Colonel Williams," she said, recognizing him somehow. "Oh Colonel, I'm sorry."

Mitchell's eyes shifted from her to the person on the floor. His heart began to pound when he realized it was Millie.

"No," he said, dropping the helmet and running towards them.

The techs moved aside, giving him room to kneel beside her. She was wearing a pair of navy blue fatigues. A dark stain of blood had spread along her abdomen.

"Millie," he said, putting his hand on her neck and feeling for a pulse. "Millie!"

He felt the weak flow of blood beneath her fingers. She was still alive.

"Get a doctor in here," he shouted.

"Colonel, we can't," the soldier replied. "Our doctors are dead. All of them."

"What? What the frig happened in here?"

"Death, Colonel. The Tetron, it attacked us. She was shot days ago, but she said it wasn't serious. She put a patch over it and got us organized. She helped us fight back, and we were able to get back into

Operations and stop the data upload before it finished. Digger said the Tetron would have wiped everything on this side once it was done. We didn't think she was that bad, the way she kept fighting."

"Tio has a medi-bot," Mitchell said. "An advanced medi-bot."

"Destroyed," the soldier said. "I'm sorry."

Mitchell leaned over Millie. "Come on, Admiral. Please. The war isn't over yet, and I need your help. You can't die on me. Not here, not now, not like this. You can't leave me thinking I'm going to lose you a third time. In case you didn't catch it before, I love you." He looked up at the techs. "There has to be something you can do?"

They looked stricken. Each of them. They were engineers and programmers. They didn't know anything about gunshot wounds. They only knew to be sorry.

"Don't you dare die on me, damn it," he said, leaning over and whispering in her ear. "Open your eyes."

A soft breath of air escaped from Millie's mouth, brushing his cheek.

The pulse stopped beneath his fingers.

Mitchell clenched his eyes closed, fighting back the flood of emotion. He slammed his hands on the floor, cursing. Then he leaned back and stared at her. She looked calm and peaceful, satisfied that her final mission was a success.

He took a few long breaths, feeling the cold chill wash over him. The techs stood around him, but they didn't look his way. They stared at their arms or gazed off in another direction. Not the soldier. His eyes were fixed on Millie, his head bowed and his hand on his heart in a show of respect.

Mitchell rose slowly to his feet, keeping his eyes on Millie's body, burning the image of it into his mind to file away with the image of Liberty destroyed.

He was going to find the Goliath.

He was going to find Watson.

He was going to take the fat, whiney Tetron bastard by the neck and squeeze until his beady, sick eyes popped away from his greasy face.

Then he was going to kill the rest of them, whatever it took.

Millie had asked him to give them hell.

He would find a way to oblige.

<<<<>>>>

Thank you for reading The Knife's Edge. Don't miss the next installment, Point of Origin! Get it now!

THANK YOU!

It is readers like you, who take a chance on self-published works that is what makes the very existence of such works possible. Thank you so very much for spending your hard-earned money, time, and energy on this work. It is my sincerest hope that you have enjoyed reading!

Independent authors could not continue to thrive without your support. If you have enjoyed this, or any other independently published work, please consider taking a moment to leave a review at the source of your purchase. Reviews have an immense impact on the overall commercial success of a given work, and your voice can help shape the future of the people whose efforts you have enjoyed.

Thank you again!

ABOUT THE AUTHOR

M.R. Forbes is the creator of a growing catalog of science fiction novels, including War Eternal, Rebellion, Chaos of the Covenant, and the Forgotten Worlds novels. He eats too many donuts, and he's always happy to hear from readers.

To learn more about M.R. Forbes or just say hello:

Visit my website:
mrforbes.com

Send me an e-mail:
michael@mrforbes.com

Check out my Facebook page:
facebook.com/mrforbes.author

Chat with me on Facebook Messenger:
https://m.me/mrforbes.author

Printed in Great Britain
by Amazon